Michael Innes is the pseudonym of J. I. M. Stewart,
who was a Student of Christ Church, Oxford, from 1949
until his retirement in 1973. He was born in 1906 and
was educated at Edinburgh Academy and Oriel College,
Oxford. He was lecturer in English at the University of
Leeds from 1930 to 1935, Jury Professor of English at
the University of Adelaide, South Australia, from 1935
to 1945, and lecturer in Queen's University, Belfast,
between 1946 and 1948.

He has published many novels – including the quintet
A Staircase in Surrey (*The Gaudy*, *Young Pattullo*, *A
Memorial Service*, *The Madonna of the Astrolabe* and
Full Term) – several volumes of short stories, as well as
books of criticism and essays, under his own name. His
Eight Modern Writers appeared in 1963 as the final
volume of *The Oxford History of English Literature*,
and he is also the author of *Rudyard Kipling* (1966) and
Joseph Conrad (1968). His other books include *Andrew
and Tobias* (1981), *The Bridge at Arta and Other Stories*
(1981), *A Villa in France* (1982), *My Aunt Christine and
Other Stories* (1983), *An Open Prison* (1984), *The
Naylors* (1985) and *Parlour 4 and Other Stories* (1986).

Under the pseudonym of Michael Innes he has written
broadcast scripts and many crime novels including
Appleby's End (1945), *The Bloody Wood* (1966),
An Awkward Lie (1971), *The Open House* (1972),
Appleby's Answer (1973), *Appleby's Other Story* (1974),
The Appleby File (1975), *The Gay Phoenix* (1976),
Honeybath's Haven (1977), *The Ampersand Papers*
(1978), *Going It Alone* (1980), *Lord Mullion's Secret*
(1981), *Sheiks and Adders* (1982), *Appleby and
Honeybath* (1983), *Carson's Conspiracy* (1984) and
Appleby and the Ospreys (1986). Several of these are
published in Penguin together with two omnibus
editions, *The Michael Innes Omnibus* containing *Death
at the President's Lodging*, *Hamlet, Revenge!* and *The
Daffodil Affair* and *The Second Michael Innes Omnibus*
containing *The Journeying Boy*, *Operation Pax* and *The
Man from the Sea*.

The Daffodil Affair

by MICHAEL INNES

PENGUIN BOOKS

PENGUIN BOOKS

Published by the Penguin Group
27 Wrights Lane, London W8 5TZ, England
Viking Penguin Inc., 40 West 23rd Street, New York, New York 10010, USA
Penguin Books Australia Ltd, Ringwood, Victoria, Australia
Penguin Books Canada Ltd, 2801 John Street, Markham, Ontario, Canada L3R 1B4
Penguin Books (NZ) Ltd, 182–190 Wairau Road, Auckland 10, New Zealand

Penguin Books Ltd, Registered Offices: Harmondsworth, Middlesex, England

First published in Great Britain by Gollancz 1942
First published in the United States of America by
Dodd, Mead & Company, Inc., 1942
Published in Penguin Books 1964
10 9 8 7

Printed and bound in Great Britain by
Cox & Wyman Ltd, Reading
Set in Monotype Times

Contents

Note

Describe the horoscope, haruspicate or scry,
Observe disease in signatures, evoke
Biography from the wrinkles of the palm
And tragedy from fingers . . . especially
When there is distress of nations and perplexity
Whether on the shores of Asia or in the
Edgware Rd.

The Dry Salvages

Part 1

Primrose Way

1

The room was void and unquickened; it was like a room in a shop-window but larger and emptier; and the man who sat at the desk had never thought to impress himself upon what he entered every day. Comfort there was none, nor discomfort either; only, did the occupant deign to qualify the pure neutrality of his surroundings, it would surely be austerity that would emerge. The spring sunshine turned bleak and functional as it passed the plate-glass of the tall, uncurtained windows.

The windows were large; the big desk lay islanded in a creeping parallelogram of light; across this and before the eyes of the man sitting motionless passed slantwise and slowly a massive shaft of shadow. Perhaps twenty times it passed to and fro, as if outside some great joy-wheel were oscillating idly in a derelict amusement park. And then the man rose, clasped hands behind him and walked to a window – high up in New Scotland Yard. He looked out and war-time London lay beneath.

With science the crane or scoop or derrick had been perched amid the skeletal remains of a large building; from this point of vantage it struck and shovelled ingeniously at a neighbouring structure whose ruin had stopped half-way down. It was possible to be sad, to be indignant; and many who walked those streets were making the biologically more useful discovery of anger. But a practical-minded man could confine himself to approving or critical appraisal of the speed with which the tidy-up was accomplished – and the man at the window looked superficially as if he might be like that. His movements were economical, impersonal, abstract. His glance, if considering, was unclouded by speculative care. But on his brow was a fixed contraction; this he had carried from desk to window, and now there was neither hardening nor relaxation as he looked out.

Hudspith looked out and took it all in. He looked out and as a practical man placed it: there was this and that contingency to fear, to hope for, next time. And as a moralist Hudspith placed it: his lips framed a word. Wicked. Undoubtedly it was that. But was it evil? He thought not; he grudged to the mere fury and blindness of it that absolute word. During fifteen years Hudspith had controlled the file of police papers which dealt with the abduction and subsequent history of feeble-minded girls. Here lay his anger, and as he looked out over London he saw, in effect, only the shadow of this. Year by year the anger had burst deeper until it was now the innermost principle of the man. He confronted sin that was double and gratuitous. For, given social conditions which were common enough, it was tolerably easy to seduce, strand, swop, sell, hire out girls whose wits were reasonably about them. And so the meanness of going for the feeble ones was – well, exasperating. Evil was exasperating. Or rather, perhaps, it was exasperating that so few people were aware of it.

Their minds stop short at wickedness – thought Hudspith, looking out over London. More of them are aware of God, of Immortality, of the Ideas of Reason, than are really aware of evil. And yet these things, as someone has said, are mere superstructure and superficies compared with the fact of evil. . . . Hudspith did not go to church, but this knowledge of evil made him, in fact, a violently religious man. He pursued his particular police job, sordid and depressing as it was, with very much that dangerous metaphysical intensity which Captain Ahab put into the pursuit of the White Whale. Other things passed him by, not impinging – like his room.

And now there was this girl – the girl with the outlandish name: Lucy Rideout. Once too often she had ridden out. . . . Hudspith smiled bleakly – unseeing and unaware – into the bleak sunshine.

A half-witted girl.

'A horse!'

John Appleby, two storeys below, looked incredulously at the old gentleman who had recently been reinstalled as

Assistant-Commissioner. 'A horse?' repeated Appleby. Never before had he been asked to go out and look for a horse.

The old gentleman nodded, indecisively; he looked Appleby cautiously in the eye. Things had changed. There were quite a lot more sahibs in lower places, and a few more rankers in higher places, than in the old days. He attached little importance to such things. But every now and then it could come awkward – if one wasn't minding one's p's and q's. 'Yes,' he said; 'a horse.' His tone was doubtful, as if some qualification must follow. He paused, as if in search of something that could be enunciated with confidence. 'Sit down,' he said.

Appleby sat down. 'There's Ambler,' he suggested hopefully. 'I believe Ambler has had a lot of experience with horses. When Crusader disappeared just before the Derby in thirty –'

The Assistant-Commissioner shook his head. 'No, no; it's not that sort of horse. Not a valuable sort of horse – not at all valuable. And, in a way, it's not really an official affair.' He began to scratch his chin doubtfully; checked himself. 'As a matter of fact, it's my sister,' he said ambiguously.

'Ah.' Appleby felt a growing dislike of this shadowy equine problem.

'My sister lives in Harrogate. Tiresome sort of place.' The Assistant-Commissioner was obscurely apologetic. 'Know it, I suppose.'

'I have an aunt living there, as a matter of fact.'

'Indeed.' The Assistant-Commissioner took a calculating glance at his own toes. 'I wonder,' he ventured, 'if she knows –'

'I believe she knows Lady Caroline quite well.'

'What a coincidence!' As he made this imbecile remark the Assistant-Commissioner scrutinized his toes more severely than before. He was not at all sure that this made the matter easier. He decided on a shift to humour. 'You don't happen to know,' he asked, 'if your aunt has a favourite cab?'

'I don't. But I think it very likely.'

'Well, Caroline has – or had. She was attached to a particularly sober driver with a particularly quiet horse. At one time when Miss Maidment rang up the stables – I should explain that Maidment is her companion – I mean I should explain that *Miss* Maidment is her companion –' The Assistant-Commissioner paused, perplexed. 'What was I saying?'

'You had got to the point, sir, at which Miss Maidment would ring up the stables.'

'To be sure. Well, at one time she used to ask for an open landau, a respectable man and a quiet horse. But latterly she has simply asked for Bodfish and Daffodil.' The Assistant-Commissioner paused. 'Bodfish and Daffodil,' he repeated. 'The former was the driver and the latter the horse. That goes without saying, I suppose. One can imagine a Mr Daffodil, but nobody ever gave the name of Bodfish to a cab-horse.'

'No, sir.'

The Assistant-Commissioner appeared dashed. 'Look here,' he said, 'I know it sounds tiresome. But just you listen. There's a quirk in it later on.'

Appleby, who quite liked this old gentleman, endeavoured to smile with cheerful interest. 'I suppose, sir, it is Daffodil who has disappeared?'

'Quite right. At first my sister was told the animal was dead. She was distressed, because the creature was a favourite, and not at all an old horse.' The Assistant-Commissioner hesitated. 'In fact, she felt rather like the poet.'

Appleby smiled – genuinely this time. 'Quite so, sir. Fair Daffodil, we weep to see you haste away so soon.'

The Assistant-Commissioner nodded his head emphatically, much pleased with the success of his cultural reconnaisance. 'Exactly. Exactly – my dear man. At first, then, they said the horse was dead – apparently feeling that the mention of anything shady would be bad for trade. Now, my sister is inquisitive – or what a politer age used to call a person of much observation. She sent for Bodfish, intending to learn the manner of the brute's death. Bodfish came to see her – and I am sorry to say he was drunk. It had taken him that way. Caroline at once made Maidment – Miss Maidment, I should say – ring up the stables for a closed cab, a respectable driver and a quiet horse. She then drove Bodfish home, gave Mrs Bodfish a receipt for brewing cocoa in a particularly wholesome and attractive manner, and went on to make searching inquiries of Daffodil's owner. When she learnt that the animal had been

12

stolen she – well, she sent me a somewhat urgent telegram. Scotland Yard, apparently, came at once to her mind. Natural, having a brother there – I suppose.'

'Very natural, sir.'

'Of course I replied that the local police were the people. So, if you please, she went to see the Chief Constable, taking her solicitor along with her. Seemingly nothing much had been done in the matter of Daffodil. And the Chief Constable, who had hard-worked officers to protect, was pretty stiff with Caroline. Not at first: I gather he tried heading her off by explaining some of the jobs he had on hand, and letting her in on a harmless war-time secret or two. But Caroline, who is even more specifically pertinacious than generally curious, held to her theme. It was *aut asphodelos aut nullus* with her. I believe her motive was quite selfish and practical: Daffodil was the only horse in Harrogate in which she really had confidence, and she was consequently determined that Daffodil should be traced. Too determined, I gather, for in the end the Chief Constable had pretty well to turn her out. So she went home, thought it over, dictated a stately letter of apology through Miss Maidment – and was thus in a position to present herself without absolute indecency on the poor chap's doorstep once more on the following afternoon. He was a bit baffled.'

'As one would imagine, sir.'

'Quite so. And I think he tried a spot of irony – suggested Scotland Yard. Caroline explained that she was already in communication with me. I fear he rather crumpled up, and really did – er – pass the buck. In short – well, it is difficult, you know.'

'Yes, sir.'

'My sister lives in the most modest way. As peers go we're nobody in particular, as you know.' The old gentleman smiled charmingly. 'But then she is the widow –'

'Quite so, sir.'

'Which means that among her brothers-in-law –'

'Clearly, sir. You would like me to go down?'

The Assistant-Commissioner sighed unhappily. 'It *is* difficult, isn't it? And, you know, you look a bit tired.' This was outrageous, but true. 'And you can't always be after those whopping big affairs. A man who manages in a twelve-month to fight a battle on a Scottish moor, and get wrecked on a desert island, and –'

'Of course I'll go if you wish it, sir.'

'Just for a week-end it's a nice quiet place enough.' The Assistant-Commissioner, here touching perhaps maximum discomfort, thrust his toes despairingly out of sight beneath his desk and looked at Appleby in frank dismay. 'You might even *find* the horse, I suppose.' He shook his head perplexedly. 'Caroline would be pleased – but then would it be tactful to the local men?' He smiled wanly. 'I leave the finding of Daffodil entirely to your discretion. The creature is said to be worth fifteen pounds. And that reminds me.'

'Of the quirk, sir?'

'Just that.' The Assistant-Commissioner brightened. 'It really is a bit remarkable. Like those tiny but disconcerting puzzles they used to take to Sherlock Holmes. In fact there's really a mystery in the Daffodil affair – and mysteries don't turn up here every day, do they? Oceans of crime in islets of anything like genuine mystification.' He paused, obscurely troubled by something in this image. 'The place is what is called a livery stables. Means just a business you hire from. But there's the older meaning of a place you put your own horses to board. And somebody was doing that. Captain Somebody who has to do with tanks down there but likes to get on a horse from time to time. In a loose-box next to Daffodil he had an animal that was worth hundreds of pounds. And this brute was stolen *first*.'

Appleby looked up sharply. 'You don't mean that –?'

'Yes. This whopping valuable brute was stolen in the night. In the morning there was a great rumpus, and nobody much bothered about Daffodil or the stable any more. Anything of the sort would have been like locking –'

'Quite so, sir.'

'And then in the course of the day up drove one of those motor-things for horses, returned Captain Somebody's brute, and carried off Daffodil instead – this without anybody being more than vaguely aware of what was happening. Apparently a mistake had been made the first time. Daffodil was the wanted horse.'

'And Daffodil is really worth almost nothing?'

'Apparently not – except to my sister's sense of security round and about the streets of Harrogate. Not very old, apparently – but broken-kneed or winded or something.'

Appleby shook his head. 'I doubt whether Lady Caroline ought to have confidence in a horse that has been down.'

'My dear man, she no doubt likes its face. Anyway, Daffofil was not a valuable horse.'

'There could be no question of pedigree, stud purposes – that sort of thing?'

'Good Heavens, man! Bodfish – I mean Daffodil – wasn't – um – that sort of horse.'

'I suppose not.' Appleby got up. 'It does seem a little queer. I'll catch the first train on Friday.' He paused by the Assistant-Commissioner's door. 'There's nothing else you can tell me about Daffodil?'

'As a matter of fact there is. It's an odd thing to say about a horse. But it appears – this despite Caroline's good opinion of the creature – well, that it was rather a half-witted sort of horse. What would you say was implied by that? Don't know much about the animals myself.'

Daffodil, the half-witted horse. Appleby wandered down the corridors of the Yard and seemed to see – for indeed he was tired – a host of these dubious creatures in his inward eye, tossing their heads in sprightly dance, curvetting and bowing to an equal number of Captain Somebody's whopping valuable brutes. A policeman could not but be gay in such a jocund company. . . .

A half-witted horse.

2

In vain the soft warm air washed over Superintendent Hudspith; he marched unmollified from one investigation to the next. It was June, and for another man Piccadilly Circus might have been filled with the ghosts of flowers: violets in little bunches wafting on bus-tops to distant suburbs; roses to be carried off by sheaves in limousines; carnations that slip singly down St James's, glow duskily from tail-coats in the bow-window of White's, adorn tweeds in the rustic Boodle's, vie with the more appropriate orchid in the Travellers' – haunt of those hardy souls who have journeyed out of the British Islands to a distance of at least 500 m. from London in a direct line. But these wraiths were nothing to Hudspith's purpose. Fleetingly he allowed himself a glance of suspicion down Jermyn Street, as fleetingly a nod of sanction at the Athenæum – and stumped down the steps and across to the park. The park was like green stuff spilt on a counter, shot with the sheen of a long fragment of blue-grey silk. The water-fowl were there as usual; statesmen paused in perambulations to observe their habits with attention; shadowing detectives, distantly known to Hudspith, exercised their corresponding vigilance behind. Hudspith marched on. His visual field was all inward and shadowy – no more than a floating wreath of cheated girls. Sometimes they had been drugged, hypnotized; and sometimes they had been robbed of nearly all their clothes. . . . Hudspith marched – as if behind Queen Anne's Mansions, beyond the Underground's clock, somewhere near Victoria station maybe, blew and wallowed that elusive Whale.

Rideout: it was not, Hudspith thought, what you would call a tony name. On the other hand the address – a block of service flats here on the fringes of Westminster – suggested substance; and if the Rideouts were substantial the more substantial would be Hudspith's severity. He had received no particulars; it was his habit to disregard the first, and often confused, report that came in; he had learnt, however, that there was a mother, a Mrs Rideout – and by this he was obscurely pleased. Mothers, when there were mothers, were commonly greatly to blame. Although Mrs Rideout could scarcely be herself the Whale, she might yet be abundantly deserving of one or two preliminary harpoons. Hudspith was accustomed to limber up in this way. He quickened his pace, turned a corner, and his objective was before him.

The Rideouts were in the humblest station: there lay something of disappointment in this. Mrs Rideout was employed as a cleaner and her daughter as a waitress, and normally they lived 'out'. But recently their home had disappeared in the night; this had moved Mrs Rideout to announce her intention of withdrawing to her sister's in the country; whereupon the management of the flats where she was employed, being much in need of such services as Rideouts supply, had provided restricted but sufficient living quarters on the premises. Through the basement, past the ironing-room and the two small store-rooms, the temporary abode of the Rideouts would be found.

Hudspith, having learnt so much from a melancholy porter whose own living quarters appeared to be in a lift, descended menacingly into the cold, the half-light and the gloom. It was familiar territory. Like the poet, but perhaps from a more pressing professional necessity, he was much aware of the damp souls of housemaids; he knew how easily perdition attended their despondent sprouting at area gates. And he knew – he told himself – all about Lucy Rideout, the half-witted waitress. Unsettlement, cramped quarters with an uncongenial parent, inadequate privacy, the constant sight of expensive or at least prosperous living upstairs, the drift of male guests – themselves often unsettled, uprooted: in all this – and in the pictures, the glamorized advertisements, the pulsing sexy music – the story lay. Had he not probed it a hundred times? And Hudspith marched on, confident in his abundant experience, his often-tested technique. Hudspith marched against the demons – all unaware of the curiously literal way in which, far in the distance, demons awaited him.

Mrs Rideout had friends. Almost might she be said, in up-stairs language, to be receiving – for two ladies were coming away as Hudspith reached the door; a third, approaching from some other angle through this subterranean world, was making a ceremonious claim for admittance; and from inside there came a murmur of voices and a chink of cups. Here however was nothing to confound the experienced investigator; it would be untoward were Mrs Rideout found enjoying her sensational sorrow in solitude.

'Good afternoon,' said Hudspith to his fellow visitor. 'A sad occasion this, marm; very sad indeed.'

'What I asks,' said the visitor, 'is – where was the police?'

'Ah,' said Hudspith. 'Where, indeed? But they're here now, missis.' With subdued drama he tapped himself on the chest. 'Come along.'

The woman, who had been about to open the door, paused round-eyed. 'Toomer's my name,' she said. Her voice sank to a whisper. 'Would it be worse than death?'

Hudspith frowned austerely. 'That remains to be seen.' And he opened the door and ushered Mrs Toomer – she was a dim-featured, almost obliterated woman – into the Rideout home.

It was possible – or it ought to have been possible – to see at a single glance all that was to be seen, for clearly in this one room consisted all the territory that the Rideouts, mother and daughter, enjoyed. It was long, narrow and of considerable size, lit by a filter of light from windows which hovered uncertainly near the ceiling; there was a bed at each extreme end, and a table and arrangements for cooking near the middle. There was little that was remarkable in this. But Hudspith, if unaware of his own habitual surroundings, had a trained eye for domestic interiors, and that eye became positively hawk-like when scrutinizing the late environment of levanting or abducted girls. Here there looked to be plenty of evidence. The influence of Lucy Rideout was dominant in the room. Her handwriting, as it were, was not only decisive at her own end; it declared itself unmistakably far beyond any fair line of demarcation, so that one immediately discerned Mrs Rideout's kingdom as a sort of beleaguered fortress within ever-contracting lines. Only here and there was evidence of a species of cautious sortie undertaken, no doubt, since the daughter's departure; a pair of elastic-sided boots had found their way to the foot of Lucy's bed; a small empty bottle of the kind in which ladies are accustomed to keep gin stood on what had served her as a dressing-table; hard by this lay a journal devoted to the celebration of the Christian Hearth and Home. All this was immediately decipherable. But there remained an element of puzzle which Hudspith at a rapid inspection was unable to resolve. And now Mrs Toomer, exalted by the fact of arriving virtually on the arm of Scotland Yard, was contriving introductions to the assembled company. 'Mrs Rideout,' she said, 'this is the police.'

18

Mrs Rideout was not much over forty and belonged to the inefficient type that contrives to get through life by the aid of a sort of massive unfocussed vehemence. She set down a teacup and looked from Mrs Toomer to Hudspith. 'That's right,' she said, largely and vaguely. 'Yes, that's right.' She exuded that repetitive and dazed acquiescence that makes so considerable a part of the social communion of the folk. 'And I'm sure they ought to do something.'

'That's right,' said Mrs Toomer – and two stout women who flanked Mrs Rideout nodded heads and bosoms in agreement. Human speech is at bottom no more than the individual's demand for reassurance in a lonely world; the sophisticated contrive to extract comforting intimations of solidarity from disagreement, controversy and repartee; the uninstructed prefer much simpler forms of mutual support. When the ritual is in course of celebration – at such a party as was now gathered at Mrs Rideout's – it is a solecism to break the grand affirmative flow of things. And indeed we none of us particularly care for the man who qualifies our suggestion that it is a fine day, or that it looks like rain, or that it is nice to see a little bit of sunshine.

All this the much-practised Hudspith knew. He nodded his head ponderously. 'Yes,' he said; 'something ought to be done. And I'm here to do it.'

'That's right,' said one of the stout women. 'That's what I say.'

'That's right,' said the other stout woman.

Mrs Rideout turned in triumph to Mrs Toomer. 'That's what Mrs Thorr and Mrs Fiddock say,' she said.

Mrs Toomer, who had turned her head in quest of the teapot, nodded skilfully backwards. 'That's right,' she agreed.

'That's right,' said Mrs Fiddock and Mrs Thorr.

Hudspith cleared his throat, preparing cautiously to intrude upon the spell. 'Acting,' he said, 'on instructions received –' The ladies all laid down their teacups, instantly impressed by this wisp of official eloquence. Hudspith slowly produced a notebook. The investigation was launched.

Mrs Rideout called God to witness that she had been a good mother. Mrs Thorr, Mrs Toomer and Mrs Fiddock responded in a sort of trinitarian chorus. Hudspith said grimly that he was glad to hear it, as in most such cases it was not so; he appeared to make a jotting on Mrs Rideout's maternal goodness as if for subsequent scrutiny. Mrs Rideout affirmed that Lucy had always been a good daughter. But everybody knew what girls were nowadays; there was no controlling them; out they would go when they pleased. Hudspith could have written down all this out of his head; he was able to spare considerable attention for a further study of the lost girl's possessions.

He saw the cheap dance slippers; he saw on a nail the pathetic wisp of white rabbit that was some sort of cape. He saw the array of photographs pinned to the wall by the bed: the usual pictures, he wearily thought, cut from the usual cinema magazines. The heroes often wore bathing-trunks now; lying under beach-umbrellas, they leered up at girls who sat with parted lips, entranced. Or in resplendent tails and hair-grease they led their ladies through exotic restaurants while little tables crowded with ambassadors and duchesses made a modest background to the scene. Or momentarily disguised as common mortals they perched, millionaire play-boys though they were, on little stools in small-town drug-stores and scooped at sundaes nose to nose with the beloved. Hudspith ground his teeth as he looked at them. Not the celebrated William Prynne, who wrote some eight hundred thousand words on the theme that stage-plays are the very pomps of the devil, could have felt more ill disposed to this fantasy-world than did Superintendent Hudspith.

It was a gentleman who had lived in the house, Mrs Rideout thought. A foreigner, she thought. And for some time she had known Lucy was carrying on. Lucy had taken to coming home later than she should. Whereupon she – Mrs Rideout – had said – and Mrs Toomer would witness that she had said . . .

Hudspith's pencil still traversed the paper. But his glance strayed now to the other walls. Over the fireplace hung Bubbles; that would be Mrs Rideout's fancy. Midway between this and Lucy's end of the room was one of those colour prints in which faintly draped figures are disposed pensively on marble terraces in a blaze of noon-tide light; behind them is a very blue lake, behind that very white mountains, with behind these again a sunset or sunrise thrown in for extra effect. Hudspith had failed to cultivate the plastic arts; nevertheless he recognized that this abomination and the magazine photographs belonged to one world. His glance ran on – and before another and smaller reproduction paused, perplexed. Momentarily disregarding Mrs Rideout's monologue, he walked over to it. A line of print on the mount told him that this aloof and lovely person had been painted by a certain Piero della Francesca. He shook his head, obscurely disturbed.

But Lucy had just gone on going out. In all that black-out too. And then the night before last she had gone out and not come back again. But she had left a note in the cocoa-jug saying . . .

Saying, thought Hudspith, that she was going to be happy and not to worry. He walked over to Lucy's bed, where stood a little book-case. Three rows of books, all nearly new. He bent down. *Sesame and Lilies*, *The Decline and Fall of the Roman Empire*, *After London*, *Cowper's Letters*, *The advancement of Learning*, *Madam Bovary*. . . . Hudspith frowned and looked at the next shelf. *Swiss Family Robinson*, *Little Women*, *Mopsie in the Fifth*, *Mopsie Captain of the School*, *Doctor Dolittle's Voyages*. . . The books were equally new; Mopsie's final adventures had been published in the present year. Hudspith turned round, aware that Mrs Rideout had said something out of the ordinary. 'Cocoa-jug?' he said. 'Are you sure it wasn't the teapot?'

Mrs Rideout was emphatic; so was Mrs Toomer, who had been present at the discovery.

'It's nearly always the teapot,' Hudspith paused, suspicious and alert. 'When do you drink cocoa, marm?'

In the Rideout *ménage* cocoa was drunk only at night. So that was it: not the breakfast teapot but the evening cocoa-jug – in other words a good twenty-four hours' start. The little piece of elementary contrivance – surprising though this may seem – placed Lucy Rideout at once among the intellectual *élite* of Hudspith's young women. And yet he had been given to understand –

The third shelf was almost on the ground; Hudspith stooped to examine it and his brow darkened. He knew *those* books, and it had not been his fault if the Home Secretary did not know them too. His eye went doubtfully back to the picture by the man Piero della Francesca, and it was a moment before he was aware that Mrs Rideout had stopped talking and that now the person called Mrs Fiddock held the stage.

With an evident sense of drama Mrs Fiddock had set down her cup. 'I seen them and I 'eard them!' she said.

It was a sensation. Mrs Fiddock looked slowly round, enjoying her triumph. Then slowly she wagged a finger at the amorphously vehement Mrs Rideout.

'I seen and I 'eard what it's my duty to diwulge in the presence of this 'igh officer of the police.'

'That's right,' said Mrs Toomer and Mrs Thorr.

And Mrs Rideout nodded her own vaster acquiescence. 'That's right,' she said.

3

Hudspith licked his pencil and congratulated himself on the irregularity of his own methods. It was contrary to correct procedure to slip in on Mrs Rideout's tea-party in this way, but what signifies a little latitude when it is Leviathan himself that one pursues? Hudspith took a final look at the very bad books on Lucy Rideouts lowest shelf and turned expectantly to Mrs Fiddock. 'Quite right, marm,' he said. 'You must out with anything you know about this poor girl.'

Mrs Rideout began to sob – energetically and very rapidly, as if bent on repairing an oversight which had only just occurred to her. Mrs Toomer, having looked round vainly for a handkerchief, handed a tea-towel. Mrs Thorr said 'There, there!' and 'There then!' and 'There now!' to everybody in turn. The tempo of Mrs Rideout's grief changed; she was really weeping; presently the discovery of this so surprised her that she fell abruptly silent. The room waited expectantly.

'This,' announced Mrs Fiddock, 'is a very painful occasion for me.'

'There now!' said Mrs Thorr.

'And I hope that none here will say I did anything I didn't ought. For I only done my duty.' Mrs Fiddock paused. 'As a citizen.' She paused again to admire this linguistic triumph.'It was in the lounge of the Crown.'

'The lounge!' said Mrs Thorr and Mrs Toomer and Mrs Rideout.

'It was more than a week back,' pursued Mrs Fiddock with dignity, 'that I had occasion to enter the bottle and jug. Now as everyone knows – or everyone except this gentleman here – there's an 'atch in the bottle and jug that gives on the private. And the private has a door into the lounge. And sometimes you sees right through.'

There was an interruption while the ladies went into committee to verify these topographical statements. Depraved old wretches, though Hudspith. Liquor, he thought. Come out on a case like this and always there's liquor round the corner. But he nodded with a large and false approval at Mrs Fiddock. 'Very observant, missus,' he said; 'very observant indeed.'

Mrs Fiddock gave a gratified bow. 'And there, Mrs Rideout, was your Lucy with that flashy furrein-looking man that was in number nine. Bold as brass, he was, and I didn't think there was any good in it.' She hesitated, momentarily confused. 'It seemed to me I had a duty to do.'

'I don't remember,' said Mrs Rideout suspiciously, 'as how you ever said anything about it afterwards.'

'I had my duty to do,' reiterated Mrs Fiddock more firmly. 'I walked round to the lounge, dispoged myself behind the haspidistra and ordered a glass of port.'

'There then!' said Mrs. Thorr. Her admiration might have been directed either to the shameless curiosity of Mrs Fiddock or to the financial solidity and social confidence which this proceeding revealed.

'And I 'eard what I 'eard. "Did you ever 'ear," 'e says, "of the isle of Capri? I got an island just like that." That's what I 'eard 'im say.'

Mrs Toomer raised her hands, instantly credulous. 'Lord!' she said; 'fancy having an island all your own.'

'"Where is it?" says your Lucy – which was the first words

I 'eard 'er say. "Where is it?" "It's difficult to describe," 'e says. "But you go to South America first."'

Hudspith's pencil snapped at the point. Rage filled him – against these awful women, against the imbecile Lucy, against the unspeakably threadbare simplicity of this professional seducer's patter. 'Mrs Fiddock,' he said benevolently, 'this is very valuable information.'

'And then neither of them said anythink, and I thought I'd best take a peep round the haspidistra. 'E was smiling at her confident like. And your Lucy she didn't say nothink. She just 'itched her skirt another hinch above the knee.'

Hudspith compressed his lips. Mrs Toomer made a shocked noise on the front of her palate. Mrs Rideout again sobbed.

'It was just then that the young fellow brought the port. "Well, ma," 'e says, "picked a winner? And shall I bring the cigars?" "Young man," I says, "I know my place, and 'opes that others does the same." So 'e went away and I listens again.' Mrs Fiddock paused. 'But what I 'eard this time,' she said dramatically, 'I can scarcely bring myself to let pass these 'ere lips.'

Mrs Thorr leant forward on her chair; the half-obliterated features of Mrs Toomer sharpened themselves in expectation; the tea-towel in Mrs Rideout's grasp suspended itself in air.

''E leaned back and lit a cigarette. And then 'e said what made my very blood run cold. "I could do with two or three of you," 'e said, –"and that's what I'm going to get!" And then 'e gave an 'orrid laugh, like 'e might give to a bit of fun that was all his own.'

A moment's profound silence greeted this appalling revelation. 'A slaver – that's what he is,' said Mrs Toomer.

'Or a regular Bluebeard,' said Mrs Thorr.

Mrs Fiddock, her imagination fired by the literary success she had achieved, leant forward. 'Do you think,' she asked hoarsely, 'he drowns them in a barf?'

Maternal solicitude is an awful power. Mrs Rideout, who had risen to her feet in agitation, took two sideways and three backward steps – and was thus able to fall upon her bed in a fit. Mrs Rideout roared; Mrs Thorr and Mrs Fiddock snivelled; Mrs Toomer gently beat her breast and uttered wheezy sighs.

It is a dreadful thing to die – or even to conduct police investigations – 'mid women howling. The hardy Hudspith looked about him with some idea of throwing water or opening a window. What his eye immediately fell on was the dispassionate gaze of the Piero della Francesca – whence it travelled involuntarily to *Sesame and Lilies* and the historical labours of Edward Gibbon. Momentarily he felt like a man who sinks through deep waters. Then he stood up. 'Be quiet!' he shouted.

Mrs Rideout stopped roaring and snivelled. Whereupon Mrs Fiddock and Mrs Thorr, as if indignant at this trespass, took breath and yelled. Mrs Toomer continued her asthmatic exhibition undeterred. Hudspith banged the table with an open palm. 'Silence!' he bellowed. 'Silence in the name of the law!'

There was instant quiet, as if the women were dispossessed of devils by the incantation. And Hudspith, learned in demonology went sternly on: 'Anything that any of you says may be taken down and used as evidence in such proceedings as the magistrate may direct. We will now proceed to inquiries on the character and habits of the missing girl.'

The crisis was over. Even Mrs Toomer ceased knocking her breast. Instead, she took the lid from the teapot and peered hopefully inside.

Lucy Rideout was nineteen; so much could be gathered from her mother – who appeared to feel, however, that this represented her fair share of such information as the assembled party might provide. On her daughter's interests and accomplishments she was vague; of her friends she knew little; among a number of photographs in a drawer she found one which, after some consultation with her friends, she was persuaded to assert was Lucy. Often, thought Hudspith, our claim upon the awareness of even close relations is surprisingly marginal and precarious. Nevertheless there was something almost pathological in this woman's attitude to her daughter; it was almost as if the child had been an intellectual problem which Mrs Rideout had long since found it simplest to give up. He scrutinized the photograph with a professional eye. Lucy Rideout was not pretty. Nor, as far as he could discern, did she possess any of the specific types of plainness which have here and there a peculiar appeal. Why, then, Lucy? Presumably because she was half-witted and so particularly easy to spirit away. Only Hudspith thought that if this indifferent photograph revealed anything at all it was the appearance of considerable intelligence. And this by no means accorded with his brief. He turned to Mrs Rideout. "I understand,' he said cautiously, 'that your daughter was never very bright at her books?'

'That's right,' said Mrs Rideout readily.

'In fact, the truth is that she isn't quite –'

'Her books?' interrupted Mrs Toomer. 'Why, she was always at her books, poor dear.'

'That's right,' said Mrs Rideout. 'So she was.'

Mrs Toomer nodded towards the bookshelf. 'See for yourself, mister. She must have bought all them since the Rideouts was blitzed. Always reading, is Lucy. But bad at her books, as you sez.'

Hudspith frowned. 'But if she was always reading –'

'That's why she was bad at her books,' Mrs Toomer looked curiously at Hudspith, as if doubting the perspicacity of one to whom this elementary point could be obscure. 'Always reading, she was. It fairly drove her teachers wild.'

'That was it,' said Mrs Rideout. She nodded, vague but decided. Suddenly she became much more emphatic. 'That and her forgetfulness. No one but me can ever know how forgetful that girl is.'

'*Was*, more likely,' said Mrs Fiddock gloomily.

'That's right,' said Mrs Rideout. 'Sometimes she wouldn't as much as know if she'd put her dinner inside her. Something chronic, Lucy's memory.'

'It comes of reading,' suggested Mrs Thorr. 'Just common reading, let alone the sort of reading your Lucy did,' She turned to Hudspith. 'Lord Bacon and Giboon,' she enumerated, awed. 'And Shakespeare and the German Gouty.'

'That's right,' chimed in Mrs Toomer. 'And fairy-stories, too, and animals what talk. Half a week's wages, Lucy would give, if she saw a nice big book with coloured pictures in a window.'

And the odd thing, thought Hudspith, is that the bookshelves bear out this fantastic confusion of testimonies. He addressed himself resolutely to Lucy's mother, 'My information is that your daughter is weak in the head. Not what they call mentally deficient, exactly – but getting on that way. Is that right?'

'Quite right,' said Mrs Toomer before Mrs Rideout could reply. 'Not mental –'

'Mentals,' interrupted Mrs Thorr, 'goes to school in a car. Lucy never did that, though her father tried for it when he was alive, poor man.'

'That's right,' said Mrs Rideout.

'Not mental,' resumed Mrs Toomer. 'Just a bit cracked like. What you might call terrible serious-minded.'

'That's right,' said Mrs Rideout and Mrs Fiddock and Mrs Thorr. It was their first piece of chorus work for some time.

'Fair childish,' said Mrs Fiddock, speaking as if offering the next logical step in a well-ordered theme. 'Creepy, it was at times. Shy and innocent and ignorant like.'

Hudspith tried something else. 'Your daughter went out to dances – that sort of thing?'

'That she did,' said Mrs Rideout. 'And that flighty she'd get that there was no holding her.'

The lips of Mrs Toomer, Mrs Thorr and Mrs Fiddock parted in affirmative incantation. Hudspith plunged again. 'What other interests had she?'

'Plays,' said Mrs Rideout.

'Ah – she went to the theatre?'

Mrs Rideout shook her head violently, apparently intimating that there were degrees of eccentricity of which even her Lucy must be acquitted. 'She made 'em.'

'Made them?'

'In bed at night. Since we came here it's fair driven me crazy. Whisper, whisper, whisper.'

'What sort of plays?'

Mrs Rideout considered. 'Diatribes,' she said. 'Diatribes and sometimes another as well.'

'You mean plays sometimes with two people and sometimes with three? What sort of people.'

'They got very queer names.' Mrs Rideout shifted uneasily on her chair, as if obliged to contemplate something she had long felt it more comfortable to ignore. 'Poppet is one.'

'Yes?'

'And Real Lucy and Sick Lucy is the others. Sick Lucy doesn't seem to know much. They're always telling her what happened before.'

Superintendent Hudspith was not a learned man. But he had read the appropriate textbooks in a number of odd fields. And now – almost as if dazzled by the great light that had come upon him – he gazed at Mrs Rideout and her friends with an unseeing eye. 'Well,' he said, 'I'll be damned!'

'That's right,' said Mrs Toomer.

Hudspith's inquiries were prolonged and it was dusk as he turned east along Victoria Street. Anyone glancing at him as he passed the Army and Navy Stores would have suspected first drink and then somnambulism – for he walked as in a trance. This beat the band; it was the very mark and acme of the evil with which he had to cope. He believed himself well-read in all the quaintness and curiosity of vice; his files were a veritable museum of *recherché* sins; he was the familiar of devils more grotesquely caparisoned than any that ever appeared to St Anthony. But the ingenuity of this – of this vest-pocket promiscuity or compendious polygamy – he had not met the like of before. . . . So he walked down Victoria Street growling, ready positively to bark – and conceivably up the wrong tree.

Sesame and Lilies and the *Swiss Family Robinson* and the books on the bottom shelf. *After London* (what would that be? – wondered Hudspith, staring fixedly and vacantly at Westminster Abbey) and *Cowper's Letters* and *Mopsie in the Fifth*. . . . And suddenly the sheer technical difficulty of what the adversary had achieved revealed itself and forced from him a sort of reluctant admiration. Did you ever hear of the isle of Capri? It was clear now that this could not have been the whole story by a long way. But then perhaps it had been a matter of simple force in the end; despite the note in the cocoa-jug, perhaps the girl had been kidnapped after all.

Hudspith looked up at Big Ben and took no comfort from still being able to read the time on it. London slid past him: high up, the last glitter of day; round him, news-boys and sand-bags, cavities and crowds; far below, the purposive hurrying of the underground and the odd pleasing smell that hangs round the stations as you pass. People glanced up at the sky, Hudspith stared through it, scanning some ultimate battle-ground of good and evil to which the heaven of heavens is but a veil.

Fetichists. Men who insist on knock-kneed women, on bow-legged women, on one-eyed women . . and now this. Hudspith climbed flight upon flight of stairs rapidly, in a sudden cold sweat. He marched along a corridor – was hailed through an open door 'Hurrying?' said a harassed voice. 'After another of the vanishing ladies?'

Hudspith snapped an affirmative reply and strode on. But the harassed voice stopped him. 'Well that's nothing. They've put me on a vanishing house.'

'A vanishing house?' Hudspith turned reluctantly round. 'What the deuce do you mean?'

'I mean that somebody's pinched a house – a whole blasted house!' The harassed voice rose to a note of extreme exaspera-tion. 'And a thoroughly crazy house at that.'

4

The best connexion was by Leeds. But Appleby, because the thing had been put to him as a holiday, went by York. The wait there was over an hour, and that would be time for a stroll up to the Minster. Also, he remembered a tea-shop with remarkable muffins; and although muffins are largely a matter of butter, he hoped for the best. With this judicious balance of spiritual and material satisfactions in mind he left the station.

The city walls were still there. Naturally so – but nowadays one went about in that frame of mind. The city walls were there, and in places as fresh as if they still expected culverins and demi-cannon to be brought against them hourly. Cromwell, thought Appleby vaguely as he crossed the Ouse. Extraordin-arily difficult really to imagine the siege of an English town. But then how oddly things lie in the womb of time: any amount of small change from Roman legionaries' pockets was dug up when they started making the railway station. A great massacre of Jews, thought Appleby as he passed the reticent façade of the Yorkshire Club. They had just time to kill their own wives and children and then the mob were on top of them. In England that was eight hundred years ago. He glanced down Coney Street. There was little traffic at this hour; shopkeepers, who had never read manuals on scientific salesmanship, stood at their doors, unashamedly at leisure; it was all very tranquil, very secure. Laurence Sterne, Appleby thought. And there is something in walking at random about a city, he thought, that makes one's mind turn thus idly over and over, like Leopold Bloom's.

On the left, a huddle of half-heartedly ecclesiastical buildings. On the right, the unbeautiful but beneficent York City Dispensary. And in front, the Minster. The poet Shelley had called it a monstrous and tasteless relic of barbarism. But then Shelley's was an appallingly rational and scientific mind. And perhaps they had been telling him about the Jews. . . . Appleby climbed the steps.

When he came out he stood for a moment blinking in the sunshine. A baker's cart rattled past; it might have reminded him of the muffins; instead, it merely recalled Daffodil and the dubious investigation in prospect. Why, he asked himself, should you prefer a quiet cab-horse to Captain Somebody's whopping expensive brute? Well, you hired a cab and you went to a party and you told the man to wait. Then you stole your hostess's diamonds, deftly wrapped them in a wisp of hay and pitched them through the drawing-room window at the creature's head. The creature at once devoured the unexpected luncheon, thus unwittingly becoming your accomplice in crime. It only remained –

Appleby shook his head at this unpolicemanlike fantasy, and found that he had wandered into that narrow and winding street which has the most interesting shops. This bookshop, for instance: *A Good Warm Watch Coat* – that was Laurence Sterne again; Francis Drake's *Eboracum* of 1736 – one would have to be fairly prosperous to buy that. And that antique shop – he crossed the road. Such places were not quite what they were in the great days of those wandering scholars, the fabulous horn-rimmed Americans of the twenties. Perhaps they will be back again in the fifties, Appleby thought; and paused to glance in. Warming-pans, coffin stools, china dogs. He walked on, passing a second shop of the same sort: china dogs, warming-pans, coffin stools. The pomps of death: dissolution had once been a comfortably solid affair. Now it was papier-mâché coffins and zip-fastening shrouds. He knew a psychiatrist who, in the early months of war, had been required to treat nervous children in a hall stacked with these conveniences. ... Another shop – and this time Appleby stared. The same sort of wares were exposed for sale. But suspended in the centre of them was something different. It was an ancient broom – the kind that is no more than a bundle of twigs or faggots bound to a handle.

Undoubtedly it was a witch's broom. And this sudden coming upon such an object in a shop window was like the beginning of a deftly told tale of the supernatural. Appleby, whose mind was perhaps no less rational than Shelley's, frowned disapprovingly. And as he frowned he became aware of somebody looking at him.

It was a shrunken and dusty man; he stood at the shop door so vacantly and patiently that he might have been something put out to purify in the sun. But he was looking at Appleby with a slowly gathering alertness, rather suggestive of a rusty machine beginning to turn. 'Good afternoon,' he said – and added mildly: 'Are you a tourist?'

The word has taken to itself a sinister quality: if you are a tourist you may well be suspected of carrying a fountain-pen filled with tear gas or a short-wave receiver concealed in your hat. And the vast annoyance of Daffodil and Bodfish and Lady Caroline lay heavily on Appleby's mind. 'No,' he said severely; 'I'm a policeman.' He looked gloomily at the broomstick. 'How,' he asked, 'did you come by that?'

The idle question had quite unexpected results. 'Oh dear, oh dear!' cried the dusty man in despair. 'I knew there must be something wrong!' He took a shuffling step backwards. 'I suppose you had better come in and see the cauldron too.'

Appleby opened his mouth to say that neither broom nor cauldron was any interest of his. But even as he did so professional instinct asserted itself. Never let any little odd thing go by. 'Certainly I must see the cauldron,' he said sternly. 'And anything else concerned.'

The dusty man ran an agitated hand through his hair, removed what appeared to be a cobweb from his right ear, and uttered a gulping sound suggestive of mingled submission and distraction. 'You see,' he said, 'one has to be on the look-out for anything that will attract the eye – of a genuine sort, of course. And there was no doubt of the provenance of the articles in this case.'

'No doubt of the what?'

'The genuineness of their history, sir, as proved by the different hands they had been through. I know the family well enough. But I should have been more careful, all the same. The whole thing was queer, I freely acknowledge. Why, even the horse was queer.'

'The *what*?'

'The horse, sir. Very queer indeed was the way that horse behaved.'

Appleby took a deep breath. 'It is about that,' he said, 'that we are going to talk.'

The first few yards of assembled antiques were reasonably well groomed; behind that everything was most woefully weighted with gathered dust. The stock-in-trade was miscellaneous, congested and arranged with a fantasy which must have been of the genuine unconscious kind. An Indian idol sat up in a four-poster bed, stretching out a multiplicity of hands as if demanding early morning tea; a row of stags' heads had Georgian coffee-pots and spoon-warmers depending from the antlers; through the half-open door of a grandfather clock peered the articulated skeleton of an ape or baboon. Your first surrealists, thought Appleby, are necessarily those who purvey curios in a restricted space. And you can achieve similar effects by dropping a bomb on a well-ordered museum. Perhaps some psychic and infantile bomb is responsible for the pictures of Miro and Dali. Perhaps – He remembered that he had come in here to listen to a confession. 'Things look rather quiet,' he said in an accusing voice.

'They *are* quiet,' said the dusty man. 'Really very quiet indeed,' he added with anxious candour.

'Still, you have sold a couple of china dogs.' On a very dusty table Appleby had noticed two oval islands such as the posteriors of these creatures would cover.

'We've been watched!' The dusty man's voice had risen to absolute despair. 'Shadowed!' He slumped down on a stool beside the grandfather clock; the door slid to; inside the bones rattled dryly, as if the whole were a nightmarish memorial of mortality and time. 'After thirty years of respectable trading, much of it with the nobility and gentry of the county – to say nothing of the Dean and Chapter. It's hard, sir; really hard.'

'No doubt.'

'And the Metcalfes are well known to be most respectable folk.'

'Ah.'

The dusty man rose heavily, and from inside the clock the bones rattled again like a sepulchral æolian harp. 'Of course there is the old story about them. I'm a Haworth man myself and I've known it since a boy. I'm far from denying the queer sort of celebrity they've enjoyed.'

'Wouldn't you say,' asked Appleby gravely, 'that as Haworth celebrities the Metcalfes have been rather outshone by the Brontës?'

'The Brontës! Let me tell you, sir, that the Metcalfes were celebrated through the whole Riding when the Brontës were still hoeing potatoes in Ireland. Why, it was in 1772 that Hannah Metcalfe barely escaped being boiled in her own cauldron. And that was just fifty years after the last recorded execution for witchcraft in these islands. As for the cauldron, it's just behind you. And now I ask you: do you blame me for giving five pounds for the lot? As a Haworth man, mark you, and not caring to see the antiquities of the district disappearing in a caravan.'

Appleby turned round and examined the cauldron. It was a massive iron affair and would doubtless have accommodated Hannah Metcalfe comfortably; certainly Turks' noses, lizards' legs and similar prescriptive ingredients would have made but an inconsiderable bubble and boil in the depths of it. Appleby peered at it more closely. 'It looks to me,' he said unkindly, 'as if it had been cast in Birmingham about fifty years ago.'

'Oh dear, oh dear!' The dusty man was even more distressed than before. 'No doubt there has been a certain element of showmanship involved. It's common enough in such places, after all. The bed in which the great man was born: that sort of thing. And if you have a celebrated witch in the family, and people regularly paying sixpence to see her kitchen, you naturally do a little fitting up from time to time. Not but what I freely admit I ought to have had nothing to do with it. Hannah Metcalfe – *this* Hannah Metcalfe – is a bit strange by all accounts. She looked strange in the caravan. What with her and the horse –'

'We must come to that. Now, I wonder' – and Appleby laid a soothing hand on the dusty man's arm – 'if you would tell me the whole story? I'm not at all inclined to think you acted improperly in any way. But the whole story would be a great help – in something, you know, quite unconnected with the broom and cauldron.'

The dusty man looked both relieved and perplexed. 'Well, it must have been a week ago last Thurdsay, and I was just taking down the shutters when I saw this caravan coming down the street. And that, you know, was rather surprising in itself. For we're a bit out of the way, and anything that turns down here is usually looking for something in particular. But from what followed in this case it didn't seem to be like that.'

'I see. But if the caravan was trying to slip through York in an unobtrusive way – might that account for it?'

'I dare say it might, sir. Anyway, the thing was going past at a quiet walk and there were two men in front and suddenly one of them calls out. "I've got an idea," he said. "Look at that shop." "Which shop?" says the other, and the first man replies, "There: number thirty-nine" – which of course is myself. And it was then that the horse – a quiet-looking horse enough – began to behave queer. It stopped – and the fellow hadn't pulled it up that I could see – and took to nodding its head like an idol. It went on nodding and the two men seemed to be having an argument. Then one of them shouted at me. "Hi," he said, "you there; here's something ought to interest you." It wasn't very polite, but then in these days' – the dusty man shook his head mournfully – 'it's something to be taken any notice of at all. So I crossed the street. "Look here," says the fellow, "you'll have heard of Hannah Metcalfe's cottage? Well, most of it's here, and for sale." And at that he reached behind him and outed with the broom. "We've got Hannah herself, for that matter," he said, "only she's already booked." "She died a hundred and fifty years ago," I said – for I thought it was some silly sort of joke. And at that there was a wildish kind of laugh from inside, and the young woman stuck her head out. It gave me quite a turn. And of course it was Hannah Metcalfe all right –the young one. "Good morning," she said. And if I remember aright, sir, it was just then that the horse stopped nodding – sudden-like. I don't mind saying that I was beginning to find it a bit strange.'

'No doubt.' Appleby was finding it a little odd himself. 'About this witch's cottage business – what are the facts on that? I gather the old Hannah Metcalfe was a celebrated witch?'

'Just so, sir. And her descendants have always lived there and made a bit out of the old story – though respectable folk enough, as I said. Of course there's the story that the witch-craft or whatever it is has been more or less hereditary, crop-ing up from time to time. It's wonderful what people will be-lieve.' And the dusty man looked round rather nervously at the cauldron.

Appleby eyed him curiously. 'Yes,' he agreed; 'it is wonder-ful. And this younger Hannah had that sort of reputation too?'

'Yes, sir – among the uneducated, of course. And I'm told she believed it herself. You see, she's the last of the Metcalfes, and has been living alone in the cottage for years, showing the cauldron and all the rest of it. Such surroundings, you'll agree, might well put uncanny ideas in a girl's head. Anyway, here she was in this caravan, sticking her head out and laughing, while these two fellows argued about I couldn't quite gather what.'

'Ah – that's a pity.'

'Well, sir, roughly it seemed like this. They'd had orders to collect the young woman and seemingly they'd collected a good many of her effects, so to speak, as well. But now they'd

35

somehow found out that these weren't wanted, and when one of them saw an antique shop it had occurred to him to turn a penny by doing a deal. The other seemed to be suggesting that this would lead to trouble – but now young Hannah put in a word. "That's all right," she said. "You turn all that stuff into beer for all I care. I'm off to something different." "There you are," says the fellow who was trying to do the deal. "All fair and square, as you see. And you can have the lot for five pounds." "All right," says the other fellow, nodding approval. And, do you know, sir, the horse seemed to approve too, for it began stamping on the ground with one of its forefeet – just as if it were giving a round of applause.'

'It sounds,' said Appleby seriously, 'as if the horse was bewitched.'

'Very good, sir – very good indeed.' The dusty man laughed with considerable uneasiness. 'And that's the whole story. This Miss Metcalfe might be behaving a bit strange, but she seemed nowise out of her wits and I knew her to be the owner of the goods. So it ended with my giving five pounds for the broom and the cauldron and two or three other things you can inspect. If the Metcalfe cottage was being broken up there seemed no harm in being in on the dispersal.'

'None at all.' Appleby was staring thoughtfully at a table weighed down with elephants' tusks, snuff-boxes and Dresden shepherdesses. 'But tell me: did you have any further talk with Miss Metcalfe herself?'

'No – or nothing with any sense to it. After the things had been brought out I did try to pass a conversational remark. "So you're off to see the world?" I said – something like that. And she looked at me mockingly, as you might say. "That's just it," she said. "Did you ever hear of the isle of Capri?" And with that she disappeared inside the caravan and I saw no more of her.'

Appleby frowned. 'The isle of Capri? It seems a far cry from Haworth. And not too easy to get to in these days.'

'I think, sir, she might be speaking in what you would call a metaphorical way.'

'Very probably.' Appleby glanced at his watch and saw that he would have to hurry for his train. He did not want to miss it; Bodfish, Daffodil, and even the Assistant-Commissioner's sister had taken on a much more beguiling colour in the past half-hour. 'It is possible that you will hear more of this.' He looked at the dusty man and remembered how outrageously he had intruded upon his little mystery. 'And meanwhile I wonder if you could sell me a – a teapot?'

But his choice was abstracted. The odd matter of Miss Hannah Metcalfe had pretty substantial possession of his mind.

5

The telephone wires rose and fell, and beyond them the dales swept past, fluid and subtly circling. It was on the white ribbons of road and lane that Appleby kept his eye – expecting always to see, symbolically receding, a caravan and a temperamental horse. There was little of reason in the expectation. But then neither had there been reason in what happened in York. Policemen rarely make long and expensive journeys in search of unimportant quadrupeds. They do not commonly come upon traces of their quarry in wholly unexpected places and in a wholly fortuitous way. And Sir Robert Peel himself still slumbered in the womb of time long after witchcraft had ceased to be matter of their serious concern.

The witches have departed, leaving no addresses; the last of them is now somewhere diminishing into distance, headed for the fields of amaranth and asphodel – and with Bodfish's Daffodil as an appropriate guide. Hannah Metcalfe has gone; down these receding vistas she has grown smaller and smaller, as did the Good Folk before her.

And so much for the fantasy of the thing. What of its sober reason? One departs from one place because one designs – or because somebody else designs – that one should arrive in another. The witches, then, are arriving – at addresses which are yet to seek. And equally Daffodil is arriving, and the problem is to find out where. For behind the abductions, thought Appleby, there was enterprise, enterprise as well as – perhaps rather than – mere caprice. And efficiency. If the removal of Captain Somebody's brute had been a piece of bungling, at least the error had been repaired with confidence and speed. And if you want to smuggle an undistinguished horse across country it is not a bad idea to clap it within the shafts of a caravan. Incidentally, you will need all the ideas you can think up. For England today is a country in which even slightly mysterious manoeuvres are singularly difficult to perform. At the top of that little church tower on the hill is the squire or the pub-keeper or the blacksmith, his imagination keyed up to suspect the ingenuities of enemy action in anything a bit out of the way. As far as interfering with Lady Caroline's carriage-exercise is concerned, or in point of persuading Yorkshire maidens that they are bound for the isle of Capri, the times could scarcely be more thoroughly out of joint. And so if the witches and the half-witted horses are arriving *now* there is likely to be some particular premium about their doing so. . . . Appleby was groping round this obscure conception when the train ran into Harrogate.

There is a pleasing element of the unknown in the approach to big hotels. They may contain an exiled court, the ghostly counterpart of a government department, a great London school, or even a thousand or so people busy making things. But Appleby found only what such an establishment normally holds out, and presently he was wandering across the Stray, somewhat at a loss. He must present himself to the local police and tactfully explain that he was the consequence of humouring earls' daughters who inappropriately demanded the services of Scotland Yard. After that he was committed to visiting this exigent lady herself, and after that again would come the tiresome business of duplicating inquiries which had doubtless already been made in a thoroughly efficient way. Finally, he could not leave Harrogate without paying a duty-visit to his aunt, a person of pronounced character and intimidating early associations.

But this was his mission only in its original or diplomatic aspect. Unless – as was, after all, likely enough – the horse of Miss Metcalfe's caravan was distinct from the horse of Bodfish's open landau – unless this was so the case had taken to

itself a certain body, a marked beguilement, in a wholly unexpected direction. Meditating this, Appleby decided to post-
pone the business of introductions until he had sought enlighten-
ment on this prior point. So he consulted a notebook and made
his way to the livery stables from which Daffodil had been
stolen.

The stables belonged – with the sort of muted absurdity which
went with this whole business, Appleby felt – to a Mr Gee; and
Mr Gee, an elderly man of cheerful appearance, was discovered
in the middle of a yard, contemplating a sleepy dog with an air
of the greatest benevolence.

'A nice dog,' Appleby said.

Still benevolent, Mr Gee swung round. 'Dish-faced,' he said
in a voice of unfathomable gloom.

'Ah,' said Appleby, rather at a loss.

'And undershot,' Mr Gee preserved his highly deceptive
appearance. 'Pig-jawed, in fact.'

'Well, yes – I suppose he is, a little.'

'She.'

'Ah.'

'Cow-hocked. No feather. Apple-headed. Pily.'

'Pily? I suppose she is. But still –'

'Pily is the only good thing about her. Apple-headed. No
feather. Cow-headed. Pig-jawed. What do you think of
the stifles?'

'I'm afraid,' Appleby said modestly, 'I don't know anything
about dogs.'

'I'm afraid you don't,' said Mr Gee gloomily. He continued
to radiate the appearance of good cheer.

'At the moment, as a matter of fact, I'm more interested in
horses.'

'You don't look as if you knew much about them either.
Taxis I should say was more your line.' Mr Gee, maintaining
his air of mild euphoria, began to move away.

'And one horse in particular. I've come about Daffodil.'

'Gawd!' said Mr Gee, and quickened his step.

'Did they try to buy Daffodil first?'

Mr Gee stopped. 'You mayn't know a poodle from a chow,'
he said. 'But you're a sensible man. It took the others half an

hour to think of that one. And of course they did. What would be the sense of all that stour to steal a horse you knew wouldn't fetch above a ten-pound note? They offered me thirty.'

'And you refused?'

'Of course I refused. Do you think I want to be taken up? It's contrary to the provisions of the Act.'

Appleby, if he knew little about horses, had necessarily to know much about the law. And this particular piece of legislative wisdom was new to him. 'You supposed it was illegal? I hardly think –'

'It was contrary to the provisions of the Act.' Mr Gee was obstinate. 'Twenty pounds for nout is certain sure to be contrary to the provisions of the Act.' He spoke as if from some depth of mournful experience. 'I'd have been taken up. What else is the likes of you paid to go about after? Taking people up over the Act.' Mr Gee's beaming eye looked very shrewdly at Appleby. 'Police everywhere,' he said. 'Gawd!'

Appleby, feeling the shoe-leather thicken under his feet and a shadowy metropolitan helmet hover on his brow, concluded that Mr Gee was a man to reckon with; he contrived to combine a mild mania with an accurate appraisal of men. 'Well, Mr Gee, we'll say you felt the thing to be irregular and would have nothing to do with it. And the result was that the horse disappeared. I don't want to know how or when, for I've no doubt at all that has been gone over already. But I want you to tell me something about the horse itself.'

'About Daffodil?' Mr Gee's cheerful face clouded, so that it was logical to suppose he was about to attempt a stroke of humour. 'Well, I always suspected rareying with Daffodil – though, mind you; it may have been galvayning all the same.' And Mr. Gee stooped down and fondled the ear of the dish-faced dog.

Appleby sat down placidly on a bench. 'My dear sir, I quite realize that an erudite hippologist like yourself –'

''Ere,' said Mr Gee, 'civil is civil, I'll have you know. And none of that language in my yard.'

'Very well, I'll say nothing at all.' Appleby took out a pipe. 'But I'm staying here until you give me a reasonable account of that horse.'

Mr Gee looked deliberately about him, plainly searching for a particularly ponderous shaft of wit. 'The trouble about Daffodil,' he said at length, 'was always in the carburettor. And for that matter I never cared for his overhead valves.' And at this Mr Gee laughed so suddenly and loudly that the pily dog rose and took to its heels.

'Come off it.' Appleby filled his pipe. 'A joke's a joke, Mr Gee. But business is business, after all. And I may tell you I hate the stink of petrol. I mayn't know about galvayning – but I'd take a cab every time, just the same.'

The effect of this mendacious statement was immediate. Mr Gee sat down on the bench in a most companionable way. 'I'll tell you what,' he said – and lowered his voice. 'I never half liked that horse. There were old parties that liked him and would order him regular. They thought him almost 'uman. But if there's one thing I like less than an almost 'uman dog it's an almost 'uman horse.'

'I see. By the way, how did Daffodil come to you in the first place?'

'I had him of a man.' Mr Gee spoke at once darkly and vaguely. 'It would have been at Boroughbridge fair, I reckon.'

'But you don't know anything about his previous owner?'

'I reckon I was told.' Mr Gee was gloomily silent. 'I suppose you come from London?'

'Yes.'

'And I suppose you've heard of the Cities of the Plain? Well, add all the lies was ever told in London, mister, to all the hanky-panky Sodom and Gomorrah ever knew – and that's a horse fair. So you may take it that anything I was told about Daffodil down Boroughbridge way isn't what you'd call evidence. I've bought horses, man and boy, for forty years. And I shuts my ears and opens my eyes.'

It was clear that on what the dusty man would call the provenance of Daffodil there was little to be discovered. Appleby tried another tack. 'How was he almost human? Was he particularly intelligent?'

Mr Gee shook his head emphatically. 'Nowise. I don't think I ever knew a horse more lacking in – well, in horse sense, if you follow me. And that's what I said to the police when they first came after him. "The horse was half-witted," I said, "and if he's gone I'll cut my losses." And now I say it again. For who wants a half-witted, almost human horse?'

Appleby looked in some perplexity at Daffodil's late owner. Mr Gee seemed to be suggesting the same relation between human and equine intelligence as Swift had expressed in his celebrated fable of the Yahoos. And yet Mr Gee was far from being a person of literary mind – nor did the quality of his humorous sallies suggest a taste for the finer ironies. So Appleby tried again. 'I find it difficult to picture this animal at all. Just *how* was he almost human?'

Mr Gee looked cautiously round the yard – very much, Appleby recalled, as the dusty man had looked round at the cauldron. 'He knew his numbers,' said Mr Gee briefly.

'How very strange.' Appleby found it difficult to hide his satisfaction. 'You mean that if, for instance, you happened to mention a number in Daffodil's presence he would stop and nod or paw out the sum of the digits involved?'

Mr Gee nodded. 'You've got it. "How much to Starbeck?" a fare would ask Bodfish. "Five Bob," Bodfish would say. And, sure enough, Daffodil would nod five times. Unnatural, I call it.'

'It sounds,' suggested Appleby cheerfully, 'as if Daffodil had once been a horse in a show.'

'But that's not all.' Mr Gee laid a hand on Appleby's arm. 'Now, listen,' he said. 'Nobody believes in the uncanny nowadays, do they?'

'Certainly not.' The proposition was extremely doubtful, Appleby thought; but nevertheless it was judicious to agree.

'Well, then, can you explain this? Daffodil knew the numbers you was *thinking* of – just as well as the others. Indeed, more accurate he was on them, Bodfish says. It would be like this. Bodfish would be driving someone to John's Well, say. And "I'll stick her for three bob," he'd think to himself. And then Daffodil would pull up and do his three times nod or stamp. When he was driving Daffodil, Bodfish had to keep figures out of his head, he says, Now, what do you think of that?'

Appleby thought it rather less remarkable than the first instance of Daffodil's powers. But as explaining this would require something like a psychological and physiological treatise, he thought it better to refrain. 'Mr Gee,' he parried, 'did it never occur to you that these peculiar powers made Daffodil an unusually valuable horse? Imagine the thing in a circus. Members of the audience are invited to come up, hold Daffodil by the bridle and think of a number. And then Daffodil taps it out. The trick would make any showman's fortune.'

'It so happens,' said Mr Gee with dignity, 'that I'm not a showman. But if Daffodil is valuable the way you suggest, then you know something about them in whose hands he was before. They weren't show people, or they wouldn't have let him go.'

Appleby got up. 'Mr Gee, you ought to have taken to my profession.'

'There's compliments you can return,' said Mr Gee, 'and there's compliments you can't.'

6

What they call a Parthian shot, Appleby said to himself as he made his way back to his hotel. And, as far as this evening was concerned, a *coup de grâce*: beguiling as the affair of Daffodil and the witches appeared, he had seen enough of it for that day.

It was the violet hour, and across the Stray the last bath-chairs were striving homewards. Conch-like and creeping, they choicely illustrated in their controlled diversity the beautiful social complexity of England. The coolie element was provided in the main by seedy old persons drawn from various strata of the deserving and undeserving poor; there was an admixture, however, of well-found private menials. These latter, Appleby noticed, tended to push, whereas the seedy old persons pulled. Pulling is more efficient, but its associations are quadrupedal and lowering; in pushing alone can a certain dignity and aloofness be preserved. With traction and propulsion the seedy persons and the servants laboured towards their goals: hydro-pathics and hotels, guest homes, boarding-houses, apartments, lodgings, furnished rooms. And the bath-chairs too had their hierarchies and orders; a system less of caste than of class – in which there is always the inspiring possibility of rapid rise and always the less cheerful probability of gradual decline. Here and there an enterprising person had contrived to smarten up his stock in trade; but more commonly these vehicles had come down in the world – the varnish cracked, the wicker-work prickly, the hood peeling, the horsehair and kapoc coming out in wisps. And through this scene of struggle moved the haughty aristocracy of the kind; bath-chairs, with doors and with elaborate windscreens of wood and glass, so that the occupants, dimly discerned, showed like dingy mezzotints in drear mahogany frames. The bath-chairs, spoking outwards like a mechanized column deploying, bore away from the focal baths and pump-rooms old women who clutched library novels, ivory sticks, triumphantly tracked packages of chocolate peppermint creams. And on the pavements, politely yielding place, were old men of respectable dress and tenuously maintained bank balances; these exercised dogs; prowled in quest of evening papers, of tobacco; cast ancient professional eyes at the multiform signs that even Harrogate stood to arms. England was carrying on

And Appleby was hurrying to dine. He would have an early meal and go to a cinema and see something really silly – something silly enough to make Daffodil and Hannah Metcalfe look comparatively sensible when he returned to them in the morning. Certainly no more of them tonight.

'John,' called a commanding voice from behind him, 'come here.'

He turned to face the roadway, and his heart sank at what he saw. It was – it could not be other than – an open landau. Two elderly ladies sat expansively and side by side on the principal seat. Opposite to them, and – although she had a whole side to herself– in a more contracted position, was a female figure in a mouse-coloured hat. And on the box, tightly wrapped in rugs like the young of some savage tribe, perched a fat man with a liquid, a frankly tap-room eye.

'How are you, aunt!' said Appleby. 'I was just on my way to call.'

'No doubt.' The disbelief of Appleby's aunt was unoffended

and matter of fact. 'Lady Caroline, let me introduce my nephew, John.'

Lady Caroline bowed. She was in the dilemma of those who must combine dignity with a bad cold; her nose and eyes were uncomfortably reddened and she had apparently chosen clothes to match: this gave her an alarmingly combustible look. 'Maidment will make room,' said Lady Caroline commandingly.

'Miss Maidment,' said Appleby's aunt politely, 'will you make room?'

The mouse-hatted lady contracted herself yet further into a corner and Appleby realized with dismay that he was expected to embark. The landau smelt of horse and dust and eucalyptus; it moved off with a creak.

'Miss Appleby,' said Lady Caroline, 'do not you think that Bodfish had better avoid James Street with that horse?'

'Miss Maidment,' said Appleby's aunt, 'Lady Caroline thinks that Bodfish had better avoid James Street. The horse.'

Miss Maidment twisted round on her seat. 'Bodfish,' she said severely, 'you had better avoid James Street with that horse.'

Bodfish, without uttering or turning round, put up a hand and raised his hat some inches above his head. Lady Caroline turned an appraising eye on Appleby. 'We are without confidence in the horse,' she explained. 'Particularly Miss Maidment. She had an experience with a horse. When young. Maidment – my bag.'

There was a search for Lady Caroline's bag. Miss Appleby took no part. But presently she spoke. 'My dear,' she said, 'remember how often you find it –' She broke off and looked meaningfully at Lady Caroline.

'Bodfish,' called Miss Maidment sternly, 'stop.'

The landau was brought to a halt and Lady Caroline prized some inches from her seat. The bag had undoubtedly been beneath her. She got out a handkerchief and blew. The equipage drove on. 'Mr Appleby,' said Lady Caroline sternly, 'you are from London?'

'Yes. I came down today.'

Lady Caroline blew again. 'The tubes are congested,' she said.

'Yes. But not so badly as they were.'

Lady Caroline frowned. 'Young man, do I understand that you are a physician?'

'Lady Caroline,' explained Appleby's aunt, 'refers to her chest.'

'I beg your pardon.' Appleby was quite unnerved by this mis-understanding. 'I'm a policeman. I've come about Daffodil.'

'You are the person' – Lady Caroline looked at Miss Appleby and coughed – 'you are the officer whom my brother was to send?'

'Yes, Lady Caroline.'

'Dear me. My dear' – she turned to Miss Appleby – 'I think Bodfish had better attend.'

'Miss Maidment, Lady Caroline thinks –'

'Bodfish,' said Miss Maidment threateningly, 'pray pay attention.'

Bodfish raised his hat. The quieter streets of Harrogate ambled past with the jerkiness only experienced in cabs and ill-projected films. Appleby, jolting hip to hip with the Assistant-Commissioner's sister's companion, reflected that carriage exercise was not altogether a contradiction in terms. And Lady Caroline, having again blown, leant forward and tapped Appleby on the knee with a decorously gloved hand, 'I must tell you that I have had more satisfaction from the Cruelty to Animals than from the police.'

'To the Cruelty to Animals,' said Miss Appleby, 'one subscribes.'

'No doubt. But one pays taxes for the police.' And Lady Caroline fixed her glance severely on Appleby's tie, an expensive one from the Burlington Arcade. 'We support the police.'

'In a sense,' said Appleby mildly, 'the police support your brother. So it evens out.'

Miss Maidment contrived a nervous sound in her throat. And Lady Caroline sat back abruptly. 'My dear,' she said, 'I believe your nephew has something of your own wit. But that he has your sufficient sense of decorum I will not at present venture to add. And now, what I was about to observe. The Cruelty to Animals have been most active. And they have arrived, so far, at the remarkable sum of one hundred and eighty-one pounds.'

Appleby looked perplexed. 'I'm afraid I don't understand you.'

'They have traced Daffodil through what may be described as a little Odyssey.' Lady Caroline paused, as if reconsidering the propriety of this word. 'What may be described,' she amended, 'as a veritable Chevy Chase. It appears that in the present posture of our affairs – Bodfish, are you attending?'

Bodfish raised his hat.

'It appears that in the present posture of our affairs –'

'In war-time,' said Miss Appleby inoffensively.

'Thank you, my dear. It appears that, at present, moving a horse clandestinely about the country is a matter of substantial difficulty. This has made it possible to trace Daffodil at least some little way. And much expense seems to have been involved. Conveyances were bought and abandoned as part of a carefully contrived scheme. That sort of thing. I am informed that at least a hundred and eighty-one pounds was spent in this way before Daffodil reached Bradford.' Lady Caroline looked suspiciously at Appleby. 'But this is information which the police already possess.'

'I haven't seen the local men yet; I determined to see *you* first, Lady Caroline.' Appleby, thinking this rather a happy stroke, allowed himself the ghost of a wink at his aunt. 'But I am surprised the animal was taken to Bradford. I knew for certain that he turned up later at York – which is pretty well in the opposite direction.'

'Daffodil was traced to Bradford, and from there some way on the road to Keighley.'

'Keighley?' said Miss Appleby suddenly. 'There is something rather interesting in that. John, you are no doubt aware of it.'

Appleby looked at his aunt with suspicion; there was that in her tone which recalled to him searching investigations into his historical and geographical knowledge long ago. 'I'm afraid,' he said, 'I can't think of anything particularly significant about Keighley.'

'No more there is. What is significant is that Daffodil should last be heard of going from Bradford *towards* Keighley. Because that, you know, would take him uncommonly near Haworth.'

'Haworth!' Appleby sat back so abruptly that his elbow almost dug Miss Maidment in the ribs.

'Exactly so. I am glad you see my point.' And Appleby's aunt turned to Lady Caroline. 'John is, of course, accustomed to putting two and two together. It is his profession. And when he brings his mind to bear upon our unfortunate loss – Bodfish's unfortunate loss –'

Bodfish raised his hat.

'– he at once asks himself what is *peculiar* about Daffodil. And the answer is this: that Daffodil is a *peculiar* horse. A *gifted* horse. In fact, a *queer* horse.'

'I cannot agree, dear Miss Appleby,' said Lady Caroline with dignity, 'that Daffodil is a *queer* horse. But *gifted*, certainly.'

'We will say, then, that Daffodil has unusual powers. And Daffodil disappears. Observe what John does. He will put two and two together if he can. He turns to his files – Scotland Yard, as your dear brother will have told you, is full of files – and seeks for any *context* in which this disappearance of Daffodil may be placed. In other words: have there been any similar disappearances of queer or gifted horses recently? And if not of horses, then of queer and gifted creatures of any other kind? He makes one significant discovery. Recently, and in this district, a young girl has suddenly and unaccountably disappeared from her home – we all read of it, you know, in the local papers. A gifted and decidedly queer girl. In fact, a witch.'

Lady Caroline blew. Miss Maidment made a noise as of muted alarm. Appleby merely gaped.

'And this young female of unusual powers lived near Haworth. How impressed, then, was John when he heard that Daffodil had last been seen moving that way!'

Lady Caroline frowned. 'This is most peculiar. And certainly above Bodfish's head.'

Miss Maidment turned round. 'Bodfish,' she said judicially, 'we do not require your attention longer.'

Bodfish raised his hat.

'But this,' continued Miss Appleby placidly, 'is only the first stage of John's inquiries. He has consulted his colleagues; assistants have been turning over press cuttings' – suddenly

Miss Appleby opened her bag – 'as I may say I have been doing myself.' She paused, and Appleby was momentarily aware of an infinitely ironical glance. 'John has been particularly struck by the case of Lucy Rideout, a young girl who recently disappeared – having been, as it would seem, procured for immoral purposes.'

'Maidment,' said Lady Caroline, 'such things ought not to afford embarrassment at your mature years.'

'Now, about this girl there is something very odd indeed.' Miss Appleby consulted the first of her cuttings. 'It appears, as the result of elaborate investigations carried out with great scientific skill by a Superintendent Hudspith, that Lucy Rideout represents a remarkable case of dissociation. She is not so much one person as two – or perhaps three – persons; and she must have been – um – correspondingly difficult to seduce. But seduced she was, having been led to believe, as it appears, that she was to be taken to Capri – a disagreeable resort, but one with romantic associations in the minds of the lower classes.'

Appleby was looking round-eyed at his aunt – much as Sherlock Holmes must have looked at his brother, the remote and quintessential detective. 'Capri,' he said, ' – to be sure. And did you say dissociation?'

'Yes. What is sometimes called multiple personality.'

'Dr Jekyll and Mr Hyde,' said Lady Caroline. 'Or consider Miss Maidment. Maidment, suppose yourself passionately to desire some unlawful delight.'

Miss Maidment wriggled on her seat – but not at all as if she were contriving to obey this injunction.

'And consider yourself as having, at the same time, a conscience which forbids such indulgence. You are torn between conflicting forces. You are like the souls of the dead in the old stained-glass windows; the angels are tugging at your hair and the devils at your toes. You follow me, Maidment?'

Miss Maidment made an indecisive noise; it acknowledged the theological trend of her employer's remarks by being faintly devotional in tone.

'The strain is great, and you let go. You let yourself go in the middle; and where there was one Maidment there are now two.' Lady Caroline frowned, apparently finding this a displeasing thought. 'But of course you still have only one *body*. The two personalities share it, each taking sole possession for a time. In this way the licentious and the puritanical Maidment each gets her turn, and a certain degree of nervous conflict is thus eliminated. You see, Maidment?'

Miss Maidment again made a noise; then – unexpectedly – she contrived speech. 'I don't understand it at all. It sounds to me much more like being possessed by evil spirits.'

'Lady Caroline's description of the condition is excellent,' said Miss Appleby. 'But Miss Maidment too has made a significant observation. I have no doubt, John, that you will take account of it. Plainly, it has its place – as has another item on which you are certainly informed. I mean the Bloomsbury affair.'

'Ah,' said Appleby.

'What the newspapers' – Appleby's aunt again consulted her cuttings – 'have been calling the Mystery of the Absconding House.'

'Miss Appleby,' said Lady Caroline severely, 'houses do not abscond. Dishonest servants abscond. You are confused.'

'I do not think I am, dear Lady Caroline. This house has undoubtedly *made off* – and very possibly to Capri. Moreover, it is a haunted house. A most substantial eighteenth-century house in a Bloomsbury square. Dr Johnson once investigated a ghost there. And now it has been stolen.'

'Houses may not be stolen, dear Miss Appleby. The proposition is absurd.'

'In normal times it would no doubt be so. But at present it is quite feasible to steal a house. This house was stolen in stages. One night it was intact; the next morning the roof had disappeared. In London at present such things are not, it seems, at all out of the way. The next morning much of the upper story had disappeared. And so on. People remarked upon it as an uncommonly unlucky house – it was so regularly hit. But by the time the ground floor was vanishing the thing had begun to excite speculation. There was so remarkably little rubble. Then one night the basement went, and there was nothing but a hole. Inquiries were made and there emerged the indisputable fact that the house had been stolen. It appears that during air-raids there is a good deal of noise and confusion. Buildings are falling and lorries are hurrying about and what are called demolition squads are at work. The opportunities for stealing a house are quite unusual. But it must be expensive. The theft of Daffodil becomes a small thing in comparison.'

'Daffodil,' said Lady Caroline, 'is a *horse*.'

'No doubt. But a queer horse. And Lucy Rideout is a queer girl. And this house of which I have been telling you is a queer house. And all of them have been stolen within a few days of each other.' Miss Appleby put the cuttings away and shut her bag. 'I am glad to think, John, that you have the matter in hand.'

'Yes, aunt,' said Appleby.

Part 2

Whale Roads

1

The ocean was empty and unruffled; it was like the sky but emptier – for sometimes across the sky would pass a small high cloud. The ocean was always empty. Every twenty-four hours, and with startling abruptness, the ship emerged from the long black tunnel of the night into this other and cerulean void; every twenty-four hours, without a glimmer of protesting light, she disappeared again. Just such a monotonous voyaging Appleby remembered in a scenic waterway of his youth; so long in a winding papiermâché tunnel, so long floating beneath some dome-like structure garishly lit from below.

With closed decks and sealed portholes the ship would nose through the night, a throb in the centre of her and a thud and a swish, a thud and a swish everlastingly at her side. And everlastingly by day the prow rose and fell, rose and fell across the horizon towards which she drove with an energy growing daily more mysterious in its evident transcendence of any merely human scale of effort. The prow rose and fell. And always there were two men watching, their immobile bodies thrown against a background now of sky and now of sea. They were looking for submarines. And now for long stretches of the day Hudspith was there beside them – Hudspith too watching, but with an eye that swept neither to port nor starboard, Hudspith looking straight ahead at the Lord knew what. Buenos Aires, Appleby thought, Rio de Janeiro, phoney social experiments vaguely reported from far up the Parana. Hudspith was one of those people upon whose nervous system the sea had a marked effect. Appleby would be glad to see him on dry land again. One does not want a loopy colleague when embarked upon so distinctly rummy an investigation as the present.

We have followed a Harrogate cab-horse across the equator, Appleby said to himself, and have no idea where it is leading us.

Wohin der Weg? Kein Weg! Ins Unbetretene. That was Mephistopheles, and ought to appeal to Hudspith – before whom it was clear that the Devil might appear in visible shape. . . . Appleby moved to the rail and looked down at the sea. The Whale Road, the Angles had called it. But the road was invisible; there was no road; the ship drove mysteriously towards a goal beyond the present reach of sense. And rather like that was the hue and cry after Daffodil.

Appleby thought of it chiefly as the Daffodil affair – no doubt because Hudspith so singly saw it as the affair of Hannah Metcalfe and Lucy Rideout. But actually, thought Appleby, it was the Affair of the Haunted House. In that lay the promise of future contact with a somewhat complex mind. For it was not as if the absconding house were a mere decorative flourish or grace note. Its theft must have cost incomparably more than the abductions of Hannah, Lucy and Daffodil put together. Not that it had been particularly difficult. Just expensive.

It sounded, said Appleby to himself as he paced the deck, like one of the impossible tasks imposed upon the heroes of fairy stories. Steal a large Bloomsbury house and walk out of England with it – this in time of war. But it had been war that made the stealing easy; when whole streets are vanishing, a single house is scarcely missed. And the walking out of the country with it depended on war too. What happens when an English port is blitzed? The rubble is promptly shipped to America as ballast and used there as the foundations of new docks and quays – a sober fact so fantastic that one would hesitate to put it in a magazine story. Your churches are bombed; whereupon they become the causeways across which AA guns are rolled aboard your waiting freighters. It is very odd; and makes it just possible for an ingenious person – or organization, surely – to make off with an edifice once critically inspected by Dr Johnson. But why steal a reputedly haunted house? Appleby could see only one reason. And it cohered with his present view of the matter – or ought he to say his aunt's view? – no better than with Hudspith's.

From somewhere aft a bugle sounded. Hudspith turned and strode across the fo'csle head. At least he still ate. Appleby stared again at the vacant horizon. One could easily lose one's bearings. All at sea, as they say. Obscurely he wished for a familiar landfall – as if that would help. Table Mountain, hanging in the sky like Swift's floating island. The litter of gigantic lettering on the quays of Manhattan; Brooklyn Bridge, Liverpool and its monster hotels. The low, dun, saurian ripple of land which Australia rolls into the Indian Ocean. If the ship could only raise one of these, he felt absurdly, then the unaccountable fragments of this business might come together in his mind. But what lay before the ship's prow was South America, and of South America he knew nothing. Nor was he sure that it was in South America that this chase would end.

The saloon was empty; he sat down and let the weeks of tedious investigation trickle through his mind. The haunted house had gone to Boston and thence to Port of Spain; after that it had disappeared. Hannah Metcalfe and Daffodil had last been heard of in Montevideo. But Lucy Rideout had been reported – though uncertainly – in Valparaiso, and perhaps there was significance in that. He looked up as Hudspith slumped darkly down beside him. 'What would you say,' he asked, 'to Robinson Crusoe's island?'

'Roast Hazel Hen,' said Hudspith sombrely. But this was to the steward.

'Juan Fernandez,' continued Appleby. 'Are they particularly immoral there? Because it looks as if our rendezvous may be somewhere in that direction.'

Hudspith shook his head and said nothing. Bodfish himself, it occurred to Appleby, would be as entertaining a companion. The truth was that Hudspith, learned in the depravities and perversities, had invented a new one – and was foundering beneath the additional burden. The seduction of feeble-minded girls he had supported for years, but the seduction of a plural-minded one was too much for him. Lucy Rideout, he believed, had been carried off for some person so vicious as to relish a mistress who was now one woman and now another. One could probably search all the volumes that booksellers discreetly call 'Curious' without coming upon anything quite so odd – and here was Hudspith obsessed by the thing as if it were an ultimate manifestation of evil. Appleby waited until Hudspith's plate was before him and then tried a little reason. For it is

desirable that policemen should be reasonable – and particularly those sent expensively across the world on detective
missions.

'Look here, I grant that your hypothesis would be sound and
sufficient if Lucy's affair stood in isolation. But it doesn't. It's
linked to Hannah Metcalfe – to begin with, by the single word
"Capri". And Hannah Metcalfe is linked to the horse; she
travelled with it. Just admit that and then ask yourself: how
does the horse fit in with your notion of the vice racket?'

Hudspith, who was eating with great intentness, paused
briefly. 'I could tell you things about horses,' he said darkly.
His eye was far away; it might have been conversing with the
shades of Caligula and Heliogabalus.

Appleby sighed. 'Lucy and Capri. Capri and Hannah.
Hannah and the horse. Hannah has witchcraft in the family.
Lucy evidences a morbid psychology of a kind which former
ages accounted for in terms of demoniac possession. The horse
has some power of hyperæsthesia which can be seen as an
uncanny ability to read thoughts. And all these and a haunted
house are picked up in England and spirited off in the direction
of South America. These are the facts, and I ask you to explain
them – particularly the house.'

Hudspith was studying the menu with a faintly pathological
concentration. 'Of course they hang together,' he said. 'Nobody
denies it. And I suppose if a man has a taste for demented
concubines he may have a taste for a crazy house to keep them
in. You don't know the lengths to which these wealthy de-
generates will go. You ought to see the private movies they
have made. You ought to see –' Hudspith broke off and sat
glowering at some inward vision. Then he fell to eating with a
slow, disconcerting avidity. Loopy, Appleby thought. St Simeon
on his pillar, with the phantasmagoria of all the sins of the
flesh circling round him. A great mistake to keep Hudspith on
that stuff all these years – particularly when he had such a taste
for it. Turn him on to forgery. Turn him on to embezzlement.
Too late.

'Hudspith –' he began, and stopped. The other passengers
had come in; with bowings and mutterings they were sitting
down at the narrow table. The ship belonged to the class of

fast cargo vessels that provide for six or eight passengers of retiring disposition – persons disliking floating hotels and averse from dances and sports tournaments. And at present there were Miss Mood, Mrs Nurse, Mr Wine, and Mr Wine's secretary, Mr Beaglehole.

'Warm,' said Mr. Beaglehole; 'decidedly warm. Not a day for woollens, Mr Appleby.'

All the passengers laughed discreetly. In time of war travellers about the world commonly cease to be travellers and become missions. And of these there are two kinds. The first, the confidential mission, everybody knows about – and everybody knew that Appleby and Hudspith were a confidential mission engaged in marketing Australian wool. The second sort of mission is the hush-hush mission. And this is the real thing. The persons here have a *mana* from which issue absolute and extensive *tabus*: their whence, their whither and their why may be neither questioned nor mentioned; they must be considered as utterly without a future or a past, as ephemerides of the sheerest sort. This makes conversation difficult and repartee more difficult still. Appleby agreed that it was a warm day.

Mrs Nurse said that the warm days were nicer than the very hot days.

Mr Wine, who seldom said anything, said nothing.

Miss Mood said nothing. She crushed her clasped hands between her knees and looked at Appleby with a penetrating glance. Really with that, Appleby thought. It was as if matter of scientific interest was being detected near the back of one's skull.

'The very hot days are rather tiring,' said Mrs Nurse.

About Mrs Nurse, it occurred to Appleby, there was something slightly peculiar. He frowned, conscious that in this lay the beginning of some obscure train of thought. Only a microscopic proportion of the human race ever crosses the South Atlantic Ocean; to do so is – however faintly – a distinction in itself; commonly this distinction is linked to the possession – however infinitesimally faint – of some specific trait or bent or characteristic in the voyager. But in Mrs Nurse nothing of the sort was detectable. It was impossible to conceive of any reason why she should now be thus floating on the waters. On the other hand it was equally hard to endow her in imagination with any more appropriate habitat. She called for nothing in particular. To posit a middling sort of suburb in a middling sort of English provincial town would be to risk far too positive an assertion about Mrs Nurse. Not that she was in the least enigmatic – that was Miss Mood's line – or in any way elusive. The apotheosis of the commonplace was a vile phrase. But it was the best that Appleby could find when considering Mrs Nurse.

'It is calm,' Mrs Nurse said.

It would be difficult to think of a more neutral remark than that, or of a more colourless way of making it. And she was physically colourless too – the colours one might see in a pool in an uninteresting place on a dull day. She was –

'Calm,' said Miss Mood tensely, 'is an illusion – a mere mathematical abstraction. It is simply an axis upon which spins the mortal storm, the great electrical flux which those who live call life.' She set down a glass of tomato juice and looked at Hudspith. 'You, I am sure, understand and agree with me.' Miss Mood's voice as it delivered itself of this gibberish was husky and glamorous, like something recorded on celluloid. Hudspith humped his shoulders, jabbed with fork and sawed with knife; he hated this awful woman as much as if she had been a celebrated bawd. But Miss Mood had clearly got him wrong; her turning to him had all the lush confidence of a tropical creeper's spiralling at the sun. 'Mind-stuff is alone pervasive,' she said. 'There is nothing else in the etheric world.'

Appleby felt a faint jar throughout his system – rather as if he had been pulled up in full career by the sudden recognition of an unexpected short cut. For between two bites of hazel hen he had apprehended the truth about Miss Mood. The woman was going where Hannah and Lucy had gone.

That was it. She and Hudspith and he were, so to speak, all in the same boat. And this was a thing likely enough – boats not being too plentiful these days. If the traffic to the pseudo-Capri was at all heavy – and already it had the appearance of being so – then parts of it were almost certain to converge quite far out on the Whale Roads. And a woman with that sort of eye and vocabulary – for there had been this sort of etheric-world stuff several times before – was just right for Daffodil's stable.

Appleby, chewing on this abrupt intuition, let his glance circle his other companions. If it were logical to suppose this of Miss Mood, then might it not –

The man called Beaglehole was looking at Miss Mood with disapproval. There was far from being anything out of the way in that. And yet about the manner of Beaglehole's disapproval it was possible to feel something puzzling. Appleby's eye travelled forward to Mrs Nurse, the commonplace and pervasively negative Mrs Nurse ... and suddenly he perceived the truth about her too. He looked at Mr Wine – there was only Mr Wine left – and as he looked at Mr Wine, Mr Wine looked at him. There are indefinable moments in which one feels that one has dropped the shutters just in time. Appleby felt this. For a second he continued to look at Wine blankly, and then he looked at Hudspith. Hudspith's eye was more discernibly than ever upon his private whale – the creature blew and spouted in the gravy. And so much for individual inspection. It remained to consider all five of his companions simultaneously and by a *coup d'oeil*. Tolerably achieving this, Appleby felt that it would be well to go up and get some air.

2

Sea and sky were as usual; the prow and its watchers went up and down as before. But Appleby paced a deck mysteriously transformed; he was like an actor who steps from the diffuse and rugged structure of actuality into the economy of a well-made play. For here, all unexpectedly, was the problem – or part of it – neatly under his nose again. Beaglehole had looked at Miss Mood with disapproval, the sort of disapproval with which a shop-walker might regard a counter ineptly piled with *demodé* goods. That was it. Miss Mood with her particular patter of the etherial world was booked for the bargain basement. Lucy Rideout and Daffodil would be much more catch.

Beaglehole, in fact, was what in commerical language is called a buyer, and Miss Mood and Mrs Nurse were his latest haul. The case of Mrs Nurse – said Appleby to himself in the sudden illumination that had befallen him – the case of Mrs Nurse was clear. She was a high-class medium – which meant an honest and peculiarly simple woman who was yet capable, in certain abnormal or trance states, of ingenious and sustained deceptions. That was it – or that was it in uncompromisingly rational terms. Mrs Nurse was just the type: a shallow pool until the waters parted and sundry problematical depths were revealed. Mrs Nurse would sit in a darkened room with bereaved mothers and sensation-seekers and inquiring Fellows of the Royal Society. Strange voices would come from her; voices voluble, hesitant, coherent, fragmentary, pathetic, pompous, fishing, shuffling. And people would listen as they had listened ever since the days of the Witch of Endor. One hears his wife speaking. One makes a verbatim report. One weeps. One smuggles a microphone. One offers banknotes. One plans tests with a manometer, a sphygmograph, a thermoscope. . . . In other words, Mrs Nurse was a steady selling line.

And somewhere over the faintly serrated blue of the horizon the spirit of enterprise was assembling a large-scale psychic circus. No other explanation would quite fit the facts – as Appleby's aunt, placidly shuffling her press cuttings, had known. The scale was large. There was no sign that Mrs Nurse and Miss Mood were aware of any special relationship with Beaglehole; if Beaglehole was buyer, there were agents in between. Among these passengers, indeed, there was only one overt relationship: Beaglehole was secretary to the gentleman down in the sailing list as Mr Emery Wine. Almost certainly this brought Wine in. In fact the hush-hush mission of these two was odder by a long way than the workaday imagination would readily arrive at. . . . Appleby, rounding a corner of the pilot-house, found Mr Wine regarding him with mild attention from a deck-chair. And momentarily his confidence flickered. The man looked so uncommonly like a hush-hush mission of the most respectable sort.

Hitherto Mr Wine had not been cordial; his attitude was one

of polite preoccupation and reserve. He was a slight man, well groomed without preciseness, and his manner at times suggested a tempered gaiety which was no doubt on appropriate occasions his most charming social card. And he smiled charmingly now. 'I am a good deal interested in your friend,' he said unexpectedly.

'In Ron Hudspith? Well, that's quite right.' Appleby's slow and easy colonial manner dated from a careful study of Rhodes scholars long ago. 'Too right, Mr Wine. You couldn't have a better off-sider than Ron.'

'You are close friends?'

'Cobbers,' said Appleby solemnly. 'And our dads before us. Ron's dad was a well-known identity Cobdogla-way. You know Cobdogla, Mr Wine?'

'I'm afraid not.'

'Ah.' Appleby contrived the kindly, if quizzical and slightly contemptuous, stare merited by one to whom Cobdogla is but a name.

'What interests me is that your friend appears to be of an unusually intense and brooding nature. To a stranger it would seem to suggest – well, almost a mild mania. I hope I don't offend you.'

'Yes?' Hearing his own richly ironical voice Appleby recalled that a pose too was necessary; he strolled forward and contrived to offer an iron pillar support. 'Ron saw a good deal of the back-blocks as a lad. He was a jackeroo on his uncle's station for years.'

'Indeed.' Mr Wine's was a civil convention of understanding.

'Boundary-riding most of the time. It marks them, you know. Don't see a soul for weeks on end.'

'Ah, I see.' Mr Wine was enlightened. 'The Bush.'

'The Malee,' said Appleby severely. 'And sometimes the Spinifex.' As he offered this refinement of fancy his glance went rather anxiously towards the companion-way from the saloon. The appearance of his cobber Ron at this moment might be unfortunate. 'You ought to meet some of the old-timers there, Mr Wine. They're so used to solitude and silence that two of them will meet and pass a night together in a humpy without exchanging a word.'

'Dear me!' said Mr Wine, and added, ' – in a what?'

'A humpy,' Appleby repeated firmly. 'Sometimes they go a bit strange. Visions – that sort of thing.'

'Indeed! And is your friend at all affected in that way?'

'You're telling me.'

'I beg your pardon?'

'Too right, he is. You're seen him up there by the bows, Mr Wine? That's where he goes when it takes him.'

'I'm very sorry to hear it.' Mr Wine was now leaning forward attentively. 'And his visions are about –?'

'Ah,' said Appleby, suddenly ironical and reticent.

Mr Wine relaxed and offered some observation on the course of the steamer. Appleby, still supporting that steamer's super-structure with his shoulders, had leisure to reflect on his own rashness of the past few minutes. He had hurled the unwitting Hudspith into a fantastic role – and this was far from being the less reckless because Hudspith at present really had a loopy side to him. He had taken upon himself the burden of an impersonation far trickier than was required to support a vague association with Australian wool. And he had done all this partly out of boredom and the residual sense of the Daffodil affair's being something of a holiday; and partly as the con-sequence of a sudden and extravagant plan. If Beaglehole was a buyer, then Wine was a talent scout – perhaps his own talent scout. And to have a friend who would score high marks in the psychic circus might be the quickest way of getting there. Hudspith, if his mind was set on tracing Hannah and Lucy, must be prepared to put an antic disposition on. And Cobdogla would be his kindly nurse.

At this moment Hudspith appeared and strode past them with all the glowering concentration that Appleby could desire. And Mr Wine watched him with what was surely the covert interest of the impresario. 'I believe,' he said, 'that a sea voyage often exacerbates such conditions.'

'It makes me feel a hundred per cent myself.' Appleby en-deavoured to exude the curious animal luxury that Cobdogla breeds. 'But I've no doubt you're right. Nothing to the out-back, though. I've known plenty men turn queer there. And beasts too, for the matter of that.'

'Beasts. You surprise me.' Mr Wine's eye was still on Huds-pith as he skirted No 1 hatch.

'Horses.'

Mr Wine's gaze swung slowly round. 'Horses? You have found horses go peculiar in the – the out-back?'

'A horse doesn't like solitude any more than a human, Mr Wine. He gets bored just like you or me – and then he'll do queer things. Why, I've known a horse teach himself his numbers just through being bored. Like counting the tiles on the lavatory floor.'

'You saw the horse gradually learn to count?'

'I wouldn't say that. It was quite a mathematician when I saw it.'

'Dear me.' Mr Wine was looking absently at the sea. 'It did simple multiplications – that sort of thing?'

'Just that.'

'Then it was one of the Elberfeld horses.'

'Elberfeld horses? It was one of the Dismal Swamp horses, Mr Wine.'

'My dear sir, it was one of the Elberfeld horses.' Mr Wine spoke with what was at once polite decision and the liveliest interest. 'They were dispersed, and I suppose one may have strayed even to your Dismal Swamp. Perhaps you never heard of Clever Hans, Mr Appleby? He was the first of a remarkable line of so-called thinking horses in Germany at the beginning of the present century. They caused quite a sensation in their day.' Mr Wine smiled faintly to an irresponsive ocean. 'Krall wrote a book about them, *Denkende Tiere*, and there was even a learned journal, *Tierseele*, taking somewhat wider ground. And now tell me: what did they think of the creature at Dismal Swamp? Were there any reactions of what might be called a superstitious sort? Old women thinking the brute inspired – that sort of thing.'

Appleby eased himself on his pillar and looked at Mr Wine with as much appearance of inattention as he could muster. An hour ago he had believed himself a week's steaming from any hope of contact with his quarry; and now here was detection at positively breakneck pace. 'Superstition?' he said. 'You're telling me. There were old women who thought the devil was in the horse.'

Wine nodded. 'The Elberfeld horses have impressed more than old women, Mr Appleby. There was Professor Claparède. And what's more there was Maeterlinck, one of the first intellects in Europe. He was convinced that the phenomena were supernormal.'

'You mean what they call psychic? I thought all that stuff had gone bunk years ago, same as table-turning and ouja-boards.'

'My dear Mr. Appleby, there are appetites which are perennial.' Wine shook a wise and indulgent head. 'Table-turning yesterday, astrology today – and tomorrow who knows what? Possibly *Denkende Tiere* again.'

'But surely you don't think there's anything supernatural about a counting horse?'

'Certainly not.' Wine's reply was dry and sharp. 'The thing is merely paranormal.'

'Yes?' Appleby contrived a promptly ironical reception for a strange word.

'These horses have one or another sense extraordinarily developed. Sometimes it is a visual hyperæsthesia; more commonly a tactual. They can be trained to act upon minute sensory impressions – imperceptible signs which a showman will give. But that is not all. They can act upon such impressions involuntarily and unconsciously given. Put your hand on such a horse's neck, or hold it on a taut rein. Then *think* of a number – say five. The horse will promptly signal five, perhaps by neighing or pawing. And the explanation is very simple. You are unable to *think* five without at the same time *acting* five. Ever so faintly, your whole organism is a pulse counting five. And the horse gets the message. Various effects of calculation can, of course, be built up on that basis.'

'Yes?' Appleby, who was far from questioning this simple physiological truth, got all the arrogant agnosticism of Cobdogla into the word.

'Yes, indeed.' Wine was almost nettled. 'And exactly similar mechanisms lie behind much so-called thought-reading. Look at any memoir of a Cambridge man in the eighties and you will find the phenomenon ranking somewhere between a solemn scientific experiment and a parlour game. Professors played it in each other's drawing-rooms. You leave the room and the company hides something. You return, lay a hand on the cheek or temple of someone in the know, and occasionally you are mysteriously guided or steered towards the hidden object.'

'Isn't that what they call telepathy?'

'Telepathy implies a certain distance – often a distance over which it is difficult to conceive any physical agency acting. This is merely a matter of subconsciously interpreting minute muscular actions.'

'Well, that's really interesting.' Appleby straightened up and stretched himself lazily. 'And you seem to know a great deal about it, Mr Wine.'

Wine smiled – so quickly that Appleby suspected something like the expunging of an involuntary frown. 'One remembers odd scraps of information and desultory reading when one is on a voyage. Don't you find it so? The empty ocean induces an empty mind, and much inconsequent stuff floats up. There is another flying fish landed on deck. It is astounding that they can leap so high.'

Appleby agreed – and was inwardly convinced that more than a flying fish had been landed since luncheon. In fact he himself had landed a very queer fish indeed. A fish with most problematical innards. And he had a strong impulse to out with a knife and venture some radical incision; to go flatly on, say, from oddly endowed horses to witches. But that would be wanton. He had already gone too far with the holiday spirit – the figure of Hudspith, once more brooding in the bows, was there to attest it. So Appleby spoke of flying fish and porpoises, and when these tenuous subjects were exhausted he took his leave of Wine and strolled down the deck. Hudspith must be spoken to presently – and the interview might not be altogether easy. Undoubtedly he would particularly object to becoming Ron. Still, it might have been Stan or Les. And policemen must put up with such things.

Twice Appleby circled the deck, and twice he passed an Emery Wine who had retreated into his habitual abstraction and reserve. But at the third time round this problematical person looked up. 'Mr Appleby, you don't happen to have seen Beaglehole.'

'No – not since lunch-time.'

'I must go and find him; we have papers to look at. An excellent fellow is Beaglehole, but we have not much except our business in common. And on a long voyage it is perhaps more pleasant to have a personal friend as a companion.' Wine rose from his deck-chair. 'I think you said that Mr Hudspith and yourself were close personal friends?'

'Yes.'

'Intimate friends?'

'Yes.'

'Very pleasant,' said Wine vaguely. 'Very pleasant, I am sure.' He looked away to the horizon – with calculation, like one weather-wise and planning to exploit a distant gale. And then he smiled his new and charming smile and walked away.

Appleby stood for a moment by the rail and looked down at the sea. Mrs Nurse's remark lay beyond dispute: it was calm. It was as placid, as unruffled as the small talk of Mr Emery Wine. And yet there was not an inch of its surface that was not in motion; the surface undulated and hung and slipped, gained momentum and lost it, flattened and tilted with a subtlety of movement defying analysis. And over the horizon was a great deal more of the same thing. A large complex affair. . . .

A large solid house, pleasantly proportioned no doubt, proclaiming still the rational good-taste of the eighteenth century. Nothing in all this obscure adventure was nearly so puzzling as the theft of 37 Hawke Square. It was here that the crux would lie. And fortunately more was known about the vanished mansion than about Hannah Metcalfe or Lucy Rideout.

Appleby went below to his cabin, took from a drawer a heavy book of severely scientific appearance and began to read.

3

... At its maximum in the summer of 1866, after which time the appearances became fewer, and finally ceased in 1871. Towards the end of this period the figure, which had at first looked lifelike and substantial, became shadowy and semi-transparent. There was also a gradual cessation of the phenomena that had occurred during these years, namely sounds of the dragging about of heavy weights, and unaccountable lights.

Here it is difficult to deny considerable weight to the evidence, for the persons concerned were well-educated for the most part and – it appears – well-balanced without exception. Indeed one of them, Sir Edward Pilbeam, was a person of scientific eminence; and it may be remarked that he came to an investigation of the phenomena not through any previous interest in psychic matters such as might be held to indicate an innately suggestible mind but simply through the accident of his extended visit to Lady Morrison. It must be observed, however, that in one particular the Morrison case cannot be classified as a true 'haunting'. Certainly the phantom appeared at different times to different persons in a particular locality. But Lady Morrison's first experience had become matter of common talk some time before her butler related his adventure in the wine-cellar; and none of those who subsequently claimed to have seen the 'ghost' did so in circumstances which positively exclude the hypothesis of suggestion or expectation.

Much more remarkable – and that on several counts – is the series of supernormal events associated with the famous No 37 Hawke Square, Bloomsbury. Here we have, what is rare in the evidential sphere, a close analogue of the traditional 'ghost-story', like that of Pliny (*see Appendix H: Phantasms of the Dead in the Classical Period*, §5, *Athenodorus*), which connects some tragedy in a particular house or place, with the vague and often confused accounts of sights or sounds which perplex or terrify the observer. We have too, as in the Morrison case, that gradual 'fading out' of an apparition which some investigators – rashly, as it would appear to the present writer – take as evidence of what may be termed the 'delayed mortality' of the spirit; its power to survive, but only for a time, the earthly tenement from which it has passed. But what more particularly distinguishes the Hawke Square case is this: that there is well-attested record of two similar, but distinct and unconnected, hauntings of the premises, *and that the second took place at a time when all record of the first had passed from any living memory.* It was not until 1911, when Dr Hayball published his well-known *Grub Street Gleanings*, that the story of Colonel Morell was recovered from a hitherto inaccessible manuscript source. Up to that date no scholar had as much as heard of it; and we must note with amusement that Johnson (who had already suffered his unfortunate experience in Cock Lane) hid the incident from Boswell as successfully as did Mrs Morell from the rest of the world. Knowledge of the Morell haunting, we repeat, was recovered in 1911. The Spettigue haunting covered the years 1888 to 1892. The evidence will thus lead many (with what degree of discretion we shall not at present attempt to estimate) to this conclusion; that certain buildings are endowed, as it were, with some special psychic sensitiveness; with an atmosphere peculiarly conducive to super-normal appearances. This has, of course, long been held of mediaeval castles, church precincts and the like. But the case of the Hawke Square house is somewhat different. Neither in 1772 nor in 1888 did the house possess any of the conventional associations of a 'haunted' place. Yet in both those years phenomena occurred. And what Dr Spettigue recorded towards the end of the nineteenth century is oddly like what Mrs Morell recorded of quite distinct protagonists in the eighteenth. *But of Mrs Morell Dr Spettigue could have known nothing.* It is this that makes 37 Hawke Square something of a *locus classicus* in researches of the present sort.

Light striking upwards through the porthole passed in endless faintly moving washes over the low cabin ceiling; the electric fan turned monotonously from side to side, as if watching invisible tennis; somewhere a bell rang remotely; near at hand a partition intermittently creaked. But Appleby, pausing at the foot of a page, heard and saw none of these things. Instead he heard banging as of innumerable doors down giant corridors; that throb, upon which the ear imposes its own patterns, of aircraft flying very high; voices in shelters saying 'It was a bomb all right, that one.' And he saw the streets of Bloomsbury in silhouette against the burning City; saw Bloomsbury under fire: here a church going, here a college library, and here – just here in this corner of a minor square – the flash and smoke and din-obscured labouring at what was surely the most bizarre activity ever undertaken by rational men.

But was it indeed rational, this genie-like purloining of 37

Hawke Square? Or was it as crazy as the world to which one might so easily be conducted by an over-attentive study of Dr Spettigue and Mrs Morell? Appleby read on.

Our only record of the first haunting is contained in a single letter made available by Dr Hayball. This, although somewhat allusive in nature, is fortunately the product of a logical mind:

To Mrs MORELL

DEAR MADAM, – I write to inform you that I have this day, together with Mr Francis Barber, terminated my three nights' sojourn at No 37 Hawke Square. The intelligence now to be conveyed – namely, that during this period no untoward appearance was observed – I know not well whether you will receive with disappointment or relief. Had the apparition of Colonel Morell in fact manifested itself we should have had some additional assurance that the matter lay beyond the grossness of imposture or the prevalence of *infectious* imagination. As it is, we are very little furthered in our enquiry and it has now to be decided what, if any, action it is proper that you should take. But first, and that you may be assured of my writing from a sufficient apprehension of the facts, I will briefly consider the course of what has taken place.

The death of Colonel Morell, although sudden, aroused in the first instance no suspicion, nor had it occurred to you in any way to connect with it his occasionally expressed anxieties about the Italian man-servant who, with his wife, has since quitted your service. And it was only after your chance communication of that anxiety to the late Colonel Morell's fellow-officer Captain Bertram that this gentleman was first visited by the apparition. Let me remind you, dear Madam, with such gentleness as this painful subject requires, that the ideas of *sudden death* and *poison* lie sufficiently near together in the *arcana* of the mind to be readily brought together when there is offered so striking a link as *absconding Italian*. Were Captain Bertram a man of fanciful mind – and of this his return to India prevents my forming an opinion of my own – the raw materials of romantic fiction lay ready to his hand.

But we are told that the apparition of your dead husband appeared not only to his old friend Captain Bertram but also to a number of other persons of respectable character who have testified to the fact; but with this difference – that whereas to the Captain the vision unfailingly called out for vengeance against his poisoner, in the presence of others it was mute or heard only to groan. The Captain saw and heard things, to him, equally familiar. Is it perhaps easier to conjure up an unfamiliar figure than an unfamiliar voice?

A total disbelief of apparitions is adverse to the opinion of the existence of the soul between death and the last day; the question simply is, whether departed spirits ever have the power of making themselves perceptible to us, and whether we are here confronted with an instance in which this has occurred. It is wonderful that five thousand years have now elapsed since the creation of the world, and still it is undecided whether or not there has ever been an instance of the spirit of any person appearing after death. All argument is against it; in its favour we must set many voluntary solemn asseverations. And even so it is in the present case.

I advise you to persevere in your resolution of selling the house; and to take no further action than this. You speak of a duty of *laying* the ghost, or doing that which will afford it relief from having to walk the earth. But this is the shadow of superstition and such as is encouraged by writings carelessly profane: as the happiness or misery of unembodied spirits does not depend upon place, but is intellectual, we cannot say that they are less happy or less miserable by appearing upon earth. Nor can I approve the argument that the apparition, being supernatural, is tantamount to a divine injunction to pursue the supposed murderer of Colonel Morèll. For the spirit, if spirit there be, is at best a *questionable shape*, bringing we know not whether *airs from heaven or blasts from hell*, and with *intents wicked or charitable* to an unknown degree. If you will but consider the painful issues which a doubtful criminal prosecution would bring you may well feel Hamlet's doubt: *Be thou a spirit of health or goblin damn'd?* I suppose, in short, that in the pursuit of merely human justice we should regard evidence only mundane and rational. But here I touch on matters so awful that I would not venture to give an opinion did I not find myself supported by my friend Dr Douglas, who, in addition to his own distinguished abilities, enjoys the superior qualification of being Bishop of Carlisle. I am, Madam, your most humble servant,

SAM JOHNSON.

JOHNSON'S COURT, FLEET STREET,
March 20, 1772.

So much for the Morell haunting. It is not remarkable in itself, or is remarkable only for the wise advice which it produced. We must credit Dr Johnson with suspecting that if Colonel Morell was indeed poisoned by his Italian servant, the wife of the Italian servant was not without her place in the affair, and from the canvassing of such a 'painful issue' he sagaciously dissuades the widow. Had he given more information on the 'persons of respectable character' we should have been grateful, but this was not to be expected in a letter of the kind he had set himself to write. For the rest we must please ourselves with the picture of the Sage and his faithful negro servant keeping their three nights' vigil in the empty house.

And now we come to the Spettigue affair . . .

Again Appleby paused in his reading. The engines had taken on the deeper throb which seems to come in the late afternoon; it was as if they were preparing for their long, tireless haul through the night. Again a bell rang and overhead there was the pad of a quartermaster's feet going forward; from the little saloon below came a chink of cutlery and rattle of plates. Dinner would be at seven-thirty; there would be the usual jokes about the metamorphoses of Roast Hazel Hen. Appleby frowned. There was over a week's steaming before them, and three times a day he and Hudspith would gather round the board with Wine and Beaglehole and Mrs Nurse and Miss Mood – with these and with the wraiths of Hannah Metcalfe and Lucy Rideout. And Daffodil. Roast Hazel Horse. . . . Appleby pulled himself awake and returned to 37 Hawke Square.

And now we come to the Spettigue affair, which is more striking in itself and gives retroactive significance to the sketchy case of Colonel Morell. At this time, more than a hundred and twenty years after the events we have been considering, the Hawke Square house was in the occupancy of Mr Smart, a merchant, who had married the sister of his close friend Dr Spettigue. There were several young children – a circumstance from which arose one of the most curious aspects of the affair. For the house, like others of its kind, had a central staircase winding round a narrow well. And Mrs Smart, like other careful parents similarly situated, had provided against accident by causing a net or lattice to be placed across the well at the level of the first and again at the third (or nursery) landing. During the summer of 1888 the whole family had repaired for a holiday visit to a hotel in Yarmouth, the servants (other than a nurse) being placed on board-wages the while. During this period nothing remarkable seems to have occurred, and Mr Smart was said to be in particularly good spirits, even playing cricket with his children on the beach. When the holiday was over – and following the usual custom of the Smarts on such occasions – Mr Smart returned to town a day earlier than his family for the purpose of 'opening up' the house – an operation of some intricacy, it will be remembered, during Victorian times. He was to await the arrival of the servants in the afternoon, sleep at his club, and his family was to return home on the morrow. This, we repeat, was the established procedure. But when the servants arrived on this occasion they found their master dead on the marble floor of the hall. The nets or lattices spoken of had been removed and there were indications that Mr Smart had fallen from the top storey.

Suicide and murder seemed equally possible as agencies in this sad affair, and at the inquest an open verdict was returned. Those taking the view that Mr Smart had been done to death saw significance in the time of the fatality: on this day of the year – and perhaps on this day only – was Mr Smart likely to be found alone in his own house. But on the other side it was maintained that this was far from weakening the case for suicide. For by taking his own life under those precise circumstances Mr Smart would so far have contrived to mitigate the shock to his family as to ensure that the discovery was made by servants and not by any of those more intimately concerned. Moreover the removal of the lattices and subsequent luring of the victim to the top of the house appeared an unnecessarily intricate method of committing murder, while the removal of the lattices by Mr Smart himself was consistent with a rational plan for taking his own life with a greater measure of decent privacy than would be compatible with, say, casting himself out of a window.

It were idle at this distance of time to speculate on the facts of Mr Smart's death as given above. Suicide appears to have been the solution at first accepted by his friends, and this chiefly on two counts: Mr Smart seemed to be without personal enemies or any irregularity of private life; and his private affairs did upon examination prove to be embarrassed. It seemed likely that, had he survived, a considerable change in his style of living would have been necessary; and this, it was felt, might have weighed unduly on his mind. As it was, this financial stringency was to have remarkable consequences after his decease.

We have mentioned Mr Smart's friend and brother-in-law, a Dr Spettigue. This gentleman was in medical practice in the vicinity and he possessed at the time a growing family which made increasing demands upon the available space at his residence in an adjoining square. It was therefore arranged that he should rent consulting-

74

rooms from his widowed sister in the Hawke Square house at a figure which should materially assist her annual budget. This estimable family arrangement was completed some three months after the death of Mr Smart, and the two houses were connected by a private telephone line, then something of a novelty in London. It was hard upon Dr Spettigue's entering in occupation of his new professional quarters that the phenomena began.

The apparition which was to appear so purposely to this competent and level-headed medical practitioner must be reckoned one of the most remarkable of which we have record – and this chiefly because of its combining the characteristics of the literary and the veridical ghost. Like most phantasms of the more respectably authenticated sort it was shy, fluid and indefinite in appearance, being commonly no more than a gliding luminous column viewed from the corner of the eye. Often, indeed, the phenomena were not visual but auditory merely, and consisted in those raps and suggestions of the movement of heavy bodies with which the reader is now so well acquainted in the better class of phantoms. On the other hand this ghost spoke, and spoke to a purpose – in this imitating those of its fellows incubated solely in the imaginations of novelists and literary men. To be brief, it was the sustained endeavour of Mr Smart's ghost to secure vengeance upon his murderer.

For some time the manifestations were perceptible to Dr Spettigue alone. Occasionally the apparition would present itself plainly in the form of Mr Smart, and then it appeared unable to speak. But at other times and more commonly – and as if conserving its psychic force for aural impression – it was a vague appearance only, an appearance from which proceeded the very voice of Dr Spettigue's dead friend – only having (Dr Spettigue thinks) 'a somewhat more settled gravity' than during life. The words were always the same. 'I was murdered, Archibald, murdered,' the voice would say. There would then be a pause and it would add: 'I was murdered by –' But at this point the voice would invariably falter and break off – in such a way that it was difficult to determine whether it was through compunction or some failure of memory that the vital information was withheld.

It will not escape the recollection of some readers that the late Mr Andrew Lang, an acute if light-hearted commentator on supernormal phenomena, at one time published a facetious essay in which it was suggested that the futile and unaccountable conduct of many supposed ghosts might be attributable to a species of *aphasia*, or inability to express certain thoughts in words by reason of some specific mental disease. Significance therefore may be attached to these facts taken in conjunction : (1) Lang's essay may have been in the conscious or unconscious recollection of Dr Spettigue; (2) Dr Spettigue was a physician, familiar with the conception of *aphasia*, a fact which might help to fix Lang's whimsical notion somewhere in his mind; (3) although numerous other observers *saw* the supposed ghost of Mr Smart, only Dr Spettigue *heard it talk*.

The subsequent history of the second Hawke Square haunting may be recounted in few words. The manifestations extended over a number of years but with diminishing definition and intensity, finally dying away into merely wraith-like appearances and feeble rappings and scratchings. But this was not before the phenomena had come within the perception of a surprisingly large number of persons, including at least two casual patients of Dr Spettigue's in whom any state of specific expectation is most unlikely. One of these, indeed, who was brought into the Doctor's surgery after having been knocked down by a hansom-cab, had that morning stepped off a boat which had brought him home from a ten years' sojourn in China. This is extremely interesting, but so too is the circumstance that neither Mrs Smart nor any of her children was ever perceptive of any supernormal phenomena whatever. The fact of the haunting, as was inevitable, became widely known, and was naturally associated with Mr Smart's mysterious death. But the words heard by Dr Spettigue were wisely suppressed during the lifetime of those concerned, the interests of scientific enquiry being at the same time safeguarded by a confidential deposition made to the Logical Society's committee for psychical investigation. The *Proceedings* of this body contain a very full report.

4

A museum, Appleby said to himself as he closed the book. A sort of ghost museum neatly housed in a rebuilt 37 Hawke Square. Lucy Rideout in the basement illustrating possession by demons; Mrs Nurse holding a seance in the drawing-room; Miss Mood crystal-gazing in the pantry; Hannah Metcalfe floating from room to room on a broomstick; Daffodil tap-tapping in the back yard; the spectres of Colonel Morell and Mr Smart toasting Yarmouth bloaters before the kitchen fire.

And no doubt there would be more exotic exhibits as well: Maori *Tohungas* and Eskimo *Angakuts*, Peay-men from British Guiana, Dènè Hareskins from North America and *Birraarks* from Australia. All with their attendant spirits: *kenaimas* and *mrarts*, *jossakeeds* and –

And Uncle Tom Cobley and all, thought Appleby, abruptly standing up. The thing was fantastic; it was as fantastic if one believed in ghosts as if one did not. And no one would believe such a story for a moment. . . . He put the book back in its drawer. Writing with a nice, dry, scientific tone. Interesting, without a doubt. And perhaps rather alarming as well.

The cabin door opened and Hudspith came in – Hudspith fresh from the rising and falling prow. And Appleby spoke at once. 'It's Wine,' he said. 'It's Wine who has made off with those women. He's forming a monstrous museum of ghosts and marvels the Devil knows where. Mediums and Medicine Lodges, bugs and bogles.'

Hudspith sat down; his eye, returning from remote distances, focused slowly on Appleby; and almost as slowly his mind focused on the significant word. 'A museum? I shouldn't be surprised. You'd hardly believe what some of them collect. There was an old man in Brussels –' He checked himself. 'Did you say Wine?'

'Emery Wine.'

Hudspith shook his head; his eye could be seen setting out again on its jong journey. 'Impossible. He's not the type – or rather not one of them. There are three types of man that traffic in women –'

'But I tell you this affair has nothing to do with trafficking in women. It has to do with trafficking in marvels. This museum –'

Hudspith nodded – very absently. 'I could tell you things about museums. There was an old man in Brussels –'

'My dear Hudspith, keep him for a limerick. We're confronted with something quite different. Wine, or somebody for whom Wine is acting, is assembling a museum of the uncanny in general. Anything within that category is welcome and no expense is being spared. And now I'll ask you two questions. Do you know why Wine has a secretary called Beaglehole?'

'Of course I don't. The question's idiotic.'

'It's an etymological matter. Beaglehole is a corrupt form of Bogle Hole, which is good Scots for the lair of the demon. Wine is very choice in everything he gathers round him, and always on the look-out for a good specimen. And that brings me to the second question. Do you know why he's particularly interested in you?'

'In me? He's nothing of the sort. I've scarcely exchanged a word with him.'

'But I have. We've become quite friendly and I've told him about your visions.'

'Visions!' Hudspith sprang to his feet. 'Is this a joke?' He sat down again abruptly. 'I don't have visions. I may look as if I do, but I don't.'

'So much the better. This is a matter in which the appearance is all. And I have assured Wine that you have visions as a regular thing – largely because of the lonely life you led among the sheep up Cobdogla way.'

'Wherever is that? And why ever –' Hudspith was staring at Appleby with the expression conventionally called open-mouthed.

'Australia, I should think. Or perhaps Tasmania or New Zealand. We must look it up at once. Anyway, that's your background.'

'I think you've taken leave of your senses. And I don't know anything about colonials.'

'Well, to begin with, they don't call themselves that. And for the rest you have just to remember that they are people of open hearts and closed minds. Stick to that and the impersonation ought to hold. And if you can really make an impression in the visionary way, I think there's a good chance of your getting an invitation.'

'Do you mean that I'm to endeavour to step into a show-case in this museum you're imagining?'

'I do.' Appleby was matter of fact. 'Simply because it's your shortest route to Hannah and Lucy – to say nothing of Daffodil. You see?'

Hudspith was far from seeing, and it took Appleby a further half-hour to expound his case. Even then Hudspith was dubious

'It's all very well,' he said, 'but you must remember I don't know anything about visions. And if this fellow is what you take him to be he's likely to have the whole subject at his finger-tips.'

Appleby nodded, and once more felt that he had, perhaps, been decidedly rash. 'Of course any analogous phenomenon would do. I suppose you couldn't levitate? Float out of one window, you know, and in at another.' He tapped the drawer before him. 'That's what the celebrated Home did in the presence of the Master of Lindsay and Lord Adare.'

'Ships,' said Hudspith tartly, 'don't have windows.'

'Or there was Lord Orrery's butler. He showed a marked predisposition to turn himself into a balloon. They locked him into a room and could hear him bumping about the ceiling. They went in and found that several people clutching his shoulders were insufficient to hold him down.'

'Look here,' said Hudspith, 'do you believe all that?'

'I do not. But does Wine? And then there was St Joseph of Cupertino. Any chance pious remark would set him off. He would give a loud yell, bound into the air and float about indefinitely. At first his superiors took a dark view of it. But later it was officially decided to be extremely edifying.'

'It had better be visions,' said Hudspith resignedly. 'Though I don't see why we shouldn't simply follow Wine up in a more regular way.'

Appleby shook his head. 'The truth is that we have only the most tenuous line on anything criminal so far. Hannah Metcalfe is of age, and at a pinch they could probably square Mrs Rideout. That means that if the girls were free agents and there was no intent to exploit them sexually there just isn't a case at all. Of course people aren't allowed to steal houses. But it would be hard to persuade a commonsense jury that a house which may plausibly be held simply to have disintegrated through enemy action has really been found at the other end of the globe. And as for Daffodil – well, everybody knows that a horse is almost as chancy a proposition in a law-court as on a racecourse.'

'In other words,' said Hudspith, 'this museum may be crazy but can't be established as criminal. So why fudge up visions? Much better go home and report no go.'

'Not at all. You may find something decidedly criminal if you get yourself favourably established there. And besides' – Appleby looked shrewdly at his colleague – 'we don't in any case know that these girls aren't getting a raw deal. Even if they were picked up primarily as museum pieces –'

Literally and figuratively, Hudspith rose. 'Very well. And as you seem to have brought a good many books on all that –'

Appleby rummaged in his suitcase, 'I think I can recommend Gurney and Myers. They describe about seven hundred decidedly queer coves, so you ought to find something to suit your type. I'm inclined to recommend bright lights and voices. They seem to crop up at any time, whereas actual phantasms are inclined to save up for special occasions – like announcing some death at a distance.'

'I see.' Hudspith, Appleby was pleased to notice, had abandoned his brooding expression for one of much cunning. 'Well, as it happens, this *is* a special occasion. It's your birthday.'

'It is nothing of the sort.'

'Look here, if you say I have visions, can't I say you have a birthday?'

Appleby grinned. 'I suppose that's fair.'

'Good. It's your birthday. And Cobdogla never knew such a party as there's going to be tonight.'

'Well, well,' said Appleby – and went on deck wondering if he had been inclined to under-estimate his colleague. Hudspith in his younger days had doubtless been constrained to drink much beer in the interests of criminal investigation, but that he should plump for conviviality as a means of forwarding the present inquiry was a surprise. Perhaps a party would be a good idea in any case, for there was now something decidedly oppressive in the air.

More than ever the South Atlantic was calm, a sort of channel-passenger's dream. The sun swam copper-coloured in a western sky which had gone strangely olive; it was like a farmer peering through a hedge, only there were no crops visible, nothing but the unharvested sea which lay flaccid and inert about the ship. The ocean, said Appleby to himself, walking aft, is our master symbol of energy. Watching it, we draw into ourselves a pleasing sense of power, as we may do from some vital companion. *There is society where none intrudes By the deep seas, and music in its roar*. And when it fails to roar there may result comfort for our stomach and semi-circular canals, but the society lapses and our spirits feel indefinably let down.

The conclusion of this marine meditation found Appleby at the after end of the short promenade deck. Here there was a sort of open-air extension of the smoke-room, glassed in on either side, with a hatch for obtaining drinks behind, and having, as if by way of diversion, a front-wise and elevated view of the little sun-deck provided for third-class passengers. Here one could sit before dinner, sip sherry or cocktails and scrutinize the unimportant proceedings of these obscure persons below. The dispositions of the human species are frequently extremely odd, and the curiosity of this instance was perhaps enhanced by the fact that the third-class passengers, like their elevated fellow voyagers, could number no more than some half-dozen. One got to know them quite well; it was like owning an aquarium or a small zoological park. For instance, thought Appleby, settling down without a drink – for the coming party was something to approach with caution – for instance there below him at the moment was the Italian girl. One could see that she was handsome; that she was dirty it was at this distance necessary only to suspect. And in a peasant girl who has beauty a little dirt is of small moment to a well-balanced mind.

Appleby watched the girl. Without positively removing his mind from conscientious reflection on the mysterious proceedings of Mr Emery Wine he watched the girl below him, and rather regretted that daylight was beginning to fail. Eusapia – he knew that her name was Eusapia Something – was alone on the little deck, and she paced it with a lithe restlessness which in this relaxed steamship environment, was extremely fetching. A gluteal type, such as would offend one's taste in a ball-dress. But that was the tyranny of the fashion-plate; Eusapia as she was, and with all Calabria behind her, was very well. Would the wife of the Italian servant of Colonel Morell – speculated Appleby, dutifully veering towards business – have been as attractive? And what would the colonel have thought in 1772? And what was Colonel Morell to Mr Wine – or he to the wraith of Mr Smart, who had so amiably sported with his children on the sands at Yarmouth? These were questions more than speculative – they were questions demonstrably meaningless – but meanwhile Eusapia there was a palpable physical fact.

She paced the deck in a white tunic cut low and tight across the breasts and a black skirt that swung to her ankles; she paced the deck with a strange restlessness and a glance that went impatiently now out to sea and now among the shadows that were losing definition and merging at her feet. It was chilly; somewhere on the starboard quarter the great bronze sun had dropped below the horizon, reddening the while; its last segment, as if suddenly molten and flowing, had spread out in a momentary line of fire that heralded the dark. This Appleby knew without turning. He was watching Eusapia still. She had moved to the side, and sat on a bollard with her back to the rail. She sat in the swiftly gathering dusk, still and isolated. Behind her was the bare rail and a sheer drop to the sea; the empty deck was all about her; and above stretched infinite space. She sat very still, and it grew darker, and she was a silhouette against the yet faintly luminous sea. Her hands lay side by side on the darkness of her lap. And Appleby saw that there was something hovering above her head.

It was white and faint, like a puff of vapour; it took more substance and might have been a dove; it circled above Eusapia's head and poised itself as no bird could do. The thing trembled, vibrated, rose and fell like a ball held in the jet of an invisible fountain. It spiralled upwards and outwards, dropped like a stone and disappeared, showed itself again motionless in air some three feet before Eusapia's knees; it rose in an arc and hung at the same distance above her head. Again it circled. Eusapia's hands, pale as acacia flowers, lay motionless on the black stuff of her dress.

Appleby sat as still as the girl below him. His pulse was not quite normal; there was an unusual sensation in the scalp; almost certainly a chemist would find in his bloodstream elements not present a few moments before. Which was interesting –for he had fallen to watching the girl with nothing more perhaps than a fleeting sexual interest; certainly with no expectation of the uncanny. And yet the performance – this performance in a strangely empty theatre – had instantaneously worked. It is strangely easy to penetrate to magical levels of the mind.

The cities of Rome, thought Appleby – keeping his eye steadily on this now so-interesting young woman the while – the cities of Rome – all the cities that ever stood where modern Rome now stands – existing still in perfect preservation, each simply superimposed upon the one preceding it: Freud had said that the human mind was like that. Well, it was possible at times to shoot right down through them like a miner plunging to his seam. . . . Now he could only just see Eusapia by straining his eyes. The thing was circling and hovering still.

It circled and hovered perhaps three feet above her head, and her hands were on her lap. Suddenly, and for a second only, one hand disappeared; and simultaneously the thing rose some three or four feet higher – it would now be touching, perhaps tapping at, the ceiling of a moderately lofty room. Appleby waited for no more; he rose and made his way cautiously forward between the deck-chairs and the davits. Perhaps the weather had helped to give Eusapia's flummery effectiveness. The atmosphere was at once chill, dry and heavy; something was in the air.

From the smoke-room came voices. People were assembling for dinner. But Appleby wanted a few minutes more of solitude, and he slipped into the deck pantry, where he could light a cigarette. It was a cubby-hole of a place, and he paced it restlessly – up and down and a step sideways to avoid the weighing-machine. . . . He stopped. About the weighing-machine there was something suggestive. The man Home again – that was it. When Home had made tables rise in the air without apparently touching them it had been shown that his own weight nevertheless went up by the weight of the table. In fact for all that side of the business there was always a simple physical explanation. Of course the machinery of Eusapia's little show was of the slenderest importance: still, it would be nice to know.

The bugle sounded and he went below – but still so preoccupied that Beaglehole had to speak to him twice on the stairway. And this pleased Beaglehole, for it opened the way to a joke. 'Wool-gathering, Mr Appleby? You know, I've seldom met a man more devoted to his profession.'

'Yes?' said Appleby, remembering Cobdogla.

There can be great power in this word, rightly inflected – and Beaglehole laughed rather uncertainly. 'But, seriously, it has been a sleepy sort of afternoon, don't you think? I haven't felt so lazy for a long time.'

'I beg your pardon?'

'I said I haven't felt so lazy –'

Appleby slapped an open palm with a clenched fist. 'There!' he said. 'I've got it.'

'Got it?'

'Only the particular wisp of wool I've been groping for.' Appleby smiled cheerfully. 'Did Hudspith tell you it was my birthday?'

5

It is very easy to pretend to be more drunk than one is; at one time or another most undergraduates have managed it. There is no great difficulty in simulating extreme drunkenness when one is entirely sober. But to pretend to all the successive stages of tipsiness and intoxication on no basis of fact is a task requiring considerable virtuosity. And it was this task that Hudspith, for reasons best known to himself, had undertaken. As dinner progressed he appeared to be getting drunker and drunker on the ship's much-tossed and shaken wines.

Appleby, in whose honour this exhibition was taking place, watched it with admiration and some trepidation. The performance was, in its way, as finished as Eusapia's, and it was clear that Hudspith had been at it before. In fact he was reviving some star turn of his earlier career and packing a great deal of science into the show. The drink was disappearing undeniably fast, and almost certainly into Hudspith's stomach. Perhaps as the level rose so too did that of some half a pint of salad oil that he had swallowed off-stage. Or perhaps he carried round some dis-intoxicant drug for use on just such occasions. You didn't know where you had Hudspith – or not once you succeeded in pushing back the cheated girls to the frontiers of his mind. For then his youth returned to him and he became a police officer with a positively alarming imaginative technique. Appleby had conjured up Cobdogla, which was probably really on the map; Hudspith was now having a great deal to say about a township called Misery, which almost certainly was not. Misery was an altogether more go-ahead place than the neighbouring Eden. Hudspith doubted if there was a rival to it short of Pimpingie or Dirty Flat. And these were a hundred miles away and over the range.

'The range?' said Beaglehole, mildly curious. 'What range is that, Mr Hudspith?'

Hudspith put down his glass. 'My range,' he said carefully. 'Mine and Uncle Len's.'

'Oh – I see.'

'But it's all mine now,' Hudspith made a wavering gesture which embraced vast distances and at the same time contrived almost to brush the nose of the intense Miss Mood. 'And I can put a sheep on every tenth acre.'

'Isn't it difficult,' Mrs Nurse asked comfortably, 'to pick them up again? Such long runs for the dogs.'

Hudspith merely breathed heavily.

'Your Uncle – ah – Len died?' asked Beaglehole.

'He didn't die,' said Hudspith. 'He perished.'

'He did a perish,' said Appleby corroboratively and idiomatically. It was he, after all, who had started this desperate masquerade, and he must in fairness back Hudspith up. 'Ron found his bones.'

'Some of them,' said Ron with heavy drunken accuracy.

Miss Mood made a sound as agonized as if her own bones were being picked in whispers. '*Which?*' she asked huskily.

'The troopers,' said Hudspith, ignoring this, 'wanted to have it that Uncle Len had been murdered. But it was just a perish, all right. You see, the blacks won't go into the range. It's haunted.'

'What by?' Wine spoke, sharply and for the first time.

There was a moment's silence, Hudspith at this juncture

finding it necessary to drink deeply. 'The Bunyip,' said Appleby. 'Haunted by the Bunyip.'

'That's right, the Bunyip,' said Hudspith.

'And what is the Bunyip, Mr Hudspith?' Wine's question was directed uncompromisingly at the late Len's nephew.

Hudspith set his glass down slowly. 'The Bunyip is something not many white people can see,' he said. His tone held a momentary sobriety which was effective in the extreme.

Miss Mood, at least, rose to it. 'And *you*, Mr Hudspith?' she breathed.

The answer was a loud bang and rattle. Everybody – except perhaps the monumentally placid Mrs Nurse – jumped. Hudspith had outrageously thumped the table and was roaring at the steward for a fresh bottle of wine. It was fortunate, Appleby reflected, that the captain appeared to prefer the company of his officers and was not dining in the saloon that night. Hudspith banged again, and there was nobody to stop him; he banged a third time and shouted, so that even Mrs Nurse looked about for her bag. But before the company could break up he had suddenly turned quiet and maudlin. 'Shame to spoil John's birthday. Man only has one birthday in the year.'

'Too right,' said Appleby, who felt that he ought not now to be quite sober himself.

'Never mind about seeing things,' Hudspith flapped a hand at Miss Mood rather as if she were a fly. 'Much better have a song. All join in song. All join in –'

'All join in "Waltzing Matilda",' said Appleby, fairly confident that this particular piece of antipodean local colour was correct. And he struck up by himself:

'Once a jolly swagman camped beside a billabong,
 Under the shade of a coolibah tree;
 And he sang as he sat and waited while his billy boiled,
 "Who'll come a-waltzin' Matilda with me?"

'Up came a jumbuck to drink at the billabong;
 Up jumped the swagman and grabbed it with glee;
 And he sang as he shoved that jumbuck in his tucker-bag,
 "You'll come a-waltzin' Matilda with me."

'Up came the Squatter, mounted on his thoroughbred.
 Up came the troopers – one, two, three!
 "Where'd you get that jumbuck you've got in your tucker-bag?
 You'll come a-waltzin' Matilda with me."'

'Rather a sinister song,' said Wine. 'Or at least with a suggestion of developing that way.'

'Is the billabong the same as the Bunyip?' asked Miss Mood.

Appleby, who was not prepared to venture an answer to this, embarked on another verse. Hudspith joined in – not very articulately, but that was explicable.

'Up jumped the swagman and dived into the billabong.
 "You'll never take me alive!" cried he.
 And his ghost may be heard if you camp beside the billabong,
 Singing, "Who'll come a-waltzin' Matilda with me?"'

'"Waltzin' Matilda, waltzin' Matilda,
 Who'll come a-waltzin' Matilda with me?"
 And his voice may be heard if you camp beside the billabong,
 Singing – "Who'll come a-waltzin' Matilda with me?"'

Hudspith applauded vigorously – so vigorously that the general attention became focused on him once more. 'Bravo!' he bawled. 'Bra –' The word died oddly on his lips. His hands, which had been gesticulating, dropped limply to his sides. It seemed uncomfortably probable that he was going to be suddenly sick. Presently, however, it was clear that he was in the grip of some other sensation. His features worked, but it was in perplexity rather than physical distress. Expectant, troubled and oddly absent, he was staring at the stairs of the saloon.

Appleby again thought the performance tip-top. But one had to remember that the audience consisted of something like a panel of experts. Perhaps it would be best to take the part of Lady Macbeth recalling her hallucinated thane to the proprieties of the banquet. 'Ron,' he said loudly, 'how does Matilda go on?'

With a perceptible but unexaggerated jerk Hudspith returned from whatever experience had befallen him 'Matilda?' he asked blankly. And then he smiled expansively at the company.

'Once knew a smart girl called Matilda.' He leered drunkenly. 'Once took a little girl called Matilda across to –'

This time Mrs Nurse gathered up her bag and rose. 'It has been a very nice party,' she said. 'And now Miss Mood and I are going into the little drawing-room to have our coffee. Good night.' Mrs Nurse put much placid decision into these last words, and Miss Mood followed her – perhaps not without a shade of reluctance – from the saloon.

Hudspith filled his glass, unbuttoned his waistcoat, lowered his voice. 'Once knew a little girl called Gladys . . .'

It was past ten o'clock. Appleby drained his coffee, put out his cigarette and left the smoke-room for a breath of air. Matilda and Gladys, girls not without interesting idiosyncrasy, were now points remote on Hudspith's amatory pilgrimage, and he was regaling Wine and Beaglehole with the fruits of more recent researches. In these matters Hudspith had, after all, a great deal of vicarious experience: more than enough to stock all the smoke-rooms of all the liners afloat. And Wine and Beaglehole were passive listeners – Beaglehole because he liked it, and Wine – conceivably – because he had designs of his own. Wine was a person who had as yet not at all emerged; he was an unpredictable quantity; and that he was really in process of being outflanked by the present fantastic procedures it would be hazardous to assert.

'Well, what do you think?' Hudspith too had come out to breathe, and his voice, disconcertingly sober, came cautiously from the darkness.

'Absolutely awful. Dirty Flat and those rangers aren't owned by people at all like you and your Uncle Len. They're owned by people rather like the lesser country gentry of Shropshire – only there are about six Shropshires to a gent. Still, I must say you do the getting tight rather well.'

'Wait till you see the getting un-tight. That's much more tricky.'

'No doubt. And will you tell me what Matilda and Gladys and the rest are all about? And do you realize that tomorrow, when we're all sober, I shall have to try to hold up my head as the intimate friend of a self-confessed lecher?'

Hudspith chuckled cheerfully. It was evident that his bogus confessions were having the most beneficial effect on his nervous constitution; he had, in fact, discovered what was virtually a new variety of psycho-therapeutic method. He chuckled again, cheerfully but cautiously still. 'Wait and see. There'll be an important moment in about twenty minutes. But the big show is timed for midnight.'

Appleby sighed, for he would have liked to go to bed. 'Very well. It's your do.'

Hudspith's shadow melted into darkness. His voice came floating back from near the smoke-room door. 'Chin chin,' it said.

The night was dark, and Appleby blinked into it. Hudspith bubbling with the raffish idiom of the nineteen hundreds was a mildly surprising phenomenon. But then so, and in an equally dated away, were a calculating horse and an Italian medium specializing in materializations. A witch and a girl possesed by demons were exhibits more 'period' still. In fact – said Appleby to himself as he paced the blacked-out deck once more – this ship has the nineteen-forties dead astern and is heading for the past at its full economic speed of eighteen knots. The Time Ship: master, Emery Wine. It sounded like H. G. Wells. . . . He took several turns about the deck and returned to the smoke-room. Hudspith's voice greeted him as he entered. 'I like them young,' it said.

'I must say I like them young,' he repeated – and Appleby saw that the process of getting un-tight had begun. For a trace of uneasiness, perhaps of shame, had come into the deplorable saga. Hudspith, though still talking defiantly, was looking at the silent Wine and Beaglehole with an occasional furtive sideways glance – as a man may do who is presently going to realize that he has been making a fool of himself. 'There was a girl in London,' said Hudspith, raising his voice with a sort of desperate and fading arrogance. 'Just a few months ago. Lucy, her name was. . .'

Rather abruptly Appleby plumped down on a settee. Perhaps he had been dull. Certainly he had not realized it was all heading for this.

'Lucy?' said Wine, profoundly uninterested. 'Do you know, I believe this is the first Lucy you've mentioned? Whereas there have been four Marys and three Janes. Beaglehole will correct me if I am wrong.'

'And you wouldn't believe' – Hudspith's voice went higher as he ignored the sarcasm – 'you wouldn't believe how young she was – sometimes.'

Wine laid down his cigar. 'Sometimes?' he echoed.

This time Hudspith lowered his voice. 'Lucy was a damned queer kid. That was what was cute about her. You never knew where you were with her. Sometimes as grave as a judge. And sometimes – well, she might have been twelve. Poor little Lucy Rideout!'

Hudspith was staring mournfully at the ceiling – which meant that he could trust his colleague to make such observations as might appear. And there could be no doubt about the palpable hit: Appleby was instantaneously convinced of that. Between Wine and his assistant there had passed a glance of the most startled intelligence. The nightmarish birthday party had justified itself at last. And the Daffodil affair, lately as ragged and flowing as cirrus clouds, stood now solid before Appleby as he sat – solid too with something of the symmetry of a carefully precipitated crystal.

And now Hudspith was shifting restlessly on his seat. Again he had the look of an uneasy man, but this time his air was not quite that of one dawningly aware that he has carried his liquor singularly ill. He had something of his old brooding appearance, and his eye seemed as if looking half fearfully into distance. 'And there's a funny thing about that girl,' he said. 'Several times today –' He broke off, rose and walked fairly steadily round the smoke-room – a rapidly sobering man. 'I suppose that's why I've been talking,' he resumed inconsequently.

There was a moment's silence. Wine was carefully relighting his cigar. 'You were saying,' he prompted, 'that several times today–'

But Hudspith had strode to the farther end of the room, poured himself out a cup of black coffee and drained it. And now when he turned back he was visibly still further chastened. 'You mustn't mind my yarns,' he said. 'Will get yarning after a party. You know how it is. Too much girl and then this damn long voyage.' He stood before them, ignoble but rational. 'Tell you snake stories now, if you like.' Again he shifted uneasily, was momentarily absent. 'Or game of cards. Fixes the mind. After a long party nothing like a hand or two before shut-eye. Come 'long, John.'

Appleby came along, noting that it was just three-quarters of an hour short of twelve. Beaglehole suggested poker; Hudspith demanded bridge and carried his point, so that presently he was demonstrating very convincingly those peculiarly rapid powers of sobering-up which some men possess. It was a dull game, for small stakes, with Beaglehole making occasional bets in the prudent manner of a commercial man, and with Wine displaying an orthodoxy so consistent as to suggest some hidden absence of mind. Hudspith himself was now as sober and normal a businessman as ever came out of Auckland or Sydney. And over the deserted bar the clock ticked steadily towards midnight.

Deep below them the engines throbbed and the slap and hiss of water came faintly up; occasionally they could hear the high note that a ship's rigging seems to take on only south of the line. Perhaps bridge does fix the mind, but bridge at midnight and in mid-ocean can strangely emphasise the isolation of a voyage. Close round about, sleeping or at watch, is the tiny company to which one is attached. Beyond, and stretching past the bounds of any concrete awareness, is the utterly alien deep. We are accustomed to think of the distances of inter-stellar space as alone baffling to the human imagination. But after a fortnight at sea we know that we have traversed distances equally transcending any realizing power of the mind. Through the night the engines drove with their mysteriously unfailing power. And the four men flipped their pasteboards on the square of green baize.

Hudspith was partnering Appleby. He was laying down his hand for dummy. And as he finished doing so he looked past Appleby's shoulder and smiled – smiled with evident pleasure and perhaps a trace of surprise. 'Lucy!' he said. 'I didn't know –' He broke off, frowned, spoke again with sudden anxiety. 'What are you doing? What are you doing with that –'

Appleby, although he ought to have been looking at Wine, swung round despite himself. The door was behind him and it was closed. Behind the door, he knew, was a curtain, and behind that an outer door, also closed. But Hudspith, it was almost possible to swear, had been looking at the deck directly beyond. And now he had sprung to his feet and was passing a hand across his eyes. 'She had a gun,' he said hoarsely. 'There were trees . . . palms. . . .' Dead sober, he looked at his companions. 'I'm drunk,' he said. 'Damn drunk – sorry.' He turned round, pushed his chair back clumsily and stumbled from the room.

As a piece of acting it was absolutely first class. Appleby, although he felt an inclination to cheer, contrived to whistle. 'Poor old Ron!' he said. 'I never knew him get it as badly as that.'

Beaglehole rose. He looked both scared and angry – which is no doubt how the sceptical do look on such occasions. And when he spoke it was more aggressively than usual. 'He'll be seeing pink and green rats next. It's a mistake to drink anything but whisky on a ship.'

'Not at all.' Wine, who was stacking cards while staring thoughtfully before him, shook his head. 'This has the appearance – at least the superficial appearance – of something rather more interesting than that. What is called, I believe, casual veridical hallucination of the sane.'

'You mean second sight?' asked Appleby.

Wine shrugged his shoulders. 'My dear man, that is a term from superstition and folk-lore. If we positively believe in such things we shall no doubt use these old words. I prefer the description science gives to something it still regards as extremely debatable.' He turned round. 'Midnight, you will notice. I wonder if your friend's Lucy is still alive? Or has conceivably just died? People who investigate these affairs would no doubt like to know.' He yawned. 'And now what about bed?'

'Sure,' said Appleby and turned towards the door. Suddenly he stopped and laid a hand with innocent familiarity on the other's shoulder. 'But say, Mr Wine, you knew all that jargon about those horses – and now you have the jargon about this. Perhaps you're a bit of a hand at investigating these things yourself?' Appleby let his hand drop, but not before he had felt Wine's muscles grow momentarily rigid. Whatever reply came would be the product of rapid calculation.

'Investigate spooks, Mr Appleby? Dear me, no.'

'Spooks and thinking animals and various sorts of mediums – that sort of thing.'

Wine's eyelids flickered. Then he smiled. It would have been a snubbing smile had it been a shade less merely amused. 'Dear me, no. Beaglehole, shall we be talking too freely if we say that we have more important work than that?' And Wine laughed pleasantly. 'Good night, my dear sir. Good night.'

6

Appleby swung himself out of his bunk and sat on the edge. His hands lay on his knees and the morning sun shone on them. 'You see?' he said. His right thumb almost imperceptibly moved. 'You see?'

'Yes, I see.' Hudspith had just returned from an early prowl on deck. 'But I *don't* see what sort of contrivance –'

'A lazy-tongs. Something that Beaglehole said put it in my head. It used to be quite a popular toy, and nowadays they make elevator doors and things on the same principle. Something rather like a pair of scissors with a piece of lattice-work pivoted to the blades. You close the scissors – a movement of the thumb will do it – and the whole affair shoots out and extends itself a surprising distance. Open the scissors and it retracts itself and folds up. Eusapia was practising with a contrivance like that.'

Hudspith shook his head. 'But surely such a thing would quickly be found out? No conjurer could get away with it.'

'A physcal medium isn't a conjuror. Or rather he is a conjurer who imposes conditions which no theatre audience would put up with. He sits in next to complete darkness. His limbs may be held, but he can claim a supernatural origin for all sorts of calculated physical convulsions. And if he is too strictly controlled – for instance if he has had to agree to a careful search before a seance – he can simply announce that the spirits are on holiday for that day. Eusapia is this special sort of conjurer and Wine knows it and is carrying her off to join his circus.

'Which places Wine. He collects frauds.'

'No.' Appleby shook his head decidedly. 'The thing is not quite so simple as that. Perhaps no known physical medium has ever been exhaustively investigated by scientists without the exposure of fraud. But there are highly intelligent investigators who maintain that with these people fraud is a sort of emergency line of defence. Mediums – roughly speaking – are paid by results. It is conceivable that they are genuinely the channels of supernormal agencies to which the methods and attitudes of scientific investigators are antipathetic. When the mediums are hard pressed by the scientists the supernormal agencies desert them. And then, to sustain their reputation, the mediums resort to trickery. There is thus a case of sorts for continuing to investigate the phenomena even of persons who have been frequently exposed as fraudulent. Wine may know that Eusapia is a little twister and yet his intentions may be those of a serious investigator.'

'Or they may be those of a showman.'

'Exactly. We may be on the track of the Strangest Show on Earth. Something of that sort. But the question is – is Wine on the track of two inquisitive policemen who have begun their dealings with him in a deplorably holiday mood?' Appleby rose and stretched himself. 'I'm going to have a bath. If I meet him I'll ask him.'

'Don't do that.' Hudspith spoke with serious concern. 'Don't, I mean, do any more forcing of the issue at present. You've claimed to know a relative of Daffodil's and I've claimed to know Lucy Rideout –'

Appleby laughed. 'My claim is quite harmless. But the laws of slander are absolutely savage against yours. And from a man whose mission in life is the defence of British maidenhood –'

Hudspith held up his hand. 'Bawdry,' he said with dignity, 'will get us nowhere. I am simply insisting that we've strained coincidence to breaking-point and must go easy if he's not to spot us. I don't think I ought to have had that vision of Lucy last night. I'm afraid I was a bit carried away.'

'Not exactly that. You did contrive to get out of the room on your own legs. And so, for that matter, did Wine. I mean that he wasn't at all bowled over. Beaglehole was much nearer

94

letting some cat out of the bag. Wine is a deep one. And just what he's thinking – or planning – at this moment I can't at all guess.'

'That's because you don't get up early enough. He's been trying to send a wireless message.'

Appleby was picking up a large sponge; he held it suspended in air. 'A wireless message? He must know he has no more chance of that than of taking over command of the ship.'

'You forget that he's ostensibly on some sort of hush-hush job. And to get a message away he's been straining any authority he possesses.'

'It looks as if we've upset him all right. Did they send him away with a flea in his ear?'

Hudspith frowned at this vulgarism – and then fleetingly smiled. 'What you might call half a flea. They told him it was absolutely impossible to send out wireless messages anyway. The atmosphere is electrical.'

Appleby stared. 'Isn't that what they say in a diplomatic crisis?'

'This time it's meant literally. I had all this from the first officer. There's some sort of electrical disturbance in the offing quite outside his experience. That's why the air felt so queer last night.'

'It's nice to know it wasn't just the drink. But isn't it pretty queer still?'

'Decidedly. I think you're quite likely to be electrocuted in that bath.'

Appleby chanced it. And as he lay in the warm salt water and watched its obstinate refusal to dip and tilt with the ship he realized how significant that attempted wireless message was. It went some way towards explaining the theft of 37 Hawke Square.

Mrs Nurse picked up the milk-jug. 'I suppose they make it out of powder,' she said. 'I'm afraid I don't think it at all nice. Particularly in tea. I don't think tea is at all nice on steamers.' She put the jug down again. 'Has anybody noticed the funny sky?'

'I never saw a sky that colour before,' said Wine.

'It's not so much the colour,' said Miss Mood, 'as the way it seems to go all wavy when you look at it.'

Beaglehole nodded. 'You need go no farther than the wireless aerial to see something damned queer. Lights like little blue devils running and jumping on the wires. Mr Hudspith mayn't believe it, but they're really there.' Beaglehole as he said this looked swiftly at Wine, as if to make sure that this was the right line to take. Then he laughed uneasily and thrust away a plate. 'Uncommonly oppressive, isn't it? Makes you feel queer. No appetite.'

'Feel queer?' said Mrs Nurse – and appeared to consider. 'No, I don't think it does that.'

Miss Mood's nervous hands played with a large amber necklace. 'The astral influences,' she said sombrely. 'It may be some great disaster. But I think one ought to eat.' And she tore the paper cover off a roll.

'These disturbances do happen in the tropics,' said Wine. 'I believe they are not yet very well understood. But I don't think Miss Mood need apprehend disaster.'

Miss Mood was clearly not reassured; instead of eating her roll she was tearing the little paper bag into fragments.

'Feel queer?' said Mrs Nurse again.

Appleby, who had been eating bacon and eggs stolidly, turned to Wine. 'A funny old day, all right,' he said. 'A real cow.'

'I beg your pardon?'

'And gets at the nerves. I've known the same sort of thing during a dust storm.'

'That's right.' Hudspith nodded heavily. 'And I've known Uncle Len say –'

'The fans!' Beaglehole was pointing excitedly. 'Did you ever see –'

It was warm and the fans were going – but now suddenly they could be seen only through a spiralling fuzz and crackle of electrical discharge.

'Did you ever see –' Beaglehole, still dramatically gesturing, was interrupted in turn by Miss Mood. Miss Mood screamed. She screamed because, from the table before her, a little snow-storm of paper fragments had risen and was circling round her head. For a moment her startled face was iike a pinnacle seen through an eddy of gulls. And then, like gulls coming to rest, the little scraps of paper had clustered on her amber necklace.

It was distinctly odd. But the behaviour of the placid Mrs Nurse was odder. 'Queer?' she said faintly, and fell back in her chair with closed eyes. A moment later they had opened again, but the pupils were upturned and only the whites were showing. 'Queer?' she said very faintly, and her body jerked itself upright. 'Near,' she said in a new voice. 'It is very near.' Her voice deepened again and took on a foreign intonation. 'The Emperor says it is near. He says Beware. No, he says Prepare. The Emperor wants you all to know that it is clear. He understands it all. The Emperor understands everything. We understand everything here. The Emperor advises prayer. It is very near now.' There was a long sigh. 'I feel all hollow,' Mrs Nurse said in her ordinary voice. 'I feel all hollow,' she said piteously.

Appleby, who had started on his last rasher, turned again to Wine. 'I expect you know the jargon of this too, Mr Wine?'

'No doubt she will come to herself presently.' Wine uttered the words non-committally and then took refuge behind a coffee-cup.

'Would you call it a trance?' asked Hudspith. 'Uncle Len once knew a woman –'

Like an erupting geyser Miss Mood went off into high-pitched laughter. Peal after peal of it rang horridly through the saloon. And then it ceased as abruptly as it had begun. Breathing rapidly, Miss Mood sat rigid and with a dilated eye.

'Now there's another strange thing,' Appleby was almost owlishly placid. 'Talking of your Uncle Len, Ron, my Uncle Sid had a cowgirl just like that.' And Appleby nodded towards Miss Mood.

'A cowgirl?' said Wine. He spoke, Appleby thought, a trifle wildly, as if the situation were becoming too much for him. There would come a point at which you could bowl over Wine.

'A cowgirl. And when she went like *that*' – and again Appleby nodded at Miss Mood – 'you could do *this*.' And Appleby's hand went to the lapel of his coat and produced a pin. 'This,' he repeated – and leaning across the table he pushed the pin firmly into Miss Mood's arm. 'Ron, have you got another?' He felt in his pocket. 'Or if one has a pen-knife –'

'Really,' said Wine, 'I don't know that you ought. Clearly Miss Mood is in a condition of hysterical anaesthesia. But you must consider –'

'There!' interrupted Appleby admiringly. 'There's the right jargon again. But does it occur to you, Mr Wine, that for a small boat like this –'

'Just look at her hand, now,' said Hudspith, pointing at Miss Mood. 'What would she be doing that for?' Miss Mood's right hand was moving oddly on the tablecloth.

'I think if I had a pencil' – Appleby felt in his pockets –'and a piece of paper she would produce automatic writing – something like that. Mr Wine, you agree?'

'No doubt,' said Wine.

'Well, as I was saying, isn't it odd that on a small boat like this there should be –'

'Where is the girl with the golden hair?' said Mrs Nurse, beginning again. 'Where is the girl with the golden hair? Where is the girl with the golden hair?'

Miss Mood, still rigid and still making scribbling movements, began to sob. There was a crackle of electricity from the fans and the atmosphere was permeated with a faint singeing smell.

'Here is Mentor to speak to the girl with the golden hair. Hurry. Mentor says hurry. There are thwarting influences. Where is the girl –'

There was a tumble of steps on the staircase and Beaglehole, who must have slipped out some minutes before, blundered in. 'That Italian!' He addressed Wine in a despairing flurry. 'She's behaving just like this in the third-class saloon. Something to do with tambourines. And a table. Turning a table . . .'

A long reverberating crash drowned his words – a crash as if some Titan had banged a tambourine, as if the very table of the gods had been upset. Again and again the thunder rolled, and daylight flickered feebly between great flashes of lightning. Then there was a hiss of falling water. The curious atmospheric conditions that had led to so much eccentric behaviour on the part of the protégées of Mr Emery Wine were resolving themselves in a straightforward tropical storm.

'I was saying,' said Appleby, 'that in a small ship like this one would hardly expect –'

'Quite so,' said Wine.

'One would hardly expect to find so many birds of a feather. Unless, of course, they were travelling together to a conference or a clinic or something of that sort. But we don't know that Mrs Nurse and Miss Mood –'

'Exactly,' said Wine. 'It is curious, no doubt.'

'We don't know that Mrs Nurse and Miss Mood believe they have anything to do with each other. And now it seems there's a similar sort of woman in the third class. It makes one think –'

Wine took him by the arm. 'My dear Mr Appleby,' he said, 'you and I must go on deck and get a breath of air.'

7

Rain gurgled in the scuppers and drummed on the sun-deck overhead; beyond, it fell in torrents from a sky watery and still lit by a faint lightning; the South Atlantic Ocean looked terribly wet.

'It must frankly appear,' said Mr Wine, 'that we are not what we seem.'

'You mean Beaglehold and yourself?'

'I mean Beaglehole and myself on the one part and Hudspith and yourself on the other part. The phrase is a trifle legal, but expresses the state of affairs very nicely. By the way, I must introduce you to Eusapia. She is quite charming. Dishonest, of course. But in pretty girls moral qualities are not so awfully relevant, are they?' Wine smiled urbanely at Appleby. 'But perhaps it is your friend whom I should introduce to Eusapia. I believe she would obliterate even Gladys from his mind.'

Appleby looked at Wine squarely. 'I don't know that our conversation can usefully take on this tone.'

Framed against a sheet of rain-streaked plate-glass, Wine gave a faint and mocking bow. 'I stand corrected. But scarcely in an idiom familiar to Uncle Sid and Uncle Len.'

'Uncle Sid and Uncle Len are all nonsense.' Appleby, thrown initially on the defensive, determined to make robust work of it.

'I wouldn't say that,' Wine was courteous. 'They seemed to me very credible – and creditable – approximations. Perhaps Uncle Len's bones were a bit steep – but then odd things no doubt do happen in those parts. May I offer you a cigarette?'

Appleby took a cigarette. 'Has it occurred to you, Mr Wine, that it is a serious matter to hold yourself out as being upon a government mission in time of war when in fact your business is quite different?'

'But we can't all of us *really* go on war missions. And unless doing so ostensibly, you know, it's now extraordinarily difficult to get about at all.' Wine struck a match. '"Some to the wars, to try their fortune there, Some to discover islands far away." The words are Shakespeare's. Perhaps they will elevate what you call the tone of our discussion. And incidentally – isn't it a discussion between the pot and the kettle? Do you and Hudspith really know much about wool?'

'Possibly not. But at least we are travelling on fairly significant business. Otherwise, and at the present time, I would rather be at home.'

Wine shook his head. 'Home-keeping youths have ever homely wits. I am inclined to recommend the islands far away. Indeed, I hope to persuade you to accompany me there. Why not? It may be we shall find the Happy Isles.'

'And meet the great Achilles whom we knew?' The words were idle, but Appleby's brain was working quickly. Some unknown factor, some odd misunderstanding, must surely lurk in Wine's proposal.

'Conceivably even that. Achilles and Hector too.'

'And other shades – like Mrs Nurse's Mentor and the Emperor?'

'Ah.' Wine frowned considerably, so that Appleby wondered if he was thinking up a little more Shakespeare. 'Now we come to business, don't we? That the storm should affect all these queerly organized people was not, I suppose, so very odd. I confess to having felt unsettled myself. But both Mrs Nurse and Miss Mood in trances simultaneously, and then word of Eusapia misbehaving too, really was a bit overpowering. As I say, it may be admitted that we are not altogether what we seem.'

'Nor are our relations what they appear to be. Neither Mrs Nurse nor Miss Mood shows any consciousness of standing in a special relationship either to each other or to yourself. And yet there can now be no doubt that, together with the Italian girl, they form a sort of convoy under the escort of you and your secretary. Perhaps they don't know about you.'

Wine nodded. 'Well, as a matter of fact they don't.'

'Such concealment is rather strange, to say the least. You have employed agents or decoys to send them travelling where you want them.'

'Just that, Mr Appleby. And of course there was Lucy Rideout too. I must admit that I was very disturbed by your friend's ostensible experience last night– very perturbed indeed. In fact it is only in the last few minutes that I have seen the thing as being an ingenious hoax. And I am disposed to think that you know about the calculating horse from Harrogate. Of what else, I wonder? Have you heard of Hannah Metcalfe? She's a witch. Indeed she is.' And Wine smiled his unruffled smile.

The thing had the speed of mechanized encounter. And the man was not confessing at random; he had an object in view; perhaps it was that of rushing one off one's feet. And – telling all this – what did he know or think he knew? Appleby put out a feeler. 'You think Hudspith never really met that Lucy Rideout?'

'I don't say that at all. I do say that last night he was very skilfully fooling us.'

Appleby threw away his cigarette and took a quick glance at his companion. There was something in the man's tone as he made this last statement – some quality of combined hesitation and emphasis – which was obscurely significant. 'In fact, Mr Wine, you think my friend Hudspith one big hoax? He isn't subject to abnormal experiences at all?'

'I think nothing of the sort. Otherwise –' Wine broke off and hauled a couple of wicker chairs across the little shelter deck. 'Shall we sit down? And perhaps go back to your own part in the affair? After all, turn about is only reasonable. And I think it is admitted that your concerns are not really with sheep –

101

except perhaps in a metaphorical sense.' Wine smiled again at Appleby – and for the first time Appleby thought it an ugly smile. It was ugly and also puzzling – puzzling because based on some misapprehension as yet unrevealed. Or was there misapprehension? Was Wine rather *feigning* a misapprehension? To arrive at a right answer to this might be vital. And perhaps the best thing would be to take a bold step.

'Perhaps, Mr Wine, you take Hudspith and myself for plain-clothes policemen?'

'Ah,' said Wine.

'In which case you wouldn't be far wrong.'

'Ah,' said Wine again. And then suddenly he sat back in his chair and laughed. His laugh was genuine and of the kind that attends the discovery of intellectual absurdity. 'My dear fellow, may we not be a little more frank with each other than that?' Suddenly he sat forward again and touched Appleby lightly on the arm.

'Listen,' he said.

Part 3

Happy Islands

1

PLOP... *PLOP*.... The waters bubbled evilly and the heavy
sound was indefinably sinister – but each time it was followed
by a delighted clapping of hands. 'Another one!' the girl cried
out. 'And another one! Oh, look at its nose – and its eyes! Mr
Wine says they have little birds that pick their teeth for them.
Oh, look at its great tail!'

The waters were dark and oily round the steamer, and
unmoving except where the great creatures dropped and
splashed. 'Another one!' cried the girl. And the man at the
wheel – who stood all day at the wheel, aloof and dreaming –
the man at the wheel laughed at her suddenly and richly.
'*Lagarto*,' he said; '*lagarto, señorita*.' He swung the wheel, and
the whole crazy little vessel creaked; swung it again so that
one of the paddles insanely clattered; gave a final tug and they
were round another bend with the interminable river stretching
before them. For some reason they hugged the south bank,
low, steamy and densely wooded. On the north the horizon was
nearly always water. They were now two thousand miles upstream, but the mind revolted at the knowledge. *PLOP*....
'And *another* one!' cried Lucy in ecstasy. Her clapping raised a
flock of pink and yellow parrots from the tree-ferns.

Reclined under an awning in the stern, Mr Emery Wine
benevolently smiled. Then a thought seemed to strike him.
'Lucy,' he called out, 'have you written to your mama?'

'Oh, yes, Mr Wine.'

'That's right, my dear.' Wine's glance turned meditatively on
Hudspith, who was gloomily scratching his jaw. 'She writes to
her mother every week – *one of her* writes to her mother – and
I try to see that the letter catches the Clipper. Mrs Rideout is a
very good sort of woman. Perhaps you know her?'

Hudspith frowned. One who had romanced so freely about

the virginal young person in the prow might well find this question embarrassing. It was true that since coming on board Mr Wine's steamer sundry mendacious explanations had been given. Nevertheless Lucy remained somebody whom Hudspith could not quite look in the eye.

'Of course,' said Wine, 'I had to act a little high-handedly in getting her away. After all *your* lot might very well have got in first if I had at all stood upon forms. Competition does make one a little unscrupulous at times. But now I believe that Mrs Rideout and I understand each other very well. It was one of the things which amused me when Appleby made his little joke about being a plain-clothes policeman. I reflected that there was really very little the police could get me on.'

'There's the horse,' said Appleby.

Wine laughed gaily. 'I stole the horse. But whoever heard of a man being convicted of absconding to South America with a broken-down cab-horse? The thing would fall to pieces as an evident absurdity. No; if you were a policeman – and if Hudspith here were another – I think you would find it difficult to nail me.' He pulled at a soft drink. 'Do you know, Hudspith, I sometimes think that you're rather *like* a policeman? But then at one time I thought you looked quite the Cobdogla type. It's never wise to let appearances count. Take Radbone, now. What would you make of him? I mean judging by the outward man?'

'We've never met him,' Appleby said.

Wine sighed. 'Really, my dear fellows, how absurd you sometimes are. Radbone employs you to keep an eye on me – and I must say I think it's carrying a healthy scientific rivalry rather far – and then when you're detected you turn uncommonly coy . . . Lucy, would you care for a glass of lemonade?'

'Oh, yes, please, Mr Wine.'

'But my point is that Radbone is a dull-looking man who is really uncommonly able. I don't mind confessing that at one time I feared he would get hold of the majority of the material. It's scarce, you know.' Wine lowered his voice. 'Take Lucy there. I doubt if there are a couple of others like that living. Or take Mrs Nurse. One can find any number of Eusapias. But a first-class non-physical medium crops up only once in a

106

generation.' Wine rubbed his hands together softly. 'First-class laboratory and clinical material, gentlemen – first-class material. And I think I have your lot beaten now. I don't think Radbone can reply. Which is why I'm asking you to come and have a look. You can go back and tell him about it.' Wine laughed with high good humour. 'I'm really most obliged to you for coming. It's a devilish long way there – and back.'

'We think it will be very interesting,' Appleby said.

'I really think you will find it so. Jorge' – and Wine turned to a servant – 'you had better fetch Miss Rideout a rug; the air is becoming a little chill. . . . I think you will find it interesting. The *Encyclopaedia Britannica* will tell you that nowhere in the world does there exist a properly equipped laboratory solely for the purposes of psychical research. You will soon know better.'

'And Lucy,' Appleby said.

Wine frowned. 'I beg your pardon?'

'She will soon know too. But why? I mean that it's difficult to see just how Lucy is orthodox psychical-research material. She represents a rare but fairly well-understood morbid condition – that of one individual split up into several personalities. Once upon a time it was thought of as possession by demons, no doubt. But I should have imagined it to be pretty well off the slate of serious psychical inquiry. Lucy is psychopathology, not psychics.'

'Ah,' said Wine – and his glance travelled over the side of the steamer, rather as if he were seeking inspiration among the alligators. 'But there is the historical point of view, you know. One must consider that.' He nodded largely and vaguely in support of this obscure statement. 'And then there are affiliations.' His voice gained confidence. 'When these strange voices speak through Mrs Nurse are we really in contact with an unseen world – or is Mrs Nurse momentarily in Lucy's case? You see?'

Appleby saw. And he saw that the man knew his stuff. Whatever was Wine's game – and it was surely not quite what he claimed – the fellow had the science of the thing adequately enough. Was he what he held himself out to be – and something more? Or was he not what he held himself out to be at all? It was conceivable that a man might devote himself to the organization of large-scale psychical research: many first-rate intelligences had become absorbed in it. It was conceivable that such a man might have a rival called Radbone, and might go to strange and even bizarre lengths to secure a sort of corner in the necessary human material. But was it conceivable that such a man should concentrate his activities thousands of miles up an appalling South American river? Was it conceivable that he should carry off to such a fastness a Harrogate cab-horse and a Bloomsbury mansion – to say nothing of two men whom he declared were spies of his rival, but as to whom there was a recurrent little joke about plain-clothes police? It was a long way up the river – and a long way back. Wine had taken them straight from the liner to his own craft. And now here they were. . . . Appleby, who did not greatly mind tough spots if only they were odd enough, sat back and sipped comfortably at his Maté tea. To all these questions – and others – answers would appear.

Lucy was having a rug wrapped round her toes; Wine nodded approvingly, set down his glass, and sighed with content. 'Poor old Radbone!' he said. 'Do you know, I think I'll send him Eusapia as a Christmas present? I could wish him a nice little crumb of comfort like that.'

Hudspith eyed his host with unforced gloom. 'You seem to feel that you've got Radbone thoroughly down.'

'I wouldn't say that. He's a smart man – though a smart man with a weakness. A weakness fatal in this particular field. The fact is, he's credulous. He doesn't know it, but he's credulous. Deep down, Radbone is hungry for wonders. And in a scientist, you'll agree, that is sheer contradiction and nonsense.'

'But isn't it a hunger for wonders which actuates you too?' Appleby had looked up sharply. 'If you don't hanker after ghosts and marvels why take all this trouble? You can hardly take much pleasure in carrying off Mrs Nurse if you regard yourself as a confirmed sceptic.'

Wine shook his head impatiently. 'My dear Appleby, you must give the matter a little more thought. My attitude is objective. And I am a scientist. That means that I am not interested in anything outside nature. If there are, in fact, ghosts,

108

then ghosts are in nature and to be brought within the rule of natural law. But Radbone has a sneaking nostalgia for something outside nature – thrills, creeps, mystery for the sake of mystery. He wants his ghosts to be uncanny to the end; to produce the same emotional effects in the laboratory as in the peasant's cottage.' Wine had risen and was speaking almost with violence. 'So his attitude and mine are poles apart. It is contended that there are certain classes of phenomena which are unaccountable. These classes of phenomena may or may not exist. But if they do exist they are certainly *not* unaccountable. The laws governing them can be discovered – and that is my job. Radbone, despite his ability and his eminence, is fundamentally no more than a silly woman at a seance. He seeks not the truth, but the thrill. You follow me?'

Appleby modestly intimated that he followed.

'You must forgive my being a little carried away.' Wine let his scientific fervour soften into a whimsical smile. 'And now I think I shall go down and change.'

Hudspith watched his immaculate panama disappear down the companion-way. Then he turned to Appleby. 'I say,' he murmured cautiously, 'do you believe in this Radbone?'

'It would be nice to. If Radbone is an invention we can hardly be his agents, can we? Which would mean that we had walked nicely into a trap. With our eyes open, of course.'

'No doubt there's comfort in that.' Hudspith was keeping a wary eye on Lucy Rideout.

'I think myself that Radbone has a sort of existence.' Appleby's eye too was on Lucy as he spoke. 'If so, it greatly complicates the whole affair.'

'Heaven forbid that it should be more complicated than at present appears. And for my own pårt I don't believe in Radbone and his rival push a bit.'

'No more do I. The existence I attribute to Radbone is – of another kind.'

Hudspith stared. 'Well, if he doesn't exist, then we've admitted to being the agents of a ruddy fiction.' Hudspith frowned at himself as he fell into this improper language. 'I've even had to vamp up some story of having angled after Lucy there as Radbone's agent before Wine got in on her. And your birthday party is supposed to have been a trap all on that same fiction's behalf.' He paused. 'Do you know, I'm beginning to take quite a morbid interest in those alligators.'

Appleby laughed. 'Whereas Lucy's interest is far from morbid. It's as spontaneous as that of a child at the zoo. But you don't think that Wine will make away with us simply because we are policemen disposed to tax him with somewhat irregular methods of assembling what he calls laboratory material?'

'I do,' said Hudspith. 'And – what's more – you do too.'

Appleby laughed again. 'As Uncle Len was so fond of remarking: you're telling me. Or, as Uncle Sid would put it: too right.'

'There are bright spots, I suppose. I'm glad that that awful woman Mood is coming up on another boat. To have her counting up the bones after the alligators had been at work –'

'There wouldn't be any bones. The digestive system of the crocodile family is the most powerful known to zoology. The bones are dissolved within a few seconds of going down.'

'It's wonderful how you can always produce the relevant information.' Hudspith stared sombrely at the clotted vegetation trailing past the port rail. 'Can we really be bound for an island?'

'We can – though it must be admitted that Juan Fernandez was a bad guess. The river runs to whole groups of islands; full-grown archipelagoes right in the middle of the continent. And of one such it appears that Wine has possessed himself.'

Hudspith heaved himself to his feet. 'Has it occurred to you what it must all cost? The thing is far more like big business than scientific research.'

'Quite so. And that brings in the alligators again. The ruthlessness of science tends to expend itself on white mice and guinea-pigs. It's in big business that you find a really concentrated effort to throw one's rivals to the crocodiles.'

Hudspith rubbed his jaw and was silent; then he turned and made his way below. But Appleby sat on under the awning and watched the mists rising along the river-bank. The day was over, and its heat and its clarity ended in noisome vapours. Steamy and miasmal, the stuff came first in scattered wisps or in the finest and least perceptible of veils. And then almost immediately it was everywhere. The landscape, familiar and unchanging through the long day, was obliterated as if some great hand had let a curtain fall. A kind of treacherously luminous darkness fell.

And that was it. Appleby sat very still, looking out over the waters. That was it. The man had chosen with a certain symbolical fitness when he pitched his lair here.

PLOP.

'Another one!'

Appleby was lost in thought; his lips were compressed and he gazed sternly before him. But now his expression softened. 'Lucy,' he called gently, 'won't you come and talk to me?'

2

'Lucy –' Appleby said, and paused. 'Young Lucy –' he said, and paused again. 'It is young Lucy, isn't it?'

Lucy Rideout nodded.

'Are you glad you came, Lucy?'

'I'm glad; I think it's fun. Do you know St Ursula's?' And Lucy looked up at Appleby, friendly and unembarrassed.

'No; I don't know about St Ursula's.'

'It's a girls' school, and it goes round and round the world in a great steamer. They have a lovely time. Of course it isn't really true. It's in a book.'

'I see.'

'But this is really true. And I do think it's fun. There's lemonade whenever you like.'

'That is very nice. But what about – about the others? Do they like it too?'

'Sick Lucy hates it. She kept on trying to run away at first. But now, of course, she has her studies. She's doing Latin with Mr Wine.' Young Lucy spoke with a sort of reluctant respect. 'That keeps her quiet.'

'And –'

'Real Lucy? Real Lucy is terribly thrilled. But she's scared too, I think. Only since you came –' Young Lucy hesitated. 'She would be dreadfully angry if she knew I told you this.'

'Then perhaps you had better not tell me.' Appleby looked at the childlike young woman beside him with considerable perplexity. Conversation with Lucy Rideout – conversation with the Lucy Rideouts – was really a job for a specially trained man. The amateur, even when he understood the situation, was constantly liable to trip. The cardinal thing to remember was that there was only one Lucy in existence at a time – a Lucy who regarded the two other Lucys commonly in an objective and friendly, but occasionally in an exasperated manner. . . . 'If it would annoy her,' Appleby said, 'you had better hold your tongue.'

'She's in love with you.'

'Oh.' Appleby was considerably at a loss.

Young Lucy's eyes danced mischievously. 'I think if you wanted –'

'Be quiet.'

Young Lucy looked hurt. 'I'm sorry. I don't know much about that sort of thing – not yet. And it's a terribly long yet. I'm twelve, you know. And I seem to have been twelve for years. Sometimes I think that the others are getting all the fun. And sometimes I'm glad and think it would be horrid to be like the others and old.' She paused and frowned, profoundly perplexed. 'But mostly I just wish it was all different and that there weren't any others. And I think the others feel that too. Since we got to know each other, that is.'

'I see. And when did you get to know each other?'

'At first there was just real Lucy, and for quite a long time after I came she knew nothing about me, though I knew about her. It was better after we did both know each other. Then after a long time sick Lucy came. We neither of us knew anything about her and she didn't know about us. Not even that we – we *were*, I mean. That was the worst time of all. Then we got to know her and hated her. And then she got to know me, but not real Lucy. That was funny.'

'It was rather strange, my dear.'

'And there was something else that was funny. It was rather

a good thing, I think. Sick Lucy was awfully clever. But she didn't remember anything. She didn't know anything about anything before she came. We had to teach her by leaving messages. We wrote things down about ourselves, I mean, and she read them, and so she got to know things. Nowadays sometimes two of us can sort of talk to each other. But it's dreadfully muddling.' Young Lucy looked at Appleby, cheerful and very pathetic. '*I* like you, too,' she said. 'May I ask you something?'

'Of course, Lucy.'

'How many are there of you?' Lucy's glance was now timid, hopeful.

Appleby looked at the deck, suddenly held by a great and growing anger. Here and there in the great cities of the world were specialists who could deal with all this; who could see their way through it as one sees one's way through a mathematical problem. The girl could be healed; made whole; made one But she was being carried off to an archipelago in the middle of South America. . . . 'There's only one of me, Lucy,' he said.

The corners of her mouth dropped. 'There seems to be *nobody* else –' Her glance wandered; she clapped her hands. 'Flamingos!' she cried. 'Oh, aren't they beautiful!' She gave a little gasp and shudder. 'Mr Appleby,' she said, 'can you tell me about the death of Socrates?'

The alligators plopped unregarded; the flight of the flamingos was now a whirr of wings. The servant called Jorge –a villainous-looking fellow – had drawn mosquito-curtains round the little deck and lit a lamp. There was a powerful smell of cooking forward, so that one could almost believe that the paddles were monotonously slapping at a great river of gravy. But Lucy Rideout appeared to have no thought of dinner; her gaze was fixed intently on Appleby.

'And he said that whether death was a dreamless sleep, or a new life in Hades among the spirits of the great men of antiquity, he counted it equally a gain to die.'

'And that is all?' Sick Lucy's face, strained and anxious, was pale in the light of the lamp.

'It is all I can remember, Miss Rideout.'

'Thank you; you are very good. I know so little. My people

were poor and without education. And I myself am subject to – to interruptions when I try to learn.'

'Indeed? But that is true in some degree of all of us.' Appleby knew that this Lucy was extremely reticent.

'Mr Wine says that he has a great library on his island. He says that he has hundreds of books' – her voice was awed – 'but still I wish that I had not come. The Latin is very hard. Do you know *amo* and *moneo*?'

'I knew them once.'

'It is for always that one must know them. I think that I know *amo* now.'

'You know what it means?'

Sick Lucy drew the rug about her. 'I love,' she said in a mechanical voice, 'thou lovest, he loves.' She was silent for a moment. 'There is so much that I want to learn.' Her voice had a painful precision of one who has doggedly studied books of grammar. 'But I am hindered – the others hinder me.'

'Very much?'

'I do not wish to speak of it.'

'Then let us speak of something else.'

'The others hinder me. Young Lucy is greedy. She is greedy for time. She would push me back – back into –'

'Yes?'

'Nothing,' said sick Lucy in a low voice. 'Back into nothing. Into not being there. I have to fight. And it is difficult. With me it is *amo* and *moneo*. But with her it is flamingos, an alligator – things felt, seen. She is young and does not know things. But she has life. I am afraid sometimes that she will win. You understand?'

'I think I understand a little.' Appleby's voice was almost as low as Lucy's. 'And –' He hesitated, for it seemed inhumane to speak of another of the Lucys as real. 'And besides young Lucy . . .?'

'There is real Lucy. I do not wish to speak of her. She is bad.'

'Bad?' said Appleby gravely.

'With her it is men.'

'I see.' Appleby found that his eye was avoiding the physical presence before him. For one who was not a professional

114

psychiatrist the thing had its occasional extreme discomforts. 'But I don't think –'

'I mean that she might go bad. It is a great anxiety. Will you – will you be careful?'

There was no more than a monosyllable in which to reply to this. But there was a great deal to find out. Mrs Nurse and Miss Mood and the beguiling Eusapia had been spirited away, and it was problematical when they would be encountered again. At the moment only the Lucys were available for interrogation. And which was the one on which to concentrate – which was the most likely to have gained any inkling of the real purposes of Wine? Not that Appleby had the technique to conjure up one particular Lucy; he must take them as they offered. And so he tried now. 'Miss Rideout, what do you recall of how this journey began? Who first suggested it? And – and to whom?'

'I do not wish to speak of it.' Sick Lucy drew the rug about her closer still. 'Mr Appleby, will you please tell me about the Golden Sayings of Marcus Aurelius?'

'. . . and that the fountain of good is inside us, and that with a little digging –'

Lucy Rideout stirred sharply. 'Hoy!' she said, 'you're not talking to *her*, you know.'

'My dear, I thought I was.' Appleby spoke gently but warily. 'It's rather an easy mistake to make. She *was* there, I promise you, only a few seconds ago.'

'Bother her.' Real Lucy's accents were unrefined but not displeasing. 'And bother the little nipper. Not that she's a bad 'un; we used to have high old times together until that prig came along. But listen. Have they been saying things about me and you?'

'Well – yes, they have.'

'You needn't kid yourself, Jacko.' Real Lucy was robustly cheerful. 'Even in the present restricted society.'

'You may call me John if you will. But if you call me Jacko I will not speak to you again.'

'John, John, whose side are you on? Shades of the prig! That's poetry.'

'I'm not on any side. I think you should all get together.'

115

'And the more we are together the happier we shall be? No, thanks. Do you know why I came away?'

Appleby shook his head. 'No – but I want to. Why?'

Real Lucy thought this a favourable moment for a move; she came over and sat on the arm of Appleby's chair. 'Probably you think it was for a bit of fun?'

'That has occurred to me.'

'Well, it wasn't. I know a thing or two about girls who have gone off like that. And at first it seemed that it *was* just that – as long as it was the foreign-looking young man, you know. But then Mr Wine turned up, John, he's a wrong 'un.'

'I know he is. But why –'

'But not that sort of wrong 'un. You see, a girl that likes a bit of life and fun has to look out for herself. And know about people. And here was Mr Wine wanting to carry me away to the isle of Capri, and yet he wasn't after – well, you know what I mean. He was after something deep of his own.'

'You were quite right, Lucy. He's after something very deep – and rather horrible. But it has nothing to do with trafficking in girls.' Real Lucy, Appleby saw, was more intelligent by a long way than her sisters; in fact she was a possible ally. 'So you saw it was something pretty deep and the mystery interested and excited you. Life was rather dull, and then here suddenly was an adventure. Was that it?'

Real Lucy laughed softly and began to stroke Appleby's hair. 'I wish we could dance,' she said.

'Stick to the point, my dear.'

'I am.' Suddenly she bent down and kissed him on the top of the head. 'I was just thinking that you are clever and rather nice, and that you would never think of me as a girl-friend because of the young 'un perhaps turning up.'

'You're quite right again. But go on.'

'Then listen. I came away because I thought I might leave those two behind. I'm tired of them, I can tell you – that silly kid and the prig. Perhaps they're good sorts in their way, but one does like a little place to oneself. I thought that if I came somewhere and did things they'd both hate that, then they might get sort of discouraged and go away. But it hasn't worked yet, has it? Young Lucy just thinks it no end fun, and the prig is

116

having a high old time with Kennedy's Shorter Latin Grammar.' Into this last statement real Lucy put a sort of whimsical venom which was not unattractive. 'No cinema, no radio, no boys – I mean, hardly any boys.'

'No need to apologize.'

'In fact this boat is a prig's paradise, and for à kid it's better than a free pass to the Zoo. So not much seems to have come so far of the plan for a change of – of –'

'Environment. I think it was a clever plan, Lucy. But rather a leap in the dark. The new environment might be all in favour of one of the others. And then where would you be?'

'Nowhere, I'd be nowhere, as likely as not. But you have to take a chance. And I'm the real one, after all. I think I've got most chance in the end. If I didn't feel that I'd drown myself – and them.'

'You mustn't do that. Nor that either; Mr. Hudspith wouldn't like it' – and Appleby removed her hand from under his chin. 'Tell me, Lucy – why did you never go to a doctor?'

'A doctor?' She stared at him. 'I'm never ill.'

'I see.' Real Lucy was so intelligent and so competently spoken that one could forget the absolute and crippling ignorance general in the Rideout world. 'It will be dinner-time in five minutes.' He had looked at his watch by the gently swaying lamp. 'Lucy, what do you think is Wine's game? Has anything ever happened that has given you any idea of what he's really about?'

She looked serious – so serious that Appleby thought for a moment that sick Lucy had returned. 'He gets together other people who – who are different.'

'I know that.'

'And also –' She broke off. 'Jacko – John, I mean – did you meet a man called Beaglehole? Yes? Well, he's one sort of man I understand – though it's not the sort that my sort of girl sees much of. Beaglehole is money. He does everything for money – just for the sake of the idea of having it. Wine is different. I expect he wants money too. But he wants something else much more. He's the kind that takes hold of you hard and pushes you about until you're just how he wants you. But also he's not.'

'Not?'

'Not that. I've said he's not that. He's that and different.'
Real Lucy was struggling with some difficult abstract conception. 'It's as if' – she paused over this unusual piece of syntax –
'it's as if he felt like that not about a girl, or about girls, but –
well about everything.'

'You mean that he has a terrific desire for power.'

'Oh, John, I knew you were clever.' She touched him on the
ear. 'If only –'

Above the plash of the paddles there sounded the chime of a
little silver bell. And Lucy Rideout sprang to her feet. 'Oh,
Mr Appleby, isn't it fun having dinner so late! When it's dark!
And will there be melon?' She clapped her hands. 'The little,
round, baby melons?'

And Appleby followed young Lucy below.

3

Like a paradox tiresomely sustained, the river widened day
after day as the little steamer puffed and paddled towards its
source. The river widened, but was filled with treacherous
shoals; they kept now to mid-channel, and sometimes there
was a water horizon on either bow. Once they passed a canoe
with fishermen – men brown and naked and lean – and once so
many canoes that Mr Wine had a case of rifles brought on
deck. But it was an uneventful voyage.

The days were hot, and by night there was a soft warmth under
brilliant stars. Mosquitoes did not come out so far; the decks
were clear of curtains and the awnings disappeared at dinner-
time; later the crew assembled on the fo'c'sle deck and chanted
to the sound of a sinister little drum. Hudpsith more than once
remarked that the alligators were becoming sparser – but without appearing to derive much comfort from the fact. Perhaps
his melancholy was coming upon him again. As he had spent
much time on the liner staring out over the prow, so now he
would gaze fixedly over the stern and down the double wake of
the steamer. Appleby supposed that the old Sirens were

operating. In Buenos Aires Hudspith had once been on terms of most profitable co-operation with the chief of police; in Rio there had occurred a notable sequel to his most famous clean-up in Cardiff. And he was growing thinner, Appleby thought; so that the alligators stood to lose by further delay.

And other things might be suspected to be growing thinner: notably the story about Radbone, the rival scientist. Not through want of the sort of sustenance which one might conceive to be afforded by the steady accumulation of cir-cumstantial detail. Wine had quite fallen into the habit of embroidering on Radbone. There was a regular saga about the man, and one with sufficient interior consistency to speak much for the intellectual powers of the story-teller who lazily and extemporaneously produced it. Unfortunately Appleby and Hudspith were scarcely in a position to give it the dispassionate appraisal of literary critics; the saga had a sort of aura of alli-gator which made it uncomfortable hearing. Nevertheless some-thing useful emerged. Emery Wine was a conceited man.

He had trapped them. He knew that they were policemen concerned with Lucy Rideout and Hannah Metcalfe and perhaps other aspects of his affairs; he believed that he had dissimulated this knowledge and convinced them of his con-viction that they were emissaries of a rival scientist – a rival scientist whom he had invented for the purpose of his trap. He was unaware that his explanations were a little too bland and his stories a little too tall. In fact he had under-estimated the perspicacity of his opponents. But then he could afford to neglect the possibility that this was so. Duped or aware, they were caught. His own problematical stronghold was in front, and beﾛind were hundreds and hundreds of miles of the alligator-infested river.

But Wine was conceited; and the fact was interesting even if not helpful. If he was a wrong 'un he was a wrong 'un on a large scale – on the largest scale that wrong 'uns can achieve, it might be. But he was not, as the largest wrong 'uns commonly are, of the double-guarded, cautious and invulnerable sort. He gave rein to an imagination in the matter of Radbone. And imagination might destroy him yet.

There would be something of imagination in a plan for

building up here, in some fastness remote from global warfare, a great organization for the study of the teasing borders of natural knowledge. The voices speaking through Mrs Nurse, the roguery and hypothetical something else in Eusapia, the ancient business of Mr Smart and the yet more ancient business of Colonel Morell: these were all but scattered examples of that class of phenomena commonly called supernatural –phenomena never perhaps convincingly and massively demonstrated but yet clinging obstinately to the fringes of human belief in almost every country and age. A spiritualist 'seance' behind the closed curtains of a modern drawing-room has very little to commend itself to an educated mind: the spirits communicate only a nauseous twaddle, and the physical manifestations have constantly the air of – and frequently a proved source in – a trivial if ingenious conjuring. It is only when the student or investigator takes wider ground, when he finds amid remote times and cultures startlingly analogous performances with the identical residuum of stubbornly unaccountable fact, that he may come to be impressed. A group of scientists, puzzled by some 'paranormal' manifestation in twentieth-century London, finds that in seventeenth-century Africa this identical quirk or quiddity in nature has puzzled Jesuit missionaries as intelligent, as acute and as sceptical as themselves. The rub is there. The rub is there, thought Appleby – and from this pervasiveness of the thing rather than from any impressiveness in individual instances does it maintain its status as a legitimate field for scientific inquiry. And there would be something of imagination in a plan for large-scale assault upon this shadowy corner of the universe.

It had never been done. Rather oddly if one considered the momentous issues which could conceivably be held involved, it had never been done. Here and there had come an endowment for such hitherto irregular investigations – but always, it would appear, there had been mismanagement or ineptitude, and the effort had faded out. Telepathy, for instance, had been studied experimentally and at considerable expense. But the investigators – Radbones of a sort, as it would seem – had inadequately meditated the terms of their problem, so that the results presented merely a new field for dispute. And yet in this strange and baffling branch of knowledge the time was probably ripe for some major clarification, and there would be imagination in a really big drive on it.

Yet all this was nothing – or was little – to Emery Wine.

Big industrialists, Appleby said to himself as he looked out across the unending river, are accustomed to keep a few 'pure' scientists in a back room. In their private and cultivated capacities they may even patronize them a little from time to time. Nevertheless the status of these workers is low; they are kept for the purpose of rounding an occasional awkward technical corner, and if they make a 'discovery' they are likely to see it promptly locked up in their cultivated patron's safe – 'discoveries' being as likely as not to jar the wheels of industry. And so perhaps it might be with Wine and any genuine science which his industry might support. For Wine had – or was going to have – an industry. That was the point. And the men in the back room were not going to be very important. Unless, perhaps, some unforeseen crisis came. There was that to be said for a world in the melting-pot. It sometimes turned the back room into the first-floor front.

There were men who would take the sword and with it conquer the world for their countrymen or themselves. Such men were a nuisance always, and in a world of high-explosive they were a calamity. But always History – a sentimental jade – would give them a little glory: that amid an ocean of tears and blood. Emery Wine was planning a conquest conceivably just as extensive. But decidedly there would be no glory. To few men – thought Appleby, looking sombrely out over the river – had there ever come a plan more absolutely bad.

There were men who had attempted to make what is called a corner in some necessity of life – say in wheat. But to this man had come the conception of making a corner in poison. The thing had a gambling element, as such cornerings commonly have: Wine had to bank on calamity and a gathering darkness. But the plan was clear. It was as if in the fourth century of our era, watching the decline and fall of world order in the empire of Rome, some cunning man had concentrated in his own hands all the promising superstitions, the long-submerged and half-forgotten magical instruments of the twilight ages of the mind.

And yet it was not quite like that; the conditions were different. Today order and science and the light of knowledge might go, but in the chaos there would remain a network of swift communications, a wilderness of still turning and pounding and shaping machines. The great presses would still revolve and the radios blare or whisper. Whole systems of mumbo-jumbo would spread with terrifying rapidity: already were not weird systems of prediction, grubbed up from the rubble of the dark ages, printed by the million every day? Grant but the initial collapse on which this bad man was counting, and the spread of sub-rational beliefs would be very swift. Power would go to him who had the most and likeliest instruments of super-stition to hand. And here – were one's organization sufficiently vast and sufficiently efficient – even a comical cab-horse, even an inwardly riven and tormented cockney girl, might have a useful niche in the new and murky temple. A corner in ghosts, a corner in witches, a corner in *denkende Tiere*. Somewhere in front of this hot and stinking little river-steamer lay the first concrete fashioning of this vast and corrosive fantasy. Round any bend now they might come upon the unholy base or depot, the laboriously accumulated reservoirs of the Lucys and Hannahs and Daffodils – unaccomplished works of Nature's hand, abortive, monstrous, or unkindly mixed. The project, if he had read it aright, was extravagant beyond the compass of a story-teller's art. And yet it was not ungrounded in the present state of the world. As a commercial venture it was dangerous; perhaps what the City used to call double dangerous. But one could write a tolerably persuasive prospectus for it should such a bizarre job come one's way.

Take the Bereavement Sentiment – take that, said Appleby to himself as he watched young Lucy fishing from the side. There are graphs of it, for insurance companies as well as sociologists find such things useful. The peak year in western Europe was 1920. And it was at that time that the papers were full of strange elysiums, cigar-and-whisky empyreans, *revenants* who reported lawn-tennis tournaments on the pavements of paradise. And it was at about that time that such bodies as did exist for the objective study of psychical evidences were inundated with members themselves far from objectively disposed. There are times when every man prays, whatever his settled belief or disbelief may be. And there are circumstances in which many men, and many women – And here Appleby stopped. The best thing, perhaps, would be to go below, and knock on the door of Wine's cabin, and enter, and shoot him dead, and possibly achieve the additional satisfaction of pitching his carcass to the alligators before his retainers interfered. That – thought Appleby with his eye still on Lucy Rideout – would be very nice. Only the train of speculation leading up to it might be all wrong after all. In a way it ought to be all wrong. The comedy of Lady Caroline and Bodfish, the episode of the York antique shop, the extravagant disappearance of 37 Hawke Square, the deplorable adventure of the birthday party, the untoward consequences of the electrical storm: none of these things alone had the quality – had anything of the key or tone – of this to which they were leading up. Nevertheless Appleby felt that the truth was assuredly here. An examination of the facts led to it as certainly as the long reaches of this river led to Wine's Happy Islands. And the mere scale of the thing made it susceptible of no other explanation.

But the man had miscalculated, Appleby thought. He was banking on what intellectuals of a high-flown kind liked to call the End of our Time. The probability was that this itself was a miscalculation. It is true that times do come to an end, but the thing happens far less frequently than people expect. History is full of periods which appeared to contemporaries agonal and conclusive, but which the textbooks were eventually to describe as no more than uncomfortably transitional. Now things were uncomfortable enough, and for the first time since the creation every continent and every sea was under fire. But in the end of his time or his country, his language or his civilization or his race, Appleby was not very disposed to believe. If Wine was counting on that sort of absolute subversion he had probably made a mistake.

Conceivably, however, all this was to attribute too great an imaginative element to his schemes. Under whatever circumstances the guns ceased fire, and whatever of his foundations Western man preserved, in the remaining superstructure there would for long be confusion and darkness, wildered wits and

123

shaken judgements enough. Once more, it simply came to this: had a bold man but his organization ready he could reap an immense harvest of wealth and power.

Think of Sludge. Appleby rose from his chair and paced the little deck. Think of the original of Browning's charlatan. In the midst of the immense solidity of the Victorian age he had been able to work up an extremely profitable hysteria in places astoundingly close to the very centres of English culture. Noblemen had solemnly sworn before committees that they had seen him float in and out of windows or carry live coals in his hand about the drawing-rooms of Mayfair. And the tone of all that – England's first spiritualist epidemic – was most oddly like the tone of more recent movements. In the period between the wars, a period in which much of stability had already gone, it had proved possible to build up – and in the same dominant social class – hysterias of essentially the same kind. This time it had not been spooks; rather it had been a species of cocktail and country-house revivalism even more antipathetic to the rational mind. But the tone was the same; one had only to read the documents to realize that. And it showed what could be done. The ranks of these unstable and disorientated revivalists were full of persons of earnest purpose and sincere conviction. But doubtless the gentlemen who had sworn to the levitating Sludge had been like that. The thing was not thereby the less aberrant, the less dangerous to all that Western man had achieved. And now, should Wine get going –

'So here we are.'

Appleby turned and found his host beside him, pointing over the prow.

'Welcome, my dear Appleby. Welcome to the Happy Islands.'

4

'My own headquarters,' said Wine, 'are on America Island.'

'America Island?' Appleby was gazing far up the river. There appeared to be a land horizon straight ahead.

'Yes. It is the largest of the islands. And then comes Europe Island. Perhaps you will be most interested in that. Particularly in English House. You see, we have found it best to organize our research on a continental, and then on a national or state basis. On America Island, for instance, different groups concentrate on the problems and – ah – possibilities of different parts of the continent. Would Radbone have carried the thing thus far? I think not.'

'Almost certainly not, I should say.'

Wine nodded, seemingly much pleased. 'Take the Deep South, my dear Appleby. The problems are naturally quite different from, say, those of New England. And so we have a Deep South House and a New England House, with a competent man in charge of each. You must prepare yourself for something on quite a considerable scale. We have been at work for a long time.'

'I see. Would it be right to say that the collecting of material, as you call it, has gone a good way ahead of the actual investigation?'

'Well, as a matter of fact, it has.' Wine had glanced swiftly at Appleby. 'When I speak of having competent men in charge of each section I am thinking in terms of field workers rather than of first-rate laboratory men. The material *is* getting somewhat out of hand. Particularly in German House.'

'Indeed?'

'It ought really to be called German Mews.' Wine gave a gay little chuckle. 'Most of the thinking Animals are there – our friend Daffodil among them. Germany was always the great place for that sort of thing. You must have a calculating horse or prescient pig if you want really to impress a Prussian academy of science. And at present we have, I must confess, nobody who really understands the creatures, or can make any headway with their investigation. And that is just an example.' Wine, now gloomy, shook his head. 'Scientists are frankly short with us. And Radbone has some of the best men.' He paused. 'Which is why, you know, I asked you and Hudspith to come and see.'

'But we are not scientists.'

'No doubt. But you have Radbone's confidence. And – well.

125

I must tell you frankly that I have the possibility of some sort of merger in mind. I hope that when you have seen how far we have got that you will go – or that one of you will go – and see if it can be arranged. Go back to Radbone, I mean, with my proposals and your own account of the place.'

'I see.' As Radbone almost certainly had no concrete existence, this was scarcely true. Appleby was far from seeing. But it was to be hoped that he was merely anticipating a truth. If Wine was to be worsted in his own stronghold it was urgently necessary to solve the riddle of such an unexpected proposal as this. But perhaps it had little or no meaning; perhaps it was merely more patter until the two men who had come so inconveniently on his tracks could be most simply eliminated. 'I see,' said Appleby again, and in as considering tones as he could assume.

'I may have spoken lightly of Radbone. But that is only an indiscretion of professional rivalry, after all. I do think that he possesses some final and serious intellectual weakness. But he is at least a magnificent deviser of experiments.' Wine looked Appleby directly but unconsciously in the eye. 'And, after all, a good experiment is everything.'

'No doubt.' Obscurely, Appleby felt disconcerted. And for a moment he had an impulse to be very frank. He would state baldly that he and Hudspith were police officers and that Wine's game was up. Even in the throes of war the British Government would not let two men disappear into the blue. They would be traced; they would be traced thousands of miles up this river. And the Happy Islands, however remote and undisturbed, were certainly sovereign territory of some friendly state. So that, in fact, the game was already up and Wine had better come quietly.... Appleby meditated this and decided: Not yet. For it was a last and desperate card, and could be played at any time.

'It will be nearly an hour before we can tie up' – Wine was looking through binoculars as he spoke. 'So do you go and find Hudspith, there's a good fellow – and we will celebrate the end of this tedious journey in a glass of champagne. With Lucy to help us. Only there had better be ginger pop, too, in case it is the young 'un who is about. Lucy is rather charming, is she not? To tell you the truth, I was rather glad to be able to send those other ladies by the first boat. Eusapia, I fear, was better out of your friend's way.' And Wine, thus gay and mischievous and considerate at once, gave orders for a little feast. The champagne was excellent, and there were tiny biscuits and a pot of caviare into which one dug with a knife. Most of the time Wine talked of Radbone still. But not quite as he had recently fallen into talking. It was as if he were now aware that there was some danger of this mysterious rival's being taken for a shade. And so he was building him up again as solid flesh and blood – establishing him as a real man to whom a real embassy might sensibly be sent. And there were no more jokes about plain-clothes policemen.

America Island was about two miles long by half a mile wide. From each of its shores it was possible to see the corresponding bank of the river, as well as something of the smaller islands farther up. Some of these lay two or three abreast, so that from the air the whole group must have presented the appearance of a single large fish leading a family of varying size downstream. There were several groups of buildings, and the island had been substantially cleared – as had also, it would seem, the river-banks beyond. Something of cultivation had been attempted, but this effort belonged to the past. From the little jetty where the steamer had drawn up there was a short, straight road to the first building. And here, sitting in the shade of a veranda, were Beaglehole and Mrs Nurse, drinking tea. For a few minutes there was an amiable and efficient bustle of welcome. The servants were greenish brown and must have been of some native tribe untouched by Spanish blood; the air was heavy with exotic scent; from the back of the house there came a species of throbbing howl conceivably intended as musical entertainment. Nevertheless, Appleby thought, it was all curiously like arriving on friends in Hampshire for the week-end.

'We chose this house,' said Beaglehole, 'because it is in the Californian style. There's something more commodious upstream, but it looks as if it were meant for Cape Cod. And one has to consider the climate. I hope you won't feel cramped here for a few days. It's been necessary to arrange it like that.'

Wine was taking round a plate of sandwiches. 'Beaglehole,' he explained, 'does all the running of things in a domestic way. We regard him as a steward or major-domo in that regard. Mrs Nurse, I believe these are gherkin. But here are tomato should you prefer.'

'*Chose* this house?' said Hudspith, who had formed the habit of regarding his hosts through a suspiciously narrowed eye. 'Didn't you build the place?'

'Dear me, no.' Beaglehole shook his head, amused. 'That would have been very poor business indeed – and not at all the sort of thing scientists can afford. We bought up the whole place for a song. It belonged to a Teuton called Schlumpf. He was going to start one of those Utopias people think up from time to time, and he got a concession on the islands and did the building. He was practically king of the place. You see, we're a long way from law and order here.'

Wine frowned. 'The Republic certainly doesn't make itself felt in these parts. So we insist that the King's law runs instead. And we have no trouble – no trouble at all, I assure you. There are some rather unruly remnants of tribal folk about, but they leave us alone. We are a very tranquil – ah – research station.'

'Ah,' said Hudspith – and added suddenly: 'What if one of your guests –Daffodil, say – announced that he wanted to go home?'

Beaglehole abruptly lowered a sandwich and raised his voice. 'Schlumpf,' he repeated. 'His idea was that there should be an island to each country concerned and that people should follow their own mode of life there, living in their own sort of houses and so on. But on the river-banks they should work co-operatively and get to know each other in that way. Of course it didn't work. And we took over.' Beaglehole grinned. 'We *do* work.'

'Schlumpf slumped.' Wine smiled engagingly as he offered this witticism. 'And we saw how usefully we could take over the structure of the place. But of course we had to give up the clearing and colonizing part of the scheme. It was quite impracticable, anyhow. For – to be quite candid – Schlumpf was a scoundrel.'

'A scoundrel?' said Hudspith. 'Dear, dear.'

'A scoundrel, I am sorry to say. The Utopia was chimerical; what his Utopians paid to be allowed in was real and substantial. So we drove a hard bargain with him without any compunction at all.'

'It must be nice,' said Appleby, 'to feel that you have turned his shady schemes to good.'

'Very nice,' said Mrs Nurse, brightening at the sound of her favourite word.

'Very nice indeed,' said Wine evenly. 'And now we must think about finding you quarters, though I have no doubt Beaglehole has it all arranged. Mrs Nurse, I expect you know your way about sufficiently well now to take charge of Miss Rideout?' Wine paused as if to emphasize the propriety of his dispositions. 'And where is Miss Mood? I am sure we are all looking forward to seeing her again.' He beamed at Hudspith and then glanced at his watch. 'But Beaglehole, my dear man, perhaps we can steal half an hour to see to a little unloading first. If you are all quite comfortable, that is.' And Wine put on his panama and led his assistant away.

Hudspith, who was holding a sandwich suspiciously between finger and thumb, looked after him frowning. 'Well, I'm damned!' he said.

'Mr Hudspith!' Mrs Nurse's glance went warningly to Lucy, and her tone was severe. Then she was placid again. 'What a nice man Mr Wine is! It was such a pleasant surprise meeting him again.'

Appleby was strolling round the veranda – apparently idly enough, but actually to discover if the party could possibly be overheard. Now he halted. 'Mrs Nurse, you had no idea that it was by Wine that you were being –' He paused, searching for the right word.

'Retained? I had no notion of it. But people do often arrange these things in strange ways. Particularly the sceptical – I suppose because they are a little ashamed of their inquiries. But I think this is going to be quite nice. Not that I like working for the researchers. Few mediums do.' Mrs Nurse was perfectly matter of fact. 'They make real communication so difficult with their conditions and their disbeliefs. You understand? Thwarting influences and all sorts of stupid little spirits break in. And that makes it so tiring.' Her voice was dispirited for a moment. 'Often I am so tired. The feeling just before and afterwards can be very dreadful, Mr. Appleby. But still' – she smiled cheerfully – 'I think this is going to be very nice.' She turned to Lucy. 'And I think you will like it too, dear. Come along.' And Appleby and Hudspith found themselves alone.

'Well,' said Hudspith, 'I *am* damned. And do you believe all that about Schlumpf?'

'I rather think I do. Wine and Beaglehole are like ourselves now, and being as economical in their fibs as may be. For instance, I don't imagine they stole this house from California and another from Cape Cod. They've stolen only one house – and stealing one house is a large order enough. But Schlumpf's fantastic notion dovetails in with 37 Hawke Square neatly enough. Do you notice that Wine has never mentioned Hawke Square? He thinks we know nothing about it; perhaps that no one knows anything about it; that it just hasn't been missed.'

'But it was in the papers.'

'For once his intelligence service must have tripped. He thinks we know nothing about it. And that is immensely important to him.'

'I really don't see –'

'But I do. I think I do.' Appleby was on his feet again and pacing restlessly about. 'And it's not at all comfortable. Still, it's a line. And a line is what we want.'

'Would you mind explaining what's in your head?'

'Not a bit; it's just what I propose. . . .' Appleby paused, walked to the edge of the veranda and stared up the river. 'Europe Island. Jungle and tree-fern and pampa and alligators and cobras. And a very substantial London mansion rearing itself in the midst of them. It's grotesque. But not quite as grotesque as if Schlumpf hadn't thought to dot the vicinity with Cape Cod bungalows and Highland crofts and Swiss chalets.' He turned back. 'Do you know what makes a first-class experimental scientist?'

'I don't know that I do.'

'The ability to exploit existing conditions. And Wine intends to do that. Thanks to Schlumpf a Bloomsbury house perching itself here is not outstanding and inexplicable in itself. It takes a sort of protective colouring from the chalets and crofts. We shall be taken there and think it nothing out of the way.'

'But –'

'Listen to me.'

And Hudspith listened. At the end he was staring at Appleby almost open-mouthed. 'I can hardly believe it,' he said. 'It's like a dream.'

Appleby smiled. 'I should put it stronger than that myself. Say a dream of dreams.' His voice sank grimly. 'And it just depends on the masons whether there will be a long, long time of waiting till my dreams all come true.

5

Hudspith took a turn about the veranda. 'But if what you say is true –'

'Let me go over a bit of it again.' Appleby held up an index-finger. 'He knows we are police.' He held up a second finger. 'But he doesn't know we know he knows.' He held up a third finger. 'He thinks he has hoodwinked us into believing that he believes that we act for Radbone; he thinks we believe that Radbone exists; he thinks we believe in the fundamentally scientific character of the whole affair. That is how the position stands now.'

'I suppose you wouldn't be disposed to call it at all complicated?'

'Only when reduced to these compressed verbal terms. The actual situation is fairly simple.'

'And we must be fairly simple ourselves – or he must think we are – if we are really to believe that the whole thing is some vast scientific investigation. Scientists just don't behave in such ways, except in strip fiction.'

'Quite so.' Appleby took a final dab at the caviare. 'And I doubt if the disinterested-investigator stuff will hold for another twenty-four hours. These islands are a sort of vast, veiled concentration camp into which Wine is packing every atom of mumbo-jumbo he can collect. Later he will purvey mumbo-jumbo – the locally appropriate mumbo-jumbo – wherever it is called for. Thames and Congo will be all one to the vast organization he is building up. But such a plan cannot really be disguised for long as a sort of grandiose laboratory experiment. He has brought us here, and if we live we are bound to find out. Think of all the contradictory baits which must have been laid; think of all the different terms on which his mediums and conjurors and prodigies must be retained here: terms ranging from full complicity through deception to duress. Apparently we are to be shown over the works – and somebody is bound to give the show away. But it won't matter to Wine.'

'Unless –'

'Unless we announce that we are police and so make it impossible for him to simulate ignorance. Then he would, in a way, be baffled. I mean in the particular little scheme on which he is at present engaged. But if we continue to appear to believe that he believes that we believe in Radbone –'

'I think it would be better without what you call the compressed verbal terms.'

'Very well. His plan – this particular little plan – requires simply this: that one of us should leave the islands while genuinely believing that there is a Radbone. We may know that the scientific business is bunkum; but we must believe in Radbone, even if in Radbone as another rascal merely.'

'Put it like this.' Hudspith frowned in ferocious concentration. 'We have to appear to be saying to ourselves: *What smart policemen we are: we have tricked him into thinking we are the agents of some other scoundrel called Radbone – and on the strength of this one of us is going to get away and bring both Wine and Radbone to book.*'

'Exactly. That will give him the conditions required for his experiment.'

'For his scientific experiment.'

Appleby laughed warily. 'Yes. The paradox is there all right. And in it lies our chance.'

'Ah. I don't know that I'd call it a chance. But perhaps that's another compressed verbal term. We'd have just as good a chance trying to chum up with the alligators.' Hudspith walked away and stared down the road to the jetty. 'No sign of them yet. What about chumming up with some of the material, or exhibits, or whatever he calls them?'

'What indeed. We might manage to start a revolt. And perhaps you'll begin with Miss Mood.'

Hudspith scowled. 'I think Mrs Nurse would be better. She strikes me as an honest woman.'

'In her everyday character I expect she is. But she is also extremely simple and somewhat lethargic. I should prefer to seek an ally in Lucy Rideout.'

'Which?' Hudspith's question was perfectly matter of fact. For long ago the minor oddities of the world of Mr Wine had ceased to surprise.

'Real Lucy. I fear her moral character will not long be of the best –'

'Ah,' said Hudspith – the old Hudspith.

'But she is lively and intelligent and would be a good pal.'

'Um,' said Hudspith suspiciously.

'And if we could get rid of sick Lucy and the young 'un – perhaps without Wine knowing it – we might find ourselves with quite a strong card.'

'My dear chap' – Hudspith stared in astonishment – 'don't you know that the curing of such a case may occupy a skilled alienist for years?'

'No doubt. But there is one fairly simple technique which might work. Lucy – real Lucy – has an inkling of it herself. You decide which personality you want to preserve and then you discourage the others whenever they appear.'

'Capital.' Hudpsith was sarcastic. 'Why not kill them outright?'

'Even that mightn't be impossible. Sometimes hypnotism is used to put the undesirable personalities to sleep. But the thing might be done by making sure they always encountered an uncongenial environment. I gather that real Lucy set off on her travels with just some such plot in mind. Now, if we could cure Lucy and make her reliable – so that she would always be real Lucy, I mean – and at the same time conceal this from Wine –'

'I don't think I ever heard a more impracticable and irrelevant scheme in my life. You might just as well set about curing that Italian girl of playing tricks with a lazy tongs.'

Appleby sighed. 'Perhaps you're right. But it would be nice to cure Lucy, and I think I'd like to try. Of course it would take time – and materials!'

'Materials?'

'Yes. A Latin grammar for young Lucy. We know that's available. And to sick Lucy I would insist on reading about Mopsie in the fifth. Sooner or later each would be disgusted and retire from the scene.'

'And real Lucy, on the other hand, would have to be pampered – quite given her head?'

Appleby nodded solemnly. 'I consider that a certain amount of giving real Lucy her head would be the right therapeutic method. Do I hear our friends returning?'

'Damn our friends.' Hudspith had strode over to his colleague and stood looking down at him suspiciously. 'And I don't like your scheme at all. Real Lucy is an extremely flighty girl. Oversexed. You can't say that I don't know them.'

'Certainly not.'

'The sort that men give dirty books to on the chance –'

'In fact, you think she should have nothing but Mopsie too?'

Hudspith relaxed. 'It's sometimes difficult to remember that you must have your little joke. I suppose it takes the mind off the alligators.'

'Ah – the alligators.' Wine's voice came cheerfully from the bright sunshine beyond the veranda, and a moment later he had sat down beside them. 'There is rather bad news about that. We have lost some valuable material to them while I have been away. The Bonteen sisters. Thought-readers with a really remarkable technique. But it appears they would most indiscreetly bathe in the river. One would have thought that a very little professional skill would have told them just what was in the creatures' minds. And now' – Wine shook his head and his smile was at once rueful and charmingly gay – 'we know just what is in the creatures' tummies.'

'You mean that the – the Bonteen sisters have been eaten?'

Wine nodded. 'And Beaglehole is particularly upset. He hates waste. Replacements are becoming so hard to get.'

'Like French wines, and the toothbrush handles that used to come from Japan.' Hudspith spoke with heavy irony.

'Exactly so; it is most vexatious. And not so long ago we lost two of our best clairvoyants. I don't think Miss Mood will be half so good. I suppose you've heard of Mrs Gladigan and Miss Molsher?'

'I can't say I have.'

'Well, they have been far our most serious wastage so far. Not that a certain amount of interesting scientific matter didn't emerge. It was like this.' Wine stretched himself comfortably in his chair. 'Mrs Gladigan and Miss Molsher were in a very remarkable physical *rapport*. It would work up to about a radius of thirty miles – a most interesting thing. Miss Molsher would go into a trance and one would stick a pin, say, into one of her limbs – much as Appleby here did to poor Miss Mood. And Miss Molsher, like Miss Mood, would be quite insensible to the pain. But Mrs Gladigan – sitting, as I say, perhaps thirty miles away – would immediately feel the appropriate sensation in the corresponding limb.'

'Very remarkable,' said Hudspith gloomily; 'very remarkable indeed.'

'Not at all, my dear fellow. Phenomena of that sort are not at all out of the way. Radbone will assure you of that. But what was exceptional was this: as soon as Mrs Gladigan felt the painful sensation to which Miss Molsher had been subjected she was able to make her way to her.'

Appleby frowned. 'You really mean that? –'

'Yes. It was simply like a bloodhound following a trail. With no previous knowledge of Miss Molsher's whereabouts Mrs Gladigan would nevertheless be guided directly to her – buying railway and tram tickets and so on as occasion required. Her explanations of how it came about were, as you may guess, vague. She seemed to imply a species of magnetic attraction between the limb of Miss Molsher actually injured and the corresponding and sympathetic part of her own anatomy. And such was the main accomplishment of the ladies when they consented to join us here – for the purpose of ruthlessly objective scientific investigation, it is needless to say.' Wine smiled. 'Well, the investigation turned out to be ruthless enough. But I don't know if you could call it scientific. Some would say that it was a little too unpremeditated for that. I think I have mentioned that we have some troublesome native tribes?'

'I think you have.' Hudspith was rubbing his jaw.

'I am sorry to say that some of them are very unpleasant – very unpleasant indeed. And before we could begin our experiments designed to test the supposed powers of the ladies, Miss Molsher disappeared. She had borrowed a canoe and very rashly gone off on a morning's expedition in it up one of the tributaries. As soon as she was missed of course we organized a search. But all in vain. We could find no trace of her. And it was about a week afterwards that Mrs Gladigan began to experience pains – somewhat sharper than usual – now in one limb and now in another.' Wine paused and glanced at his watch. 'Dear me!' he said; 'how pleasant. It will soon be quite a feasible hour for a glass of sherry.' He paused again. 'What was I saying? Ah, yes, about poor Miss Molsher. Well, we got out the launch, and a gun or two, and Mrs Gladigan steered. But it was soon apparent that something had gone wrong. She was quite at sea. Or perhaps a hunting man would say that she was at fault – badly at fault. We cast – that would be the word – now up the river and now down. And when at length we landed Mrs Gladigan was in yet more evident distress. She appeared attracted now to one and now to another point of the compass. Hudspith, my dear fellow, you look pale. I fear you have had a tiring day. This wretched heat! – it is the one great drawback to the place.'

'That and the savages,' said Appleby.

'The savages? Oh, yes, of course. That evening we heard that they had dispersed. Some had gone in this direction and some in that. Cannibals? Yes, I rather think they are. And Mrs Gladigan too did not survive. Brain fever carried her off a few days later. Of course without Miss Molsher she was a person of very limited utility. Still, it was sad. And the experiment itself – if we may be allowed to call it so – was tantalizingly inconclusive. One could hardly venture to send it to a learned journal, do you think? As I remarked to Beaglehole at the time: if only she had been able to lead us to an abandoned limb! But here are Mrs Nurse and dear little Lucy come out to join

136

us again.' He rose and clapped his hands, and instantly a servant appeared with a decanter and glasses. 'We dine late. It is the Spanish habit. And to give one an appetite there is nothing, I always feel, like lingering talk over a glass of sherry.'

6

The following morning was given to a tour of America Island. Besides the buildings put up by the unscrupulous Schlumpf there were several, more strictly utilitarian in appearance, which were the work of Wine. And of these the most impressive was his private research block. It comprised a library, a museum, rest-rooms and living quarters for the subjects under observation, a room for the projection of films, and a laboratory. It was of this last that Wine was particularly proud.

'My dear Appleby,' he said, 'pray notice the floor.'

Appleby looked at the floor. It appeared to consist of polished slabs of wood some eighteen inches square.

'Now walk across it.'

Appleby walked – somewhat gingerly, but without noticing anything untoward.

Wine moved to the wall and touched a button. 'Now try again.'

Appleby tried again, not without memories of boys' stories in which, upon such an occasion as this, yawning pits would incontinently open beneath the hero's feet. And decidedly there was now something odd about the floor. Nevertheless he got safely across.

'Later I will take you into the basement and show you the mechanisms. But at the moment I need only explain that each of these slabs is actually a tolerably accurate balance. Should we place a table here and sit round it in the dark, and should you then be prompted, say, to tie a thread to your handkerchief and pitch it to the other end of the room, the fact would be recorded down below – and so would the trailing return of the handkerchief as you hauled it back across the floor. And here

137

is the cabinet' – Wine had moved to where a heavy black curtain cut off one corner of the room – 'and behind it the rest of the paraphernalia that physical mediums are so tiresomely insistent on. As you may guess, our best cameras are here. You notice that everywhere the roof is high. That gives scope for the wide-angle lenses. I wonder if Radbone has learnt much from the technique of aerial and infra-red photography?' Wine smiled charmingly. 'I have.'

'Very interesting,' said Appleby. 'But do the mediums like it?'

'Commonly they know nothing whatever about it. And now notice this.' Wine opened a cupboard in the wall and revealed some intricate electrical apparatus. 'I have no doubt you know that one of the grand difficulties in a long seance is distinguishing between one hand and two. Hudspith, when you rub your jaw in that way I know you are a little at sea. So let me explain what happens during a typical experiment. The laboratory is almost dark, and the medium sits at a table just before the cabinet. I am on one side, and one of my assistants is on the other. My right foot is on the medium's left foot, and my assistant's left foot is on her right foot. And each of us holds one of her hands. The medium writhes about; she is allegedly in the grip of some supernormal force. And I assure you that presently, although my assistant and I are convinced that we each are in contact with a separate hand, it may very well be that we each have got hold of the same one.' Wine shook his head. 'There is really nothing like a little psychical research for convincing one of the fallibility of the human senses and of the difficulty of really unintermittent concentration. But, fortunately machines are inexorable. I dare say you've seen in the shop windows radio sets that can be set going by a passer-by simply waving his hand in front of a particular spot on the glass? This machine refines a little upon that not very difficult principle. Let the medium get one hand below the level of the table – –which unfortunately is what she probably wants to do – and at once this machine –'

'Poor little Eusapia,' Appleby interrupted. 'I'm afraid she hasn't a chance. And that she should be brought all that way for this.'

'Eusapia is said to be full of the most elementary wiles. But it's just possible there may be something else as well.'

And it's just possible, thought Appleby, that there may be at least a little green cheese in the moon. But who would build a costly observatory on what he held to be the off chance of making such an observation? Or who, wishing to convince others of the fact, would build in the middle of nowhere? Yet this laboratory, in which Eusapia's lazy tongs would presently be exposed with the aid of balances and infra-red light, was no mere flimsy screen. It really was an elaborate unit for the research Wine professed. And in this lay the truth about Wine.

If there were three Lucy Rideouts, there were – in a sense – three Emery Wines also. And the name of one of these Wines was – again in a sense – Radbone. When Wine spoke of the insufficiencies of this fictitious scientist he was simply drawing a picture of one of the Wines. Perhaps consciously, or perhaps unconsciously. But there it was.

There was a Wine who was a scientist, a Wine who really wanted to know. And there was a Wine who was a gangster, a Wine who wanted to exploit and grab. But to these two Wines, the scientific and the predatory, there must be added a third: an imaginative and credulous Wine.

Out of spiritualism and allied interests of the mind he was going to form a vast racket. The thing was feasible: nevertheless it was bizarre and extremely out of the way. What had led him to so remote a project? The same bent that really led the scientist into such territory: an obscure impulse to believe – an impulse which would dispense with intellectually respectable evidence if it dared. When Hudspith had simulated seeing an apparition of the sort traditionally associated with the death of the person seen, Wine had been so far carried away as to attempt to verify the thing by radio. The attempt had been entirely futile, for a cast-iron regulation had been against him; it therefore demonstrated something other than a coolly critical mind in face of a possible supernormal occurrence. In fact on that morning Wine had given much away. Again, he had revealed this streak in his make-up through the picture he had drawn of Radbone. And he had revealed it once more in his fondness for putting across tall stories – of which surely the tallest and most irresponsible was that recent one of Mrs Gladigan and Miss Molsher.

And yet, later than morning – and as he and Hudspith were being conducted somewhat hastily over other parts of America Island – Appleby thought a good deal on the history of those unfortunate ladies. The mortal remains of Miss Molsher departing to stew-pots at various points of the compass and the resulting bafflement of Mrs Gladigan's psychic perceptions: the notion was rather more absurd than horrible. Wine had spoken of it in terms of an abortive experiment, and though it was doubtless a fantasy, yet the conducting of experiments by Wine was a fact – a fact to which the elaborate laboratory testified. There was something in Mrs Gladigan and Miss Molsher: they were a sort of allegory. Appleby told himself, of that aspect of Wine's activities with which he himself was scheduled to be most intimately concerned.

'We have half a dozen rather interesting people over there' – Wine was pointing to a long, low building near the water's edge – 'but I think we had better not visit them just now. The fact is that they are really rather tiresome.' He sighed. 'A few will prove to be interesting, but all are rather tiresome. It is one of the depressing conditions of our work.'

'You mean,' asked Hudspith, 'that they're discontented? They'd like to get away?'

'To get away?' Wine looked politely puzzled. 'Of course they would leave if they wanted to. Actually I believe that most of them feel they have fallen on their feet. All have some rather special nervous organization in one way or another, and the result commonly is that they are misfits in the workaday world. Here we provide a special and carefully-contrived environment which I doubt if they would wish to change. They are tiresome simply because they are an edgy and temperamental lot. And I'm not sure that working with them one doesn't take on something of the same trying nervous organization.' Wine turned to Appleby and smiled blithely. 'If you find me – or Beaglehole – a bit queer, you know, you must put it down to that. Perhaps we shall come back here another day. I should at least like you to meet Danilov. He promises some most interesting results. On the other hand, he is perhaps the most temperamental of all.'

'A medium?' Appleby asked.

'It is really difficult to say. He has the gift of tongues – an endowment common in legend and folk-lore, but which I have never met elsewhere. A language will come to Danilov perhaps for an hour, perhaps for a day or even a week. Then it will vanish and another will take its place. Curious, is it not? There is never more than one language at a time – or rather never more than one in addition to his basic Russian. The speaker of whatever is the strange language of the moment understands himself but has no Russian. The Danilov who speaks Russian understands none of the other languages spoken.'

'Very odd,' said Appleby.

'Suppose Danilov to be visited for the moment by French. You can converse with him in either French or Russian, but you can't converse in French about what has just been said in Russian, nor in Russian about what has just been said in French. You see? Either the man is indeed visited by tongues in some supernormal manner, or the different languages contrive to exist in separate compartments of his mind.'

'Do you know anything of his history?'

'Yes, indeed. He was born in Denmark, his mother being English and his father a Spanish engineer. When he was four the family moved to Greece, where he had a German nurse who went mad and ran away with him to Egypt. Later he was adopted by a wealthy Russian who had married a Dutch lady long resident in France.'

'I see.'

'But later on his life became somewhat unsettled and he roamed about the world a good deal. He was back in Russia at the time of the Revolution and was wounded in the fighting. In fact a bullet passed through his brain, and for some time he couldn't talk at all. It was when he recovered from this that he began to exercise his peculiar gifts. But he himself is firmly convinced that it is spirits.'

They were walking uphill, perhaps it was because of this that Hudspith could be heard breathing heavily.

'And of course spirits it may be. One ought never to jump to conclusions on the strength of fragmentary evidence.' Wine chuckled. 'I am taking you this way so that we can get a

141

bird's-eye view of the islands. This hill in front of us rises to about four hundred feet.'

'I'm inclined to think,' said Appleby, 'that you expect Hudspith and me to rise to more than that.'

'Ah.' Wine walked some paces in silence. Then he chuckled again. 'I think we are getting to know each other very nicely.' Again he walked in silence. 'Just think, my dear Appleby, what one could do with Danilov as a sort of evangelist. He roves about the world – perhaps with a little choir or orchestra – and languages come and go as he moves. It's tremendous.'

The breathing of Hudspith became heavier still. Appleby, glancing sideways as they walked, noticed with some alarm a fixed contraction on his brow. It seemed only too likely that the cheated girls had been usurped. Hudspith had found a new Whale.

7

They climbed higher. America Island took form beneath them: an irregular oval of blotched green and brown framed in the yellow of the incredible river. On the summit was a little clearing of which the borders were low palmetto scrub and Papaw trees and feathery palm. Parrots flew chattering over them; unknown butterflies hovered; and everywhere was the sweet scent of the Espinillo de Olor. That the island had been cultivated could be seen – but the orange groves, laid out in quincunx form, were now eroded and forlorn, yielding to a stealthy pincers movement of which the spear-heads were a tangled monté of low trees wreathed in creepers; this with a marching army of crisscrossed bamboo behind. Unguarded, nothing human would last here long; nature would sweep in with something of the pounce of Eusapia's lazy tongs, and the Happy Islands would be as they had been before ever Domingo de Irala and the Conquistadores had come this way.

Upstream, the other islands stretched westward; the nearer appearing securely anchored in the flood; those farther away floating uncertainly between air and water. Each was blotched and brown and green, featureless and scrubby except for here and there an aracá or a commanding palm, but with many of the strangely assorted buildings of Schlumpf's fantasy showing clear in the shadowless light of noon. That queer project had been ragged and untidy and evanescent; superimposed upon it could be seen evidences of the yet queerer but efficient and considered project of Emery Wine. Plain frame buildings had been added here and there; each island had a small uniform jetty; a purposive network of wires ran between the houses and spanned the channels on high-masted buoys; here and there a launch darted on the obscure business of the community. For it was a community of sorts; man dominated this corner of the wilderness and nature took second place.

But the majestic river floated on, and a few miles downstream the world was a solitary haunt of tapir and capibara, of vizcachas sitting at their holes and of flamingos contemplative on stilt-like legs. The river was an unending world of yellow water and Pampas-grass and willow, of strange birds – macaws and Magellanic swans – and stranger fish – bagre and dorado, pacu and surubi. The river and its multitudinous life was a world unending. But the river also was no more than a dully-variegated thread winding through the immeasurable monotony of what from this eminence could be clearly seen: the great green ocean of high and waving grass which made the larger world of this part of the South American continent. It was a far cry from Lady Caroline and the dusty little antique-dealer of York.

Wine seated himself in the shade of a solitary Ñandubay. 'You are looking down,' he said, 'on all the kingdoms of the world.' The words were spoken without magniloquence and without either the irony or the gaiety that the man was wont to affect. Appleby, withdrawing his gaze from the farthest verge of the rippling pampa, looked at him curiously – as one may look at somebody interesting and new. 'And the glory of them,' said Wine. His finger made a circle in air – a small circle which seemed to define no more than the group of islands below. 'So why should you and I pretend to each other any longer?'

'It does seem unnecessary,' said Appleby. And Hudspith

143

nodded – not at all like a man who believes that only such successful pretence stands between him and the incomparable digestive system of the crocodile.

'Radbone and I are after the same thing; so let us admit it. And let him admit that here' – and again Wine's finger circled – 'I have got ahead of him. Let him admit that and come in. He sent you to spy out the land. And now' – and a third time Wine's finger circled – 'it is before you. All the kingdoms of the world, graphed and taped.'

Appleby looked down on the islands and electric wires and launches, on these as a stray and tiny atom of human activity in that great void of green. And he saw the atom as a rebel cell in the vast organism of human civility, a minute cell or nexus of cells, definable still by a circling finger, but having the potentiality for unlimited and disastrous proliferation. Here the thing was growing in treacherous concealment, and presently it would send off down the great river, as if through a bloodstream, armies that should attack every weakened centre of a riven and exhausted planet. It was a large picture, and not a pretty one. 'Certainly there seems no necessity to pretend,' Appleby repeated.

'Did I once remind you that home-keeping youth have ever homely wits? When I was a young man I visited Egypt and I visited Rome. And I saw how the resolute man invents gods to put his fellows in awe. I saw what of splendour and power could be built out of the infantile recesses of the mind. I looked at what Milton accurately calls the brutish gods of Nile – and then I looked at the pyramids. By observing how children irrationally fear a dog or a beetle, by probing a little the vast unreason of the unconscious mind, able men had gained all that overlordship and command. I saw it as men must often have seen it before me. I saw it as Faustus saw it.'

'Ah,' said Appleby. 'Faust. But there are those who believe rather in Prometheus.'

'And I went to Rome.' Under the shadow of the Ñandubay, Wine sat staring unseeingly before him, far too absorbed to heed an obscure interruption. 'My plan came to me there. It was as I sat musing in the ruins of the Capitol, while the bare-footed friars sang vespers in the temple of Jupiter –'

144

The man was the soul of charlatanism, Appleby thought. Spouting Gibbon. Always making a tall story of it. And yet practical and efficient and ruthless. In fact – But better hear him out.

'– that I saw it could all be done again. I saw how such a dominion could be built up more rapidly and surely, because more scientifically, than ever before. Two things were necessary. First, a command of – or better a corner in – all those oddities and abnormalities which must be the instruments for building up a popular magical system. Mrs Nurse and her voices, Eusapia and her conjuring, Danilov and his gift of tongues; all that material one must hold ready and organized. And, second, there must be a softening process. All successful attack, unless it is to rely on sudden and devastating surprise, must be preceded by that. And alone one could not manage it. There must be the hour as well as the man.'

But the point, thought Appleby, is this: is the man, without knowing it, himself the product of the hour? And is the softening process not the source of the plot as well as its instrument? Was not Wine in some measure involved in his own twilight – and was he not vulnerable in terms of this? The point lay there.

'But the solvents had been at work long before my mind contacted the situation. For decades the great institutional systems of belief had been crumbling You remember Christianity?'

Hudspith, to whom this flamboyant question appeared to be addressed, glowered darkly. But Wine was not in an observant mood.

'How exquisitely the rational and the irrational were held together there! What an instrument it was!' Something of Wine's gaiety had displeasingly returned, and he spoke as a connoisseur might speak of some rare vintage which had passed its allotted span. 'But things fall apart. The centre cannot hold. Mere anarchy is loosed upon the world.' He paused, apparently because this was a quotation and to be savoured. 'And so we can begin again.'

There were times at which the man had a certain impressiveness of perverted imagination. But at other times he was merely odious. And this, no doubt, was only another facet of the fact that there were several Wines. 'And so,' said Appleby, 'you begin again.'

'I begin wherever the softening process yields an opening. And there are openings in almost every country. There are openings in all classes – or sections, as I believe your Uncle Len would rather say. The different fields have, of course, been carefully studied; just as carefully as if we were proposing to market a new face-cream or soap. In the main it will be spiritualism for the upper class and astrology for the lower. Spiritualism is comparatively expensive – and can be extremely so – whereas astrology is quite cheap. The middle classes will have the benefit of a little of both. For rural populations we shall rely chiefly on witchcraft. What is sometimes called the intelligentsia has exercised my mind a good deal. Yoga might do, and reincarnation and the Great Mind and perhaps a little Irish mythology. But the problem is not important, as there are likely to be singularly few of them left. What we shall have to consider – and that, gentlemen, from China to Peru by way of Paris, London and Berlin – is simply Barbarians, Philistines and Populace. The classification is not one of the most up to date, but I fancy it is sufficient. I may say that the United States, in which even Barbarians are lacking, is going to be the simplest proposition of all.'

'Do I understand,' asked Appleby, 'that you are going to start your own Church?'

'Hardly that. But I may say that it will be more like a Church in some countries than others. For instance, in America, we shall gradually take over the churches – the buildings, I mean – themselves. But in England I believe that they would be useless to us, even those that still have roofs to them. In England we shall take over the Music-Halls. Have you ever sat among an English audience during a good variety show? A favourite comedienne singing a sentimental song, with a ventriloquist and a bit of conjuring to follow, can get pretty near the sort of atmosphere we want to achieve. The audience fuses into one cheerful and gullible monster. It is true that the Music-Hall has fallen into a decline, but into nothing like so steep a decline as the Church. We shall make it one of our major centres. And the other will be the Pub. Do you remember Wells's story of the man who tried to perform a miracle in a pub – and it worked? I think he ordered a lamp to turn upside-down. We shall see to it that all our pubs have lamps like that.'

Hudspith stirred uneasily, as if particularly outraged at the thought of hanky-panky in pubs. For some moments nobody spoke; in the heat of noon the viuditas and cardinales had ceased to sing; there was silence except where, directly beneath their feet, a tuco-tuco pursued its subterranean monologue like a gnome.

'The inverted lamp.' Wine had taken off his panama – and with it had shed his facetiousness, so that he was staring across the river, absent and absorbed once more. 'It might be our emblem. One by one what men have taken to be the true lamps are going out, and only the topsy-turvy ones will give any light at all. But are they topsy-turvy, after all? Or have we followed false lights for a thousand years or more?'

The fellow had taken the trouble, thought Appleby, to provide his rascality with a sort of philosophy. And they were going to be treated to it now; if only Hudspith had his professional notebook and pencil a valuable treatise might be preserved. He settled his back against the great tree. Suddenly overhead a teru-tero was calling – the plover of the pampa – and obscurely the tuco-tuco answered from below. Between them the well-modulated voice of Wine held the middle air.

'Take a piece of paper and make a pin-hole and look through the hole at a lighted lamp. Move the pin, head upwards, between the lamp and the paper until it is within your field of vision as you peer. What happens?'

Hudspith, whose eye appeared to have been probing after the tuco-tuco, looked up frowning. 'You see the pin-head upside down.'

'Exactly. Actually it is the image of the lamp which is inverted upon the retina. But our intellect rejects this and insists on seeing the pin head-downwards. It thinks a pin upside down less unlikely than a lamp upside down. And what the intellect rejects shall be our emblem: the inverted lamp.' Wine's voice dropped – dropped as if dipping towards the burrowing creature below. 'Light after light goes out, fire after fire is extinguished. And this gathering darkness has been the work of Science. That is the paradox. The Christians had a very clear picture of things. The simplest peasant could take it in and the subtlest school-man could spend a lifetime interpreting it. It was simple and permanent. But then Science came along and substituted something difficult and provisional. Decade by decade the picture became more complicated and shorter lived – until now neither the learned nor the simple at all know where they stand. And it is thus that Science puts out the lamps of reason; it is thus that Science is a vast softening process, a vast clearing the way for world-wide superstition. Science offers no fixed points of belief. And Science, in the popular mind, is the sphere of the un-accountable and the marvellous. Have you studied the strip serials? Nothing could be more significant. The Scientist is always there, and he is nothing more or less than the old Magician. He belongs to our camp. And we shall use him. Under our control he will become part of what the world most needs.'

Appleby got to his feet. 'And that is?'

'A handful of simple and thorough-going superstitions, backed by conjurers, freaks and prodigies.' Wine too rose. 'What a pleasant gossip we have had! But now I must go down to the boat. I think you will find luncheon waiting for you. And will you make my apologies to the ladies?'

They watched him go briskly down the hill. And Hudspith snorted – so vigorously that the tuco-tuco beneath his feet fell silent. 'Softening process!' he said. 'I'll soften him.'

'On the contrary, it is only too likely that he will soften us, Light after light goes out, including two luminaries from Scotland Yard.' Appleby stretched himself in the sunshine. 'Or, if you prefer it, light after light has gone out already, including several in our friend. As the old books used to say, his mind is darkened.'

'You think he's mad?'

'What is the test? If his fantasies are unworkable – as I rather think they are – then he is mad. But if he could bring his scheme off, or even bring a sizeable fragment of it off, we should have to allow him a sort of perverted sanity of his own. I thought he might have made a little more of that stuff about science and superstition – because of course there's something in it. And if

148

he isn't quite so impressive as he ought to be it's because he fails as the thoroughly objective exploiter of the situation as he sees it. He reckons the uncanny can move the world. Why? Primarily because it can move him. The truth is, he's the kind that would blench before a ghost.'

'And I would beam before roast mutton and a pint of bitter in the Strand. But I'm as unlikely to have occasion for the beaming as he for the blenching.' Hudspith stopped as if to scrutinize the syntax of this. 'We can't whistle up a squad of ghosts to corner him.'

'I suppose not.' Appleby took a last look at the islands and started off down the hill. 'But as far as the roast mutton goes there is likely to be some quite reasonable substitute cooking now. One can't complain of short rations.'

'Talking of short rations' – Hudspith had fallen into step beside him – 'has it occurred to you that in all this business nothing much has happened so far?'

'Nothing happened?'

'No one pulled out a gun or smashed a window or pushed someone else over a cliff.'

'Over a cliff? I don't think I've seen any. But perhaps we *have* been rather quiet.' Appleby paused to watch a charm of humming-birds mysteriously suspended at the lips of flowers. 'Would it be a good thing, I wonder, to take the initiative in brightening things up?'

8

Half-way down the hill Hudspith halted. His indignation had got the better of his appetite. 'The cheek of the man!' he said. 'Telling all that to people he knows are police officers.'

'He doesn't know that we know that he knows.' Appleby tramped on and made this familiar refrain a marching song. 'He thinks we think we have tricked him. We are Radbone's men. *We* have persuaded him we are agents of a man of whose existence *he* has persuaded us. And that gives the basis of his

149

plan – or that little bit of his plan which concerns you and me. If we believe in Radbone, and believe Wine believes we're his men –'

'The experiment will work.'

'Just that. It will be colourable that he should send one of us off to do a deal, while the other remains as a sort of hostage. But any suspicion on our part would be a spanner in the works.'

'A spoke in the spook.'

'Just that.' Appleby nodded placidly at this cryptic remark. 'But, talking of expectation, I really must insist on luncheon. So come along.'

Luncheon was excellent; nevertheless it was consumed in an atmosphere of gloom. Something had bitten Beaglehole, who glowered at his companions with frank dislike. Mrs Nurse was tired and without spirits even to pronounce things nice. Opposite to her sat sick Lucy in an abstraction, her mind turned perhaps on *moneo* and *audio*, perhaps upon Socrates or Marcus Aurelius.

'This Schlumpf,' said Appleby, cheerful amid the glumness, '– did he build European-looking houses on what you call Europe Land? Did I once hear Wine say something about English House?'

Beaglehole looked up warily. 'English House? Yes – and damned odd it looks. It's the larger part of the sort of house you might find in a Bloomsbury square.'

'What an odd idea! Surely something rural would have been more in the picture?'

'The man was loopy.' Beaglehole spoke ungraciously but carefully, with evident knowledge that for his employer here was delicate and important ground. 'And there it is. One of those big houses built about a gloomy sort of well with a staircase going round and round.'

Mr Smart's staircase, Appleby thought – and Colonel Morell's before him. 'It sounds,' he said aloud, 'a very costly affair to erect.'

'Enormously so, no doubt. But the whole house isn't there.' Beaglehole caught himself up. 'I mean, they build just a sizeable part of such a house. And with old materials, I fancy. In places it looks quite genuinely old.'

'Dear me.'

'Dear you, indeed.' Beaglehole, still unaccountably disturbed, was openly rude. But he continued to give his explanations with care. 'As a matter of fact, the constructing or reconstructing or whatever it was seems to have been uncommonly badly done. We had a storm some months ago, and a good part of it came down. Awkward, because we have a lot of material for English House. Men are just finishing working on the repairs now.'

Appleby felt an impulse to smile confidentially at the savoury mess of fish before him. As an explanation of the awkward fact that 37 Hawke Square was still going up this was no doubt as good as could be contrived. 'It sounds pretty queer,' he said. 'I'm rather looking forward to seeing it.'

Beaglehole put down his knife and fork. 'You'll see it, all right. And damned nonsense it is. Bah!'

'Bah, indeed,' said Appleby cheerfully. It was plain that there were matters upon which Beaglehole and his employer failed to see eye to eye. And it was not difficult to guess what these were. With the proposition that a good experiment is everything Beaglehole had no patience at all. 'And you have a certain amount of what Wine calls material waiting to move back into English House? The exhibits weren't blown away in the storm?'

Beaglehole pushed back his chair; he was even more irritated than before. 'One's gone,' he said. 'A confounded –'

'Gone? More wastage?' Wine had returned and was standing in the doorway looking at his assistant with a sort of easy dismay. 'Don't tell me that the alligators have got old Mrs Owler – or the Cockshell boy – or little Miss Spurdle?'

'The alligators have got nobody. But that Yorkshire vixen has decamped. I told you there would be trouble with her. They lost her after a couple of days. She's been gone for weeks.'

Wine frowned, now genuinely displeased, and turned to Appleby. 'The girl called Hannah Metcalfe. I sent her on a couple of sailings ahead of us. A mistake. An intractable person I ought to have kept an eye on.' He smiled wryly. 'You can tell Radbone we're at least not a hundred per cent efficient.'

'And it's not her alone.' Beaglehole was calmer now. 'She took a horse with her.'

Wine sat down, his brow darkening. 'Not Daffodil?'

'Yes. That's how she managed it. She sneaked over to German House in the night, nobbled the brute and a saddle, and swam the river with him. After that she had the pampa before her. But she wouldn't go far with an old cab-horse, you may be pretty sure. The Indians will have got her by this time. There's some consolation in that.'

Mrs Nurse, vaguely apprehending, looked distressed. Hudspith was concealing signs of massive disapprobation. And Appleby looked dubiously at his fish. *Did you ever hear of the isle of Capri?* She had said that. *The Happy Islands.* Well, at least the girl had made a break for it. Perhaps it would be well to follow suit.

'I find no consolation in the poor girl's death.' Wine was looking sternly at his assistant, and it occurred to Appleby that he was speaking the simple truth. 'Such talk is vindictive nonsense. Her death is useless to us.'

'At least it means that nothing will be given away.'

'Rubbish. If she got through to the coast she would be judged merely demented. And alive she was valuable – very valuable indeed. She might have been brought round. And she had guts. There was the makings of a Joan of Arc in her – our own sort of Joan of Arc.'

'Tell me,' said sick Lucy plaintively, 'about the voices of Joan of Arc.'

No one replied, and in the brief silence Appleby felt an uncomfortable pricking of the spine. 'After all,' he said at random, 'she mayn't be dead.'

'I hope not,' Wine reached for a decanter. 'Death is sheer waste – *useless* death.' For the fraction of a second he looked Appleby straight in the eye. 'Do you know, I think we'll all move to Europe Island in the morning?'

There was murder in the air. And that afternoon Appleby committed two murders. It was time to take the offensive, after all.

Near the upper end of the island the departed Schlumpf had caused a bathing-pool to be constructed – an elaborate little place, presumably in the Californian style. To this Lucy Rideout – young Lucy Rideout – had betaken herself shortly after luncheon, and here Appleby later found her practising diving with only a modicum of skill. For a time he watched her – watched that which was common to the Lucy Rideouts – flopping into the water and scrambling out. Sometimes she chattered to him, and her chattering was a twelve-year-old child's. But the body which curved and slid and panted before him was a grown-up woman's – the body of a grown-up woman and of a woman spontaneously physical. In fact, real Lucy's body. In that tenement of clay the other Lucys were misfits. . . .

Lucy Rideout flopped and scrambled and panted; tired and gasping, she lay on warm concrete and closed her eyes against the sun. She opened them, and suddenly they were sick Lucy's eyes – strained eyes which looked disconsolately down at a bright red bather, at a full and abounding body. She reached for a towel and wrapped it round her shoulders. 'About Socrates,' she said, 'and what he said about being dead –' She looked up – pathetic, unhealthy, tiresome. And Appleby found that he had murder in his heart.

There had been such a lot of sick Lucy lately; it was as if real Lucy had miscalculated in her notion of what a change of environment might do. Sick Lucy was winning. And although an interest in Socrates and the Sages is generally accounted highly estimable, Appleby was tired of it. He was tired of it as would be – he believed – a physician by this time. And he would take the responsibility of killing it if he could. This Lucy's head he would hold under that glittering pool until it breathed no more. Or he would do some equivalent thing. 'About being dead?' he repeated. 'Socrates was interested in what happens after death; in whether anything happens. But he wasn't like Wine. He wasn't prepared to kill people in order to find out.'

'What do you mean?' Sick Lucy had sat up and was looking at him with dilated eyes, suddenly trembling and deadly pale.

'Wine wonders if there are really ghosts. He has stolen a house where twice in the past the ghosts of murdered men are said to have appeared to friends. He himself is going to have a man killed there in order to find out. I am going to be killed without Hudspith knowing or suspecting – and will Hudspith see my ghost? Or the other way about. It is what Wine calls an experiment '

'I don't believe it. I don't understand it. I don't wish to hear it or speak of it.' Sick Lucy was cowering horribly in upon herself. 'I wish to continue my Latin, to be told about –'

'You didn't know Wine was like that? You didn't know the world was like that?' Appleby had leant forward and was almost whispering into Lucy Rideout's ear. 'It is only one of Wine's experiments. Others will be on you. He teaches you Latin just to keep you about – to keep you alive until he is ready. You understand? He has to keep on encouraging you, or the others would drive you away – drive you into nothing. They are stronger than you. For a long time now you've only been kept alive by believing in Wine and the things he teaches you. Well, they are all false. That stuff isn't even Latin at all. You could never learn Latin – only gibberish. Your mind is too feeble. Your whole life has only been a sick flicker. But it has interested Wine because it is a freak life. What would happen if you died? Would there be three ghosts? He is interested in that sort of thing. You see? And there are other things about the world that I will tell you too. Listen . . .'

She had given a last little cry . . . infinitely horrible. And he looked down on her sprawled body and felt himself faint with compunction and fear. But, ever so faintly, the body was breathing. Perhaps – The breathing was less perceptible, less perceptible still, had surely ceased. Seconds stretched themselves out interminably. He turned away his head in despair.

'Jacko.'

He looked at her, and she was still pale as a corpse. But her eyes were open; were awed; were full of intelligence and life.

'Jacko – John' – the voice was faint, excited, alive – 'something's happened; something's happened to the prig.' Her voice rose in sudden triumph, complete conviction. 'She's dead.' Real Lucy sat up and laughed – happily and exultantly laughed. And then she was weeping uncontrollably – bewildered and bereaved.

But Appleby sat still and waited, like a fantastic sniper beneath the Tree of Life. Presently young Lucy would appear. She was tougher than sick Lucy had been; it would be less easy to hold her head beneath the glittering pool. He sat still and waited, thinking with what words a child could best be killed.

·   ·   ·   ·

'Dead?' said Hudspith and paused, startled, in climbing once more the little hill.

'Dead.' Appleby looked westwards to where the farther islands were swimming into evening. 'You remember how I suggested that two of the personalities might be systematically discouraged? That's slow murder, though it's an orthodox clinical method. In this case quick murder proved possible. Single lethal doses of discouragement sufficed. And two things are left: an extremely curious moral problem and a valuable ally. Ought I to be hanged? The question will have significance only if the alligators are cheated of their due. As for the ally, there is no doubt of her. Real Lucy – sole Lucy, as one will think of her for a bit – may be a little lacking in modesty. But she has plenty of intelligence and resolution. Wine's plan pleases her very much.'

Hudspith puffed as the ascent grew steeper. 'Then I don't think much of her taste.'

'I mean that her mind can cope with it. It gives her intellectual satisfaction, just as it does you or me.'

'It's not likely to give you any other.'

'Be thankful for small mercies.' To the west the sky was molten, so that the great river seemed to pour from a cauldron of gold. 'I still keep on remembering things that fit in. I remember how Wine once told me Beaglehole and he were only acquaintances – something of the sort. He wanted to make sure – Cobdogla or not – that you and I were fast pals. Friendship was a prominent element in both the Hawke Square hauntings; it was to a more or less intimate friend that the full manifestations were accorded. The ghost of Colonel Morell spoke only to his friend Captain Bertram, and the ghost of Mr Smart only to his brother-in-law and friend Dr Spettigue. So when Wine saw that we were troublesome policemen and at the same time friends, he took the opportunity of killing two birds with one stone.'

'Or of throwing two birds to one alligator.' And Hudspith laughed – morosely but at greater length than the witticism justified. 'Not that one brace of friends would yield sufficient material for the great Hawke Square experiment. I don't doubt that a whole series of incidents is planned. Come to think of it,

155

what about Mrs Gladigan and Miss Molsher? Perhaps they were really used that way. Perhaps Miss Molsher's ghost and mine will play hide and seek up and down that staircase.'

Hudspith, it struck Appleby, was developing quite a vein of fantasy. Doubtless it was the exotic environment at work. They were at the top of the hill now, and the river, still golden to the west, flowed dark and unreal beneath them. Mamey and Papaw, castor-oil plants and feathery palm were casting long shadows; the chatter of the chaja and the bien-te-veo was dying; soon it would be night and a universe of fireflies and stars – fireflies multitudinous and fleeting; stars remote and enduring, like the abstract ideas of these, laid up in a heaven of dark deep nocturnal blue. 'Miss Molsher?' said Appleby prosaically. 'But Hawke Square has only just gone up. You and I are guinea-pigs one and two.'

'Unless –'

'Unless he can be headed off the whole thing. After all, this geniune experimental side to the man makes only part of the picture. His racket, his Spook Church, his preparing his grotesque instruments of power: the greater part of the man is in that. And all of Beaglehole; he cares wholly for the practical and nothing for the speculative side. He regards it as the boss's weakness, and so perhaps it is – though it is his fascination too. Now, suppose the major project in some sort of danger –'

Hudspith shook his head. 'At the moment it appears to me invulnerable.'

'Don't be so sure of that. If the major project were imperilled, then Hawke Square, costly though it must have been, would no doubt go by the board for a time.'

Hudspith sat down and leant his back against the now almost invisible Ñandubay. 'Would you say,' he asked dryly, 'that you and I are making plans?'

'Certainly. And we have a good deal of freedom of action – and shall have as long as we succeed in giving the impression we believe in Radbone. We are unlikely to do anything desperate so long as we think one of us is to be let leave this place to negotiate with him. For instance, here are you and I conspiring together in solitude and nobody trailing us. I have a revolver in my suitcase and nobody has rifled it. We could kill Wine. We could kill both Wine and Beaglehole. Might not that break the back of the whole thing?'

'Not necessarily.' Faintly Appleby could see his companion shaking his head. 'We don't know what able lieutenants, what carefully nominated successors, what absentee directors there may be. But it would certainly be the end of us. There must be a pretty big gang of scoundrels scattered over these islands to control what Wine is pleased to call his material. We'd never shoot our way out.'

'I agree.'

'Of course we might contrive a revolution and organize the material behind barricades. But for the most part it's unknown. loopy and unreliable. Except for Lucy – and she's material no longer, according to you.'

Appleby said nothing. It was very quiet on the island and the river made no sound. Within scores of miles there might have been stirring nothing but the indefatigable mole. And yet the island was full of noises – the obscure noises of the South American night, seeming to come always from unknown distances, like murmurings indistinguishable whether of hope or fear.

'The sober truth,' said Hudspith, 'is that we must hope for something from without. A *deus ex machina* to wind the thing up happily after all.'

Again Appleby said nothing. It was dark and, far below, the mole was groping like a spirit perturbed.

PLOP.

Perhaps Hudspith shivered. 'Alligator,' he said.

But Appleby put a hand on his arm. 'Listen.'

And there was a new sound – a near-by sound from the river below. Silence succeeded and then it came again. There could be no mistaking it.

'Yes,' said Hudspith soberly. 'A horse.'

Part 4

Everlasting Bonfire

1

The horse whinnied in the dark. At the sound, a third time repeated, the tuco-tuco beneath their feet ceased like a demon charmed. Stillness was round them like an unruffled pool – a pool beyond whose margins hovered uncertain presences, the enigmatic murmurings of vagrant winds through distant colonnades of grass. The horse coughed.

'It's swimming,' said Hudspith.

Below – far below, it seemed – lights shone in the late Schlumpf's residence in the Californian style. One light might be Wine's and Beaglehole's; they would be sitting with papers before them, augmenting their strange plot. One might be Mrs Nurse's – Mrs Nurse feeling nice, felling all hollow, feeling tired. And one, Appleby knew, was Lucy's – illiterate real Lucy with a big book before her, spelling out with concentrated intelligence the significant history of 37 Hawke Square. Lights shone on farther islands. Far away a beam of light briefly circled as a launch moved about the upper fringes of the colony – Australia Island, Asia Island, the lord knew what. Something splashed. Something slithered and heavily respired. A single clipped word was spoken by a human voice. Silence fell again and was prolonged.

'A horse and rider.' Hudspith spoke low. 'But who would put a horse in that infested river?'

Against darkness the fireflies flickered, tiny inconsequently-roving points of light like a random molecular peppering revealed by some laboratory device.

'Who indeed?' said Appleby. 'Or who but a crazed Yorkshire girl!'

They waited, straining their ears. Somewhere on the island a radio had started disgorging the hollow and bodiless bellowings of an announcer tuned too loud – news from the China

161

Sea, from Samara, from San Francisco ceaselessly circling the world, flooding it at the flick of a switch. The faint and hollow bellowing came up to them like the sound of water aimlessly bumping and bouncing in distant caves, but they listened only for a footfall or the quick clop of hoofs. They heard still the bodiless booming and the distant pampas sounds, and once the tuco-tuco stirred briefly below, and then, startlingly near, they heard in the darkness an intermittent short crisp tearing crunch –a noise baffling for seconds, and then suddenly not misinterpretable; the noise of a graminivorous creature cropping as it moved. And then they smelt horse.

The creature stood beside them: a presence, a faint whitish cloud – a warm horse-smelling cloud. If it was saddled and bitted it had been wandering with the reins on its neck; if it had a rider the rider was invisible, dark against the night. Appleby's eye followed the uncertain upper outline of the cloud and rested where the background lacked its powdering of stars. There was indeed a rider, a rider who sat immobile, gazing down on the scattering of lights which marked the headquarters of Emery Wine.

'Good evening,' Appleby said.

A faint jingle, as if a hand had tightened on a rein, was the only reply.

'Good evening,' Appleby repeated. 'Do you remember the shop in York, where they sold the things from old Hannah Metcalfe's cottage? It must be nearly four months ago now.'

Again there was no reply, but the whitish cloud moved. The whitish cloud which was horse elongated itself at the tip and four times dipped in air. The Daffodil of Bodfish and Lady Caroline had not lost his skill.

'And now,' said Appleby, 'here we are on the isle of Capri.'

'Mock.' The voice was husky and deep and not unmusical. 'Go on mocking. But come no nearer. I am not alone.'

Hudspith was scrambling to his feet. But Appleby put a restraining hand on his arm. 'Not alone?' he said. 'Well, there's Daffodil, of course.'

'There are the demons of earth and water and air.' The girl's voice was deep, assured, level. 'You think that in your little room with the cameras and the trembling floor you command the demons. But you are wrong. They are commanded by me.'

'We are not the friends of Wine. And we have no interest in demons. We don't believe in them. We are going to get you safely away – back to the Haworth you were foolish enough to leave.'

The answer was a low laugh, and when the voice spoke again the laughter was in it still – malicious, triumphant. 'You are the friends of Wine. All here are the friends of Wine – or all except the demons in whom you don't believe.'

Obscurely the invisible girl was having it her own way. A spell was forming. Appleby tried to break it. 'My dear Miss Metcalfe –'

Her laugh came again. His words broke against it. 'Listen,' she said. 'Listen to the demons of earth.' Slightly the patch of starless sky shifted, as if the girl were leaning over the neck of her horse. And Daffodil whinnied. And instantly from far below, from beyond the banks of the yellow invisible river, from round the farther islands came a deep faint throb – a throb so deep as to be less a sound than a mere muscular sensation in the ear. 'The demons of earth,' Hannah Metcalfe said. And the throbbing – like the distant beat of many drums – died away.

It was odd; it was so very odd that Appleby found himself cautiously testing the control of his vocal organs before he spoke again. 'And the demons of water?' he asked.

Once more Daffodil whinnied – and whinnied again. And instantly upon the deepest darkness where the great slow river flowed there floated a hundred streaks of pale fire. The streaks curved to arcs, to circles, to rolling and intersecting wheels of phosphorescent fire. 'The demons of water,' said Hannah Metcalfe, 'and the demons of air.' As she spoke the dark sky beyond the river became alive as if with meteors, became alive with red and angry smears and shafts of fire. They rose, curved and fell, and the stars were uncertain and pale behind them. For seconds only the thing lasted, and then Night resumed her natural sway. Out of it came Hannah Metcalfe's voice, graver now. 'Is one of you Beaglehole?' it asked.

'Neither of us is Beaglehole.' Appleby's voice was steady. 'We are the enemies of Beaglehole and Wine.'

'I do not believe you. Here all except the victims are the friends of Beaglehole and Wine. Are you victims?'

'We are police officers.'

'That is nonsense. You are the friends of Beaglehole and Wine. Tell them. But tell Beaglehole above all. Tell him I do not forget. About the ship.'

'We know nothing of the ship.'

'The little ship which sailed from Ireland. I would not go. I did not like the men. Beaglehole made them bind me. And he had a whip. Tell him I do not forget. Tell him that only the victims shall escape and be given their rightful place. All the rest of you the demons are going to take.'

'Miss Metcalfe –'

She laughed. The cloud – the cloud which faintly smelt of Bodfish's open landau – stirred, faded, dissolved. There was a long silence and then the voice, grave and malicious at once, came faintly up to them. 'The demons,' it said. 'The demons of earth and water and air.'

They groped their way downhill, sober and silent. It was only when the lighted windows took definition before them that Hudspith spoke. 'I don't suppose –'

'Of course not.'

'In that case –'

'Quite so.'

Perhaps Hudspith was rubbing his jaw. 'We don't know quite when she escaped. But she's a quick worker.'

'And with decided powers of organization.'

'Joan of Arc.'

'Ah.'

'The horse would help.'

'The horse?'

'Tricks. A magic horse. When the Spaniards first came quite ordinary horses created no end of a sensation.'

'Um.'

The veranda was in darkness but from a corner came the glow of a cigarette – a cigarette rapidly and nervously puffed. Appleby addressed it. 'Hullo,' he said cheerfully.

The cigarette dipped and took flight into the night. Beaglehole spoke. 'Is that you two? You're prowling late. Where have you been? I thought I heard something damned queer. And did you see something in the sky?'

'We walk by night,' said Appleby. 'What could be more appropriate in a haunt of ghosts and spirits? Of course it's dangerous. The right-valiant Banquo walked too late.'

Beaglehole swore. 'Did you hear anything, I say? Did you see anything?'

'We heard the owl scream and the crickets cry. Is Wine about? He would enjoy a little culture. But perhaps it's time to go to bed – to sleep, perchance to dream.'

'Damn you,' said Beaglehole. 'What the devil are you talking about?'

'Something queer. They say five moons were seen tonight.'

'Five moons!'

'Four fixed, and the fifth did whirl the other four in wondrous motion.'

'Bah! You must be tight.' And in the darkness Beaglehole turned away.

'Take care,' said Appleby softly. 'Take care, sirrah – the whip.'

There was silence. They were alone again. 'Well, well,' said Hudspith. 'I never knew excitement took you that way. Quite like Prince Hamlet putting his antic disposition on.'

'If a man were porter of hell-gate ...'

'What?'

'I suppose he would be rather like Beaglehole. Don't you dislike Beaglehole much more than Wine? It's because he's without a metaphysical – or superstitious – side to him. A porter of hell-gate with no belief in the everlasting bonfire.'

'No doubt,' said Hudspith vaguely, and yawned. 'But I think we'll call it a day.'

2

The launch pushed off; the engine spluttered and roared; above the Ceibas with their bunches of great purple flowers rose macaws, blue, red, and yellow, to hover against a morning sky of amethyst and gold. Nature was in one of her painfully frequent gaudy and tasteless moods. But Lucy Rideout clapped her hands and shouted. 'Oh, look at their wings!' she cried. 'Oh, look at their lovely beaks!'

Out of the corner of his eye Appleby saw Hudspith shiver. The real and only Lucy Rideout had still a substantial memory of her deceased sisters; she acted them, as one might say, to the life. Wine, debonair and amiable in the stern, could have no inkling of the latest wastage in his material. But to one in the know Lucy's impersonations were a little eerie. And were they not perhaps hazardous as well? Thus encouraged, might not Lucy's ghosts walk; sick Lucy and young Lucy indeed revisit the glimpses of the moon – even achieve some shadowy resurrection in that now glad and eager body in the bows? But by such thoughts Lucy herself was clearly untroubled. She was single and whole; she was in on such counter-plot as could be contrived; she was having a marvellous time. And now she turned to Hudspith with suddenly serious eyes. 'Mr Hudspith,' she said plaintively, 'tell me about the Discourses of Epictetus.' She wriggled a little nearer Appleby. It was all outrageous fun.

And Hudspith rubbed his jaw and frowned – but before he could offer any suitable reply Wine leant forward. 'You can see it now,' he said. 'English House. Or perhaps it should be called Schlumpf's Folly.'

Fantastic against the morning, rectangular amid the curved and coiled luxuriance of the place, soot-begrimed in the clear air, 37 Hawke Square reared itself somewhat shakily before them. A large house hastily demolished and in its old age transported across the Line can never look quite the same again – particularly when originally designed as a unit in the middle of a row. But there it stood, discernibly something out of

Bloomsbury, and presumably carrying with it sufficient of the spirit of place to justify the psychic experiments of Mr Emery Wine. It might have been simpler to endeavour to take over the house where it originally stood and try out a murder or two on the spot. Perhaps Wine had mistrusted the metropolitan police. Or perhaps he had simply obeyed a collector's instinct to have everything cosily around him. Anyway, there was the house – and so pitched that the yellow and unending river almost laved the vestigial remains of its basement storey. Here had died Colonel Morell and that unfortunate Victorian merchant, Mr Smart. The place looked, too, as if its conscience might be heavy with the doing to death of sundry general servants; their ghosts, brandishing brooms or ceaselessly hauling scuttles of coal from floor to floor, might well haunt the premises with obstinate venom.

'I am particularly fond,' said Wine, 'of the simple and severe lines of the front door.'

Appleby looked at the front door – the door through which, nearly two hundred years before, Dr Samuel Johnson and his negro servant Mr Francis Barber had departed from their fruitless vigils. And of course the bodies must have been brought out that way. But where hearse and mourners had stood there were now only reeds and water and alligators. In fact the front door – it had been given a new coat of green paint, and in the centre, very shiny, was the brass head of a lion champing a ring – the front door had more of Venice than of London: one would have found the appearance of a gondola more appropriate than that of a Sedan-chair. Still, it was all very colourable, and there was even smoke coming from the chimneys. And Appleby looked at it steadily. Then he turned to Wine. 'The man who did that was quite, quite mad.' He paused. 'Don't you agree?'

Wine looked thoughtfully at his finger-nails. 'Well – of course I should not care to defend the sanity of old Schlumpf. I scarcely knew him. And the thing looks pretty mad. But one can never be quite sure. There may be something more to the maddest-looking project than immediately meets the eye. Don't you think so? Hudspith, my dear fellow, don't you agree with me?' Wine smiled whimsically at the inarticulate reply given to this last appeal. 'But at least one would not have it otherwise; the thing is so pleasingly odd. Of course there is a good deal that is odd about our own project – Lucy, my dear, I think you should put on your hat – and Schlumpf's anterior oddities make perhaps too much of a good thing. That is why Beaglehole there is such a comfort. There is nothing odd about him. A solid businessman who keeps our feet on earth – or on deck as we puff up and down our interminable river.' Wine was talking gently and apparently at random. 'Which reminds me: the steamer is going down with Beaglehole tomorrow. So I fear you will not have much time to explore more of our oddities or of Schlumpf's. One of you, that is to say.'

'One of us?' said Appleby. The launch was curving inshore; presently 37 Hawke Square would tower above them like a menacing cliff.

'Either Hudspith or yourself. I want one of you to go and contact Radbone just as quickly as you can. Have you listened to the news lately? There really isn't much time to lose; our merger, if we can agree upon it, had better be soon.'

'Perhaps we ought both to go?'

Wine cocked his head, as if this were a sound suggestion which had not occurred to him. 'Perhaps so. And yet I don't know. There is so much that I could discuss with one of you. I think we could draught a complete plan. No' – his voice was politely final – 'I really think not. We must save all the time we can. But which of you had better go?'

'I don't think it makes much difference,' said Hudspith.

'No,' said Wine amiably. 'I don't think it does.'

Deserted and echoing, and with its ill-assembled doors and floors and wainscoting rattling and creaking in the dry wind of the Pampas – it was thus that Appleby had instinctively thought of the new 37 Hawke Square. But it proved to be more than fully occupied. Miss Mood seemed, since her last appearance, to have multiplied herself by some process of fissure natural to the lower forms of life; she was to be found on every landing. And – although Mrs Nurses are rare – there were several Mrs Nurses. It had to be remembered that 37 Hawke Square was also English House, and that in material for operating in England Mr Wine was peculiarly rich. Mediums and thought-readers and prodigies wandered on every landing and popped in and out through numbered doors. Moreover it was probable that for every person thus visible there was another altogether too odd or erratic or unreliable for present view. The place was, in fact, crammed like a cheap lodging-house. And this, thought Appleby as he stood on the first-floor landing after luncheon, made the situation more than curious. Perhaps it offered un-expected scope for manœuvre. Certainly it straitened the enemy's plans.

'Jacko!'

He looked up and saw Lucy beckoning from the next landing. She was conspiratorial and happy. He went up and joined her. 'Have they given you a decent room?'

'Not bad. In the attics. It's funny about this house. Come up to the top.'

They climbed.

'It's funny about habit.'

'About habit?' Real Lucy's English prose, Appleby reflected, had a touch of young Lucy still. It was at once infantile and cogent, like the more lucid performances of Miss Gertrude Stein.

'It's funny about a step you think is there in the dark when it isn't – isn't it?'

'When you try to take a step down that isn't there? It can give you quite a jar.'

'Yes. Well, I get a jar when I keep on trying to go below-stairs and there isn't a below-stairs. You see, the house we all lived in before the blitz –'

'All lived in!'

'Mum and me and the others.'

'Of course.'

'It was just like this, and of course below-stairs and the attics were our parts. And now there is no below-stairs; just three or four steps and then it ends off. I suppose it was all they managed to steal of the basement. Still, there's all the attics. Let's go right up.'

They climbed higher. The English material of Emery Wine flitted past, banged doors, talked, sang, somewhere played a piano. It's funny about this house, Appleby thought. It's funny –

'Jack – about Mr Smart.' They had reached the top, and Lucy leant over the balustrade. 'This is where he fell from. It's not really a well, is it? Not much more than a slit.'

They stood approximately on the spot from which, in the London of 1888, an unfortunate merchant had fallen to his death. A cross, thought Appleby, looking down, marks the spot. It was funny about Mr Smart. And it was, indeed, hardly a well. What one saw far below was a narrow rectangle of tiled floor.

'Of course,' said Lucy, 'you'd go right to the bottom. But not quite – quite clean. There'd be bumps.'

The observation was correct; probably there would be bumps probably the body would go bumping down like a ball on a pin-table. And this, somehow, was nastier than a single plunge; and smash.

'Of course,' said Lucy, 'he may try poison, like the other man – the colonel. But I don't think so.' She was frowning down at the tiny pattern of tiles below. He looked at her curiously. 'But I don't think so,' she repeated.

'Why not?'

'Because the – the case of Colonel Morell is less certain. I think he'll try to – to reproduce the more striking one.'

Striking, thought Appleby, was the word. He glanced round the landing. There appeared to be nobody about. 'You're probably right.'

'Though of course he might just do something quite different. The – the –' She paused, at a loss for the right abstract words.

'The conditions of the problem would still hold.'

'Yes. But somehow I think it will be the staircase. So think what he has to do. And suppose it's Hudspith.'

'Suppose it's Hudspith,' said Appleby gravely.

'Well, Hudspith has to go off with Beaglehole on the steamer as if for a long journey. That means no more Beaglehole for weeks. And that's important – if we can work it.'

Appleby was looking at her with narrowed eyes. He had colleagues as competent and economically-minded as this. But not many of them.

170

'And then Hudspith has to be brought back – or persuaded to come back. And nobody here must know. And he must be pitched down here and killed, and still none of all these queer people must know, and then there must be a lot of waiting while you think he is just sailing down the river. It was ages before Dr Spettigue –'

'But that was because Dr Spettigue didn't move into his new consulting-rooms for quite a time.'

She shook her head. 'That's not quite right, Jacko. I mean, we don't know the ghost would have appeared any quicker even if Dr Spettigue had moved in at once. Perhaps ghosts take some time to pull themselves together. Particularly after –' And her glance went down the long drop to the hall below.

'You're quite right. Wine must be prepared to wait weeks or even months for results from this particular experiment. And, mind you, it's no more than a side-line with him; a little weak hankering after pure science in a predominantly practical man. Interesting chap, Wine.'

Lucy shook her head impatiently. 'Don't be cool and detached, Jacko. It's just showing off. And – and beside the point.'

Appleby looked at his late patient and victim with respect. 'Go on,' he said.

'The point is this. Hudspith is pitched down there and killed and nobody must know. That means getting rid of the body quick. What will they do? Feed it to the alligators, if you ask me. And what about Beaglehole? He must make himself scarce and keep himself scarce. If you saw him or heard he was about it would be all up with the experiment. The whole thing turns on your not suspecting anything. If you suspected that Hudspith was dead, then you might begin to *expect* a ghost. And the experiment has to be so that there isn't what that big book calls specific expectation.'

'You've got it all up, Lucy. Have you anything to suggest?'

'Well it's pretty clear what *might* be done, isn't it? The question is, can it be worked? We'll try.' She sighed and grinned at him, pale and excited. 'You know, it's a good thing the young 'un and the prig are out of this. They'd be scared stiff.'

'And you, Lucy?'

She stretched herself luxuriously and perilously against the balustrade. 'Me, Jacko? Well, I don't think I'll ever bother to go to the pictures again.'

3

It was dusk among the chimney-pots. Half-close the eyes and it was possible to imagine a whole forest of them; possible to conjure up a whole London below. And perhaps one day London – perhaps one day all the great cities would be like this: some single surviving battered building perched above swamps and grasses which stretched everywhere to the horizon. *After London* . . . it had been one of the books of one of the Lucys – the story of a sparse feudal culture scattered over home counties from which the industrial heart had vanished in some unnamed catastrophe. . . . Appleby peered out over the darkening Pampa. There too, on those last and inaccessible reaches of the monstrous river, were spears and bows and arrows; were the remnants of some primitive and tribal organization. Perhaps the savages would have the laugh on the more complicated and showy structures in the end. Perhaps –

A smut falling on Appleby's nose interrupted this reverie. Down in the bowels of 37 Hawke Square they were burning real coal. Soot and coal-dust were no doubt the appropriate incense of the place and peculiarly necessary while the right psychical atmosphere was being worked up. There was something very close to ritual sacrifice in the fantastic experiment being prepared by Wine. Indeed, a psychologist would say that his conduct was purely atavistic – a mere throw-back to primitive magic – and that the ingenious notion of an unusually drastic experiment in psychical research was the merest rationalization. But whatever it was – thought Appleby, sitting on the laboriously transplanted leads of 37 Hawke Square – whatever it was, it *was* – and in a very pretty state of forwardness. And there was only one thing to do.

They must go to Wine and tell him that his experiment was

pointless – pointless because they knew all about it. They must tell him that they knew Radbone to be nonsense; that they were known to be policemen; that they were policemen with a powerful backing behind them; that they had accompanied him up the river knowing all about his game; that their superiors knew all about his game; that diplomatic means were being taken to smash it now; that his best chance was to fade out quietly without committing a capital crime. Government would step in and liquidate his enterprise, but with luck he himself would not be successfully pursued.

Appleby reeled it off in his own mind – and disliked it. The perfection of Wine's experiment, it was true, they had power to smash. To no unsuspecting friend in that house would the ghost of a murdered man ever appear, or fail to appear. At their first word spoken all that laborious project of Wine's would be in atoms. But beyond that the position was bleak. Wine was very little likely to be intimidated. He would know, almost as well as they knew themselves, how long and tenuous was the track from the Happy Islands to Scotland Yard. In a world at peace the pursuit of two missing officers would be inexorable indeed, but would be slow. Under present conditions Wine – whose whole vast project was a gamble – might well reckon that his own powers would be deployed and triumphant long before they were run to earth here in their vulnerable cradle.

The river flowed past the front door of 37 Hawke Square. The alligators plopped within earshot of its dining-rooms. Such incongruities, deliberately contrived by a logical if perverted mind, had an insidious power to paralyse the will, to baffle the intellect. But not Lucy Rideout's. Lucy enjoyed a saving ignorance. She knew far too little of the world to be in danger of sitting back flabbergasted. And she knew enough of melodrama and had enough of native wit to contrive sufficiently surprising answering stratagems of her own. One might do worse than give Lucy her head.

A shadow moved among the chimney-pots. Wine had emerged on the roof – an incongruous figure in his quietly immaculate tropical clothes. 'Appleby, is it you? I am glad you have found this amusing vantage point.' Wine sat down easily on the leads. 'Who would ever think to survey the heart of

173

South America from the roof of a London tenement? And yet here we are, and there South America is.' He waved his hand whimsically before him. 'Utterly irrational, but a fact. And all the most potent facts are utterly irrational. That is our theme. Men made steam engines by observing and exploiting the way things actually work. We are going to make far more potent engines by observing and exploiting the way things are spontaneously imagined to work. Consider the stars, my dear man.'

Appleby looked up at the darkening sky. In a few minutes now the stars would be hanging there, would be hanging there whether one was considering them or not. . . . 'The stars?' he said vaguely.

'Consider the stars. What is it natural to believe of them? What notions about them come spontaneously into men's minds? Clearly the notions of judicial astrology. Compared with them the notions of Copernicus and Newton, of Kepler and Einstein, are temporary, local and eccentric in the highest degree.'

'But the notions of Copernicus and his followers work. Their predictions come true. Whereas with the astrologers –'

Wine interrupted with a wave of an amiably dismissive hand. 'The human race, my dear Appleby, is much too shock-headed, and has much too short a memory, to take much notice of whether predictions are fulfilled or not. All it wants is a certain quality in the predictions themselves. They must have a magical and irrational element of sufficient substance to satisfy the magical and irrational appetencies which make up nine-tenths of the content of the human mind. That is what we are going to provide – Radbone and you and I.'

'And Hudspith.'

'And Hudspith, of course.' Wine was silent for a moment, as if his mind had gone off on some other train of thought. 'Has one of you by any chance got a revolver?' he asked suddenly.

'I have. But I don't think Hudspith has. Would you care to borrow it?' Appleby spoke easily, but with a mild unconcealed surprise. If Lucy's hair-raising plan was to be adopted it was necessary to appear utterly unsuspecting of danger.

'Dear me, no. It has simply struck me that some rough census of weapons is desirable. The truth is, there are rumours about the surrounding natives which I don't quite like.'

'I hope they haven't caused any more wastage?'

'No: the trouble is rather that they appear to be lying very low. It makes me think they may be meditating some attack. And though they are not visible by day, there are stories going round of rather queer things being seen and heard at night.'

'Queer things? That sounds right up your pitch. Perhaps they just want to pull their weight in your brave and irrational new world.'

Wine laughed – perhaps a shade uncertainly. 'After so much of Beaglehole it is really delightful to talk to somebody who can make a joke. But, seriously, I am a little perturbed. They undoubtedly ate those two women who were so interestingly *en rapport*.'

'Miss Molsher and Mrs Gladigan?'

'Yes. And now they have most certainly eaten the Yorkshire girl who escaped with the horse. That is most upsetting in itself, for really she was a most promising witch. But what I am afraid of is that the thing may give them an ungovernable taste for white man in the stew-pot. I believe it does sometimes happen that way.'

'No doubt. In fact, an abstention from cannibalism, if one takes a broad enough view, is probably temporary, local and eccentric in the highest degree. And if the savages turn really spontaneous we are all likely to be turned into cutlets.'

Wine's laugh was perceptibly harsh this time. 'Quite so. We don't want magical practices *too* near home. Perhaps Hudspith may congratulate himself that he is going downstream in the morning. He, at least, won't be eaten by cannibals.' Wine paused. From the river below came the faint *plop* of an alligator.

'But for us who remain you think there is real danger?'

'Only of inconvenience and a tiresome scrap. The savages are believed to exist in quite considerable numbers, and in these upper reaches have never been brought under control. But fortunately they are quite without any sort of directing intelligence.'

'Ah.' Appleby knocked out his pipe and looked up at the heavens. Yes, the stars were there – armies of unalterable law. And, perched obscurely on his grain of dust in space, he winked at them. 'Fancy,' he said. 'Fancy a Yorkshire witch ending her days in an American savage's cauldron. Irrational, isn't it?'

Hudspith snapped down the locks of his suitcase. 'I wonder why it should be me?' he asked composedly. 'Of course Wine came to realize that my having a vision of Lucy that night was a hoax. But I feel he went on believing those stories of yours about my being that sort of man.'

'In a way you are that sort of man.' Appleby, sitting on his bed in the small hours, spoke softly across the room. 'You're a moody devil with an abstracted eye and a bee in your bonnet about abducted girls. It gives you quite a distinguished air. And I don't doubt Wine regards you as psychically sensitive. Nevertheless you are going to supply the ghost and I am going to be the percipient: there's no doubt of that. Probably the theory is that only psychically peculiar people have the makings of good ghosts. Come to think of it, ghosts are seen by all and sundry in the most unselective way. If they're seen at all, that is.' Appleby paused in order to give some attention to loading his revolver. 'Whereas as often as not a ghost has been a person of some mark. I think you must take it as rather a compliment that you have been cast for that particular role.'

'Cast is the word,' said Hudspith. 'But not so much a role as a bump.' He laughed loudly at this complex of puns, and then checked himself as the sound echoed startlingly in the night. 'You know I can't help feeling an element of waste in the thing.'

Appleby laid the revolver on his bed. 'Very natural, I'm sure. All condemned men must regard the projected execution as a quite unjustifiably lavish expenditure of life. They must feel that a decent regard for economy positively requires that the thing be commuted to a kindly rebuke.'

'I don't mean quite like that. Do you ever read detective stories?'

'Lord, lord! What sort of talk is this? No, I haven't read a detective story for years.'

'I read quite a lot. Recreative, I find them.' Hudspith had

176

switched off the light and was speaking out of the darkness. 'They quite take one out of oneself, if one's in my line.'

'I see. No ruined girls.'

'Not many ruined girls. They don't sell. How many people would you say have written detective stories?'

Appleby yawned. 'Hundreds, I should imagine.'

'Quite so – and some of them have written scores of books. Folk with intelligences ranging from moderate through good to excellent. A couple of women are quite excellent; there's no other word for them.'

'Is that so? I say, Hudspith, it must be deuced late.'

'And what would you say those hundreds of folk are constantly after?'

'Money.' Appleby's voice, if sleepy, was decided.

'They're constantly after a really original motive for murder. And here one is. I'm being murdered to further the purposes of psychical research; murdered in order to manufacture a ghost. It's a genuinely new motive, and none of them has ever thought of it.'

'Probably someone.. ..as. You just haven't read that particular yarn. Good night.'

'But I haven't explained what I mean. About waste, that is.' Hudspith's voice continued to come laboriously out of the night. 'Here is a perfect detective-story motive, and yet we're not in a detective story at all.'

'My dear man, you're talking like something in Pirandello. Go to sleep.'

'We're in a sort of hodge-podge of fantasy and harum-scarum adventure that isn't a proper detective story at all. We might be by Michael Innes.'

'Innes? I've never heard of him.' Appleby spoke with decided exasperation. 'You might employ your last hours more profitably than in chatter about the underworld of letters. Go to sleep. Go to sleep and dream of the nice boiled egg they send to the condemned cell on the fatal morning.'

Hudspith sighed and for a time was silent. 'It's all very well rotting,' he said at length. 'But about this idea of Lucy's – do you think it will work?'

Silence answered him.

'Do you think it will? After all, it's a matter of some importance from my point of view.'

But again there was silence. Appleby was asleep.

4

Boiled eggs had been prominent on the breakfast-table, and while discussing them Wine had gone over in considerable detail the terms which Hudspith was to propose to his employer Radbone. Hudspith had made jottings in a notebook, scraped out his second egg and gone stolidly on board the little steamer. And no one could have guessed he guessed he was flirting with death. He stood beside Beaglehole in the stern, and sometimes he waved and sometimes Beaglehole waved, and quite soon they were indistinguishable dots far down the river. Wine, whose farewells had been openly affectionate, retired to administrative duties for the day. And once more Appleby climbed the little hill and sat himself down beneath the Ñandubay.

Hudspith was gone. A policeman who believed himself not to be known as such, he was gone as the result of what he believed to be a successful ruse – was gone, as he believed, to bring back troops and police and the rule of law to the Happy Islands. But in all this he was deluding himself. Radbone was a fiction successfully imposed upon him. And he was going to his death – a curious death, useful to science.

Such was the picture of the affair as it presented itself to Wine now. And how did Wine see Appleby? As another policeman who believed himself not to be known as such, a policeman who had only to go on pretending to believe in Radbone, a policeman who had only to sit tight in unsuspicious-seeming ease until his colleague returned with abundant help. But in all this but another deluded policeman. For to Appleby no Hudspith would ever return in the flesh. Only to an Appleby wholly unapprehensive, whole unsuspicious of his friend's death, there might one day appear Hudspith's ghost – a ghost calling for

178

revenge. To others as well the ghost might manifest itself, but it would be to Appleby, as to Captain Bertram and Dr Spettigue, that some definite revelation would be attempted. Hudspith was to die, and thereafter the unsuspecting Appleby would be under scientific observation. Has he seen anything? Has the spirit of his murdered friend managed to communicate with him? These would be the questions asked. And all this as a sort of side-line to Wine's vast organization. The man sat down there, marshalling and docketing his growing army of clairvoyants and astrologers and miracle-workers to strictly practical ends. But he had this little weakness for real science. And hence the strange transplanting of 37 Hawke Square and Hudspith's present voyage. . . . Appleby gazed down the river. The little steamer had rounded a bend. There was only water, yellow and empty, to be seen.

Appleby filled his pipe. He lit it and puffed and thought about Hudspith's death. It was important to get this melancholy event quite clear.

Hudspith must die here. It would be no good cutting his throat fifty miles down the river– else might his ghost vainly haunt a solitude broken only by the flamingos and the scissorsbirds. And not only must he die here – here in 37 Hawke Square – but here too must violence first be offered him. Wine's scientific thoroughness would insist on that. The murder must, so to speak, begin and end here.

Hudspith, then, must be brought back all unsuspecting. And quietly; nobody must know. Not one of the teeming occupants of the house must know. Even thoroughly reliable accomplices must be at a minimum – for the more of these there were the more possible would it be that the experiment might be vitiated by the operation of telepathy. Minds knowing of the murder might communicate to Appleby an obscure alarm.

Hudspith must be murdered here. *And he must know it.* Appleby frowned as he hit upon this point. If you do not know that you are being murdered it is conceivable that your ghost will never know that you were murdered. Hudspith must be brought back all unsuspecting; he must be made aware that his murder is imminent; he must be murdered with the knowledge of as few persons as possible; his body must be disposed of safely and instantly; all must be as if he were still smoothly dropping down the river in the company of Beaglehole.

These were the conditions of the experiment. Most of them Lucy had worked out already; and Lucy had seen how drastically they limited the enemy's power of manœuvre. How could the thing be done?

Appleby looked up into the empty South American sky. It needed an aeroplane, he thought.

The steamer could not come back. But Hudspith must come back. Suppose, then, that Beaglehole affected to remember some vital point in the proposed deal with Radbone which Wine had not cleared up. Suppose that, some way down the river, a plane of Wine's opportunely turned up. Suppose Beaglehole proposed a quick hop back in this to the Happy Islands and then a return hop before the steamer had gone much farther on its way. This would serve to bring an unsuspecting Hudspith back and – what was equally important – it would serve to get Beaglehole quickly away again after the murder. For nobody must know of Beaglehole as mysteriously returned and hanging about. The moment Hudspith was murdered it would be desirable that Beaglehole should make himself scarce. And for this a plane would be the thing. An amphibian plane could come and go in darkness. And Wine was almost certain to possess one. It all combined to bring Lucy's plan within the fringes of the feasible. . . . Appleby knocked out his pipe and started down the hill. Lucy Rideout was all right. One knew where one was with her – now. But what of Hannah Metcalfe – and Daffodil? He looked out over the dark luxuriant fringe of the river to the infinite spaces beyond. An army could manœuvre there.

Black coffee is the best vehicle for administering a surreptitious sleeping draught, and at half past eight that night Appleby gave the appearance of drinking a good deal of black coffee. An hour later he told Wine and Mrs Nurse that he was feeling sleepy. And half an hour after that again he was in bed. He was in bed and in darkness – for the night was very dark. He lay in bed thinking of the curious turn which it was proposed that things should take. Finish was required; there must be a constant care for convincing detail. And Appleby put out his arm and turned on a little lamp by his bedside. He tossed an open book, spine upwards, on the floor. It would be thus with a man whom an opiate had surprised

Everything was very quiet by eleven o'clock; so quiet in this over-populated house that it was tempting to believe there must have been laudanum all round. The sluggish river slapped half-heartedly at the stone steps before the front door of 37 Hawke Square; a light wind intermittently clattered in some metro-politan chimney-top contrivance overhead; far away the creatures of the South American night called to each other sparely and without conviction – the call of wild things per-petually half awake on the off-chance of alarm or catastrophe. For Appleby it was an off-chance too; it would mean a hitch if he were called out into the violent stream of things that night. But he was very wakeful.

Wine came at twenty past eleven. He tapped at the door – lightly; slipped into the room – softly; spoke – very quietly indeed. 'Appleby, my dear fellow, I hope you don't mind –' He was across the room and by the bed; and now he said nothing more. Appleby, breathing heavily, sensed him as sitting down. And then he felt a touch, light but purposive, on his wrist. Wine was feeling his pulse.

Constantly one had to remember that it would all be very scientific. The way to avoid surprises was to remember this. Doubtless this pulse-business would be repeated at frequent intervals during the next hour or so. For, hard by the sleeping man, stirring events were presently to accomplish themselves. How interesting – how scientifically interesting – if that pulse quickened to some obscure intimation of drama from the waking world!

Wine must be watching him intently. And as Appleby visualized that intent glance he felt his own eyelids flicker as those of a man heavily asleep ought not to do; he contrived to stir uneasily, groan, and bury his head in the pillow. And what, in fact, would his pulse tell? Wine was a hard man to cozen.

The light from the bedside lamp still seeped faintly through to Appleby's retina; outside the room, on the second-floor landing, another faint light would be burning. But everywhere else there would be a velvet blackness now; only from high over-head the river would show, perhaps, as a streak of dullest silver. No doubt a skilful pilot – Appleby listened. From far down the river came a murmur of sound that grew momentarily in volume and then faded away. There was silence and then far off a bird cried. A bird cried and another answered; many birds were calling, and the blended sound made the same murmur but louder, so that it drowned the sullen slap-slap of the river and the creak of the London chimney-pot overhead. But again there was silence, and then again the murmur grew, louder still. Colony by colony up the long reaches of the river the birds were coming awake and crying and then once more sinking to rest. High above them something was passing – and now a new vibration could be felt, a new sound heard. The faint quick throb of the engine grew. And again Appleby felt the touch on his wrist.

The engine cut out. Seconds passed. Now the plane must be on the water. But nothing more was heard, and the lengthened minutes crawled interminably by.

'Appleby!' It was Wine's voice, sudden and commanding hard by Appleby's ear. But this was something abundantly to be expected, and the sluggish movement of the head which alone resulted must have been convincing enough. For now Wine took Appleby's right arm and cautiously pushed up the sleeve above the elbow. Something cool, firm, binding was applied and faintly the arm began to throb. More science. A mere finger on the pulse was not enough; here was one of those gadgets which gives much more accurate information on how the human engine behaves.... Minutes passed again, and then a sharp jarring sound came up and in through the open window. That was a boat, thought Appleby; Hudspith and Beaglehole had arrived. And *that* – there was a click and a distant bang – was the front door opening and closing. And in a moment there would be footsteps on the stairs.

Mr Smart's stairs – the stairs up which that respectable merchant had mounted on returning from his good-humoured holiday at Yarmouth. And now Hudspith was coming up, with Beaglehole, maybe, a couple of treads behind him.... The throb in Appleby's arm changed its tempo;

182

nothing could be done about that; Wine must make what he might of it. And now they were outside on the landing and there seemed to be a pause. Here they would have to halt if the proposal was to knock up Wine in his bedroom. Would they go higher? Beaglehole had a room on the next floor – the floor where Mr Smart's nurseries had lain. Could a pretext be manufactured out of that? Appleby strained his ears. Yes, they were going up. Wine sat very still.

A murmur of voices floated briefly down. Voices in talk – and then a voice in surprise, in anger, in alarm. There was a split second's silence, and then a queer crack or smack followed by a thud. Silence flooded the house, was broken by a deep gasp as of a man raising a burden. Then a brief slither, a bump, a slither again and again a bump. And finally, from below, one single and very horrible sound.

Appleby rolled over, groaned and again lay still; the performance gave some little ease to his nerves. Probably there were beads of sweat on his face; of that too Wine must make what he would. Steps were descending. They went past the landing and down again without hurry but without pause. And then the front door must have been opened once more. For from outside came up a heavy splash. The incomparable digestive system of the crocodile genus was being invoked – and perhaps the affair held no worse moment than that. . . . A very long pause followed. On those smooth marble slabs, transported so far for this far-fetched destiny, a good deal of mopping up would have to be done. But presently that too was over, and up from the river came the low plash of oars cautiously plied. The sound died away, and as it did so the pressure on Appleby's arm relaxed. Wine was packing up his instrument. Now, with the quiet satisfaction of an investigator who has successfully laid the foundations for an important experiment, he would take himself off to bed.

Breakfast was even better than usual. There was melon in monster slices which the servants had cut so as to give an appearance of quaintly serrated teeth, and Wine, though a modest host, had to confess himself quite proud of the grilled trout. Mrs Nurse placidly poured coffee at the head of the table.

Behind her, through the incongruous urban window, the morning showed fresh and lovely, an almost English affair of cool breezes and fleecy clouds. On one of the nearer islands, nestled in greenery, there could just be distinguished a *schloss* and a *chalet* pleasantly recalling the curious fantasy of the late Schlumpf. Everything was smiling and cheerful. Only Lucy Rideout looked a little worn and pale. Sick Lucy had looked rather like that

'How charming it will be,' said Wine, 'sailing down the river this morning. I declare I quite envy our friends. Mrs Nurse, another trout? They are toothsome but small. Or will you take a boiled egg?' He looked round the table in momentary perplexity. 'I am sure I saw boiled eggs. But here is what looks like quite a capital ham. Lucy, my dear, a slice of ham will certainly help you on with your Latin later in the morning. We seem quite to have dropped our Latin lately. And quite soon we must begin German. A language full of interesting shades. What do you think, now, is the difference between *essen* and *fressen*?' Wine looked gaily round the table. 'It's *essen* when we eat the trout and it's *fressen* when the alligators eat us. I wonder if they thought to put some of these delicious little fish on board the steamer? Hudspith, I am sure, would be not unpartial to them.'

The man had a macabre imagination which seemed at the moment too much even for Lucy's robustly melodramatic taste. She pushed away her melon – it had rather an alligator-like look – and slipped from the room. Wine watched her go without curiosity; already it was on Appleby that most of his interest was concentrated. How long did a ghost take to get going? Perhaps there would be a preliminary period of obscure intimations. Or perhaps it would walk in as promptly as the shade of Banquo. Appleby, like Wine looking round vaguely for the boiled eggs, frowned sombrely. *Fail not our feast. . ..* What if the dead man should really walk? And he in turn pushed his plate away – a gesture more expressive than elegant – and left the table. The dead man. . . . Appleby disliked the idea of homicide.

Lucy was on the veranda, and he went up to her with a question in his eye. She nodded – cautious, careful and excited. 'Dead,' she said.

'Instantaneously?'

'Quite.' Her glance became troubled. 'Jacko, about those eggs –'

'Eggs?'

'Was it too risky to pocket them? After all, he must –'

Appleby smiled faintly. 'One must take risks.' He paused. 'Do you know, Lucy, I'm rather troubled about – well, about the ruthlessness of the whole affair.'

She looked at him, wondering. 'But it was one or other of them. Or probably it was him or all of us. And I'm certainly not going to be done for if I can help it. After all, you must remember I'm only just beginning as – as a person.'

'That's true, Lucy. And good luck to you.'

'And now we've gained a lot of time, and perhaps we'll be able to wind the whole thing up. All we have to do is to keep on stealing eggs and things without being noticed.'

Appleby laughed 'This ghost must eat By the way, where is he?'

'I've got him hidden in my room. And we've got the plane hidden too.'

'There was a pilot?'

'No. Beaglehole piloted it himself. So afterwards we just taxied up the river and into a creek.'

'But, good lord, he's never –'

He seemed quite good at it. But he's worried about being concealed in my room. He doesn't think it quite – quite proper.'

'No more it is. But, bless him, I don't suppose anyone since Casanova has had more frequent occasion to hide himself in girls' rooms than Hudspith.'

'Who was Casanova, Jacko?'

'Never mind.'

5

Undoubtedly time had been gained. The liquidation of Beaglehole at the moment when Hudspith was to be liquidated had been a master stroke in its way. Hudspith, preserved, could live on filched boiled eggs indefinitely. And Wine, by the very conditions of his experiment, was obliged to wait patiently upon events. No doubt there would be a limit to the scope of the deception achieved. The Beaglehole who was to have flown down the river again had presumably tasks to perform and reports to make; when these were unachieved Wine's suspicions would be aroused; and although various explanations of Beaglehole's disappearance could be imagined, something like the true explanation would certainly present itself to his late employer as one of the substantial possibilities.

Time had been gained, thought Appleby – and once more he frowned over the way the thing had been done. Beaglehole – disagreeable wretch that he was – had been murdered by an aggressively moral policeman and a green and engaging girl. It was true that he had been murdered in the act of committing murder; true that the killing of him had been in a certain sense an act of self-defence. Any other way of attempting to deal with the situation would probably have been fatal to the ultimate interests of law and order. Still, Beaglehole had been deliberately killed as the result of a course of action carefully and ingeniously thought out beforehand. Legally that was homicide in some degree. Morally it was murder. Or so Appleby thought it wise to think. A policeman, if forced to essays in manslaughter and assassination, ought to view them somewhat on the sombre side. . . . And Appleby looked out over the green and yellow of the incredible river. Anyway Beaglehole's death, whether criminal or not, had been all one to the alligators.

Time had been gained – but was it certain that the commodity was a useful one? Time to reconnoitre the full strength of Wine's organization but did they not already know that it was too strong to fight through? They had played for time while know-

186

ing that time was not a particularly attractive proposition; had played for it because there seemed nothing else to play for. They had won it, and it remained a dubious gain. But in the same match they had won something else. They had won not an indeterminate extension of the affair, but an instrument for abruptly writing *Finis* to it. An instrument, thought Appleby, out of the very last chapter of a schoolboys' story. In fact, an aeroplane.... And Appleby, strolling across Europe Island, glanced over his shoulder. Not far behind him Wine was taking an after-breakfast walk in the same direction.

And likely enough Wine or another would always be there now. In this fantastic community Appleby had become an object of major scientific interest, something far more beguiling to the psychic investigator than Miss Molsher or Mrs Gladigan had ever been. A man who at any turn may encounter a veridical ghost is abundantly worth keeping an eye on. And this is likely to be annoying to one whose thoughts turn much upon a conveniently hidden aeroplane.

Appleby paused and waited for Wine to overtake him. Had it fuel and oil? Of course Hudspith should slip away with it in the night; that would be the ideal thing. Only Hudspith, by whatever inspiration he had contrived to taxi the craft into hiding, was certainly incapable of controlling it while air-borne; that, tiresomely enough, was an accomplishment which only Appleby himself possessed. And his skill was their best chance. Once get the thing into the air and it should be possible, however unfamiliar a crate it was, to get some sort of flying start down the river. It would be a matter of dodging surveillance – surveillance which would be particularly carefully maintained at night. For it is then that ghosts and spirits walk. Perhaps, thought Appleby, as he prepared to receive one of Wine's most cordial smiles, perhaps the dodging could be done. But somehow his faith in the aeroplane was small. He had tried to terminate adventures in the simple fashion of juvenile fiction before. And always something had gone wrong. It was as if the adult universe wasn't constructed that way. Of course there was one other method of concluding this deplorable adventure of the Happy Islands – a method much too odd to commend itself to the realism of youthful minds. But a method he had better get going on now. 'A pleasant day,' he said; 'but with a hint of something rather oppressive, don't you think?'

'Perhaps so.' Wine looked absently at the day. 'I hope you slept well?'

'Thank you – yes. Rather heavily, in fact. I suppose it is the Pampas air.'

'No doubt.' Wine shot out a hand which neatly caught a mosquito on the wing. 'I do not always sleep well myself on the Islands. I find them a great place for dreams. And dreams – after one has thoroughly studied them, I mean – are tiresome when they come in legions. Do you dream?' The question dropped out casually. 'Or dream here more than usual?'

Appleby appeared to consider. 'No, I don't think I do.'

'Last night, for instance, when you say you slept particularly heavily: did you dream at all then?'

'I'm sure I didn't. Or I think I'm sure. But I suppose one has many dreams one doesn't remember. I believe people have been studied and examined while asleep in an effort to discover whether they really dream all the time or not.'

'Indeed?' Wine was more vague than a man of science ought to have been. He pointed up the river. 'I take particular delight in those Magellanic swans.'

They walked together for a time in silence. Time. They had gained time. But obscurely Appleby was sure that he didn't want it – or not much of it. Why not push straight ahead? They were passing through a little grove. Not a bad spot, a grove. For some seconds he walked in an abstraction. Then suddenly he stopped, swung round, stared behind him. It was the evolution of a moment, and he was pacing forward with Wine once more. 'Those mists,' he said casually; 'they seem to hang about quite late among the trees.'

'Mists?' Wine's eyes faintly widened. 'Ah – to be sure.'

Not that one must go too fast. There was the prime difficulty that something like this trick had been played on Wine before. He had been credulous over Hudspith's supposed vision on the night of the birthday-party; surely he would be on his guard a second time. Still, the point was that the credulous side to him was there. And it might be played upon to the point of complete nervous upset. The experiment – perhaps it ought to be called the counter-experiment – was not easy. But it was beguiling. And a fairly direct road to it might be best. Appleby lit his pipe. 'What would you do,' he asked, 'if you saw a ghost?'

Wine's eye followed a humming-bird. 'A ghost?' he said. 'What a curious question!'

'I don't know what put it in my head.' Appleby frowned. 'I suppose this. Here you are proposing to trade in superstition – to batten on it in a very large way. In fact you are going to cash in on the uncanny on a hitherto unthought-of scale.'

'Well, I suppose it will be some time before I rival our theological friends in their heyday. But on a fair scale, certainly. Incidentally, I don't think you put it very prettily. Batten is a horrid word.' Wine smiled cheerfully. 'But I think you were saying –'

'That you are proposing to exploit the supernatural for profit.'

'Just like Radbone and yourselves.'

'Quite so. Has it occurred to you that it is all rather disrespectful?'

Wine came to a halt. 'I'm afraid I don't follow you, my dear fellow.'

'You claim to have an open mind on the whole thing. You conduct experiments in a thoroughly scientific manner. You wouldn't do that unless you supposed it possible that the whole supernatural structure of traditional superstition and belief may, in fact, exist. Suppose it does Suppose your experiments yield unmistakably positive results. Suppose, as I say, you see a ghost. Where does that take you?'

'Some way farther along the path of science, I suppose. I have added to human knowledge.'

'You have indeed. You have demonstrated to yourself that you live, after all, in a magical universe. Not a materialist and rational universe, in which we clearly do the best for ourselves by grabbing what we can of the here and now. On the contrary, you live in an unaccountable universe, one much more like that of what you call our theological friends. Really believe that you see a ghost, and you are bound, on reflection, to see that you see a great deal behind it: malignant spirits, jealous powers.

189

Suppose Hamlet really saw his father's ghost: where did that ghost come from?'

'From sulphorous and tormenting flames – if we are to believe Shakespeare, that is.'

'But if a real ghost were to appear in your laboratory, could you say it didn't come from the same place?'

'I don't know that I could.'

'In fact you would find yourself in a new universe, and one in which the practical side of your enterprise would look much less smart than it does at present. For if the universe is, after all, a spiritual or spiritualist universe, then exploiting spirits and spiritualism for material ends is –'

'Disrepectful was, I think, your word.'

'Just that.' Wine, Appleby reflected, was not to be easily bowled over by a nerve-war. Still, some undermining might be going on. 'Think of Faust. He peered too far into the way things work.'

'And was carried off by demons.' Wine chuckled and resumed his walk. 'As a matter of fact,' he said presently, 'I do at times think of Faust. Your train of thought is not unfamiliar to me. But you put it rather well.' He walked for some time in silence. 'And after all, my dear Appleby, you are in the same boat. I wonder what *you* would do if it was *you* who . . .'

He paused, and Appleby looked at him innocently. 'If it was I who –?'

'Nothing, my dear fellow; nothing at all.' They had turned back and were now in the little grove in which their conversation had begun. 'Mist?' he said. 'Do you know I didn't notice it?'

'Mist,' said Appleby. 'I saw a wisp of mist where there wasn't any. And I felt the morning obscurely oppressive when it was quite lovely. I don't know that you could have done better yourself.'

'Ah,' said Hudspith.

'I'm sure he couldn't,' said Lucy. 'Not that I don't think Mr Hudspith very clever.'

'But it was a mistake.' Appleby shook his head sombrely. 'One wants to go after an element of the unexpected. The ghost of Hudspith appears to his friend Appleby. It repeats the pattern of the other Hawke Square affairs. The experiment yields a result which has been envisaged. And though it may not be comfortable for Wine to have to decide that the universe does, after all, contain unaccountable powers, still, the disconcerting result has been foreseen by him, and there will be a certain reassurance in that. His equilibrium is much more likely to be upset by something which is both supernatural and *unexpected*. *He* sees the ghost of his victim; *I* fail to see the ghost of my friend. Something like that.'

'Ah,' said Hudspith again. Somewhat gloomily, he was peeling the shell off a boiled egg.

Lucy crossed the room from the door where she had been listening. 'It's a pity about the sheets,' she said.

'The sheets?'

She pointed to the bed. 'Nice pastel shades. But one wants a good old-fashioned white sheet for a ghost.'

Appleby sighed. 'Somehow I don't think we'll ever catch Wine in a sheet, however snowy. What's our plan? Nothing less than to make him repent. It's almost absurd.'

'Faust was scared into deciding to burn his books.'

'My dear Lucy, wherever did you learn that?'

Lucy frowned. 'I don't know. But I could tell you quite a lot of funny things like that. Things about Socrates and Marcus Aurelius and –'

'I see.' Her former sisters were rapidly growing dim to Lucy Rideout; already they had merely the quality of intermittently remembered dreams. In another twenty-four hours it looked as if they would have joined Miss Molsher and Mrs Gladigan on Wine's somewhat rapidly growing list of wastages. Which was satisfactory, but not immediately to the point. Appleby rose. 'I must be off. There's a fellow watching for me at the end of the corridor, and he might get curious if my visit to Lucy lasted too long. Wine won't repent. Ghosts won't make him believe that trading in ghosts is disrespectful and dangerous. He won't shake hands with us and retire into private life. But even one ghost – and that merely in pastel shades – might cause him a bit of a flutter for a time. Remember the birthday-party and how het-up he must have got for a bit.' Appleby turned to Hudspith. 'This plane – will it have gas?'

'Presumably so. Beaglehole was certainly going to fly straight back in it. That, of course, is what Wine thinks has actually happened. Beaglehole was going to fly straight back without anybody except Wine knowing that he and I had as much as been here. It would be the obvious thing to have enough fuel to begin with to make the double trip.'

'It depends on the capacity of the tank. But we'll hope for the best. The plane is our real hope, such as it is. While everything runs smoothly here it's no go; I'm watched much too carefully to get away. But tonight we'll spring our ghost and hope for fifteen minutes' chaos. Then we make a break for it.'

Hudspith nodded. 'But must it really be a sheet? I doubt if that's at all the current fashion with ghosts.'

'Nor has been for centuries. No, this ghost shall have risen dripping and bloody from the river.'

'It doesn't sound at all comfortable.'

'There will be a reek as of the inside of a charnel-house – no, of an alligator. And a rush of chill air.'

'I don't see –'

'To say nothing of a phosphorescent glow. I think Lucy and I can work it all out this afternoon.' Appleby moved to the door. 'And now eat your last egg – my dear fellow, as Wine would say.'

6

Positive seduction would be immoral. And under the present conditions of constant surveillance it would be moreover, if not impracticable, at least of a daunting impudicity. So what had it better be? A cash proposition was a possibility. Or one could try threats. Or contrive some sort of appeal to professional vanity. . . . Appleby, strolling over Europe Island, shook his head. If he knew anything of the type, sex it would have to be. The promising beginnings of a vulgar intrigue. Hudspith could offer much technical advice. But then Hudspith would disapprove. For that matter Appleby disapproved himself. He was prepared to admire, but reluctant to pursue – in this being like the majority of prudent men past the first flush of youth's irresponsibilites. Still, the girl must be nobbled. Appleby strolled on.

She lived in a sort of convent. This was an initial difficulty, though likely to be an eventual advantage – for decidedly she must be feeling rather bored. And probably annoyed: the food would be wrong and, likely enough, they made her take baths. This last would be all to the good. But meantime there was a high, white wall. Appleby climbed it and sat on top. He waved cheerfully. And the dark-skinned person who unobtrusively followed him everywhere this afternoon, and who had quickened his pace as he began to climb, grinned sardonically and sat down on a tump of panicle grass. Appleby waved again; or perhaps it might be better said that he made a gesture of a frank and Latin sort. For there she was. He jumped down on the other side and advanced upon her. Whereupon the dark-skinned man got up, scaled the wall in his turn and settled down to a grandstand view from the top. Well, let him. '*Buenos tardes,*' he said.

It was long after dinner. A little fire – a real coal fire – had been lit in the small ground-floor room used by Wine as an office and study. And he and Appleby were alone, sipping whiskies and sodas in the soft light of a standard lamp. Wine was growing increasingly affable. 'I hear,' he said, 'that you have been visiting our Southern European friends.' And he chuckled good-humouredly.

'I really don't know how you can have come to hear that.' Appleby did his best to reply with a sort of shame-faced caution.

'My dear chap, I must really apologize. With so many queer fish about the place – scores and scores of them, I am happy to say – we have necessarily become something of a police-state. The staff are all spies by instinct, and they keep a smart eye on new-comers in particular. I fear one of them has been zealously trailing your good self. It is very absurd, of course – but that's how my little piece of information comes to me.' He chuckled again. 'I hope you found it interesting? And not too tiring?' Wine threw another piece of coal on the fire. He was being very man-of-the-world.

'It struck me as rather conventual.'

193

'Exactly. It is what I aim at over there. With half a dozen or so girls brought up in Mediterranean conditions it seems the best way to cope with what might be a difficult situation. Not that I at all object to their having a visitor from time to time, my dear chap. There is some very promising material over there – I mean from our professional point of view. Some very promising mediums of the lower class. And well-behaved on the whole. Just sometimes I have to threaten to bring over one of the Fathers to give them a talking to.'

'One of the Fathers?'

'Our nearest neighbours.' Wine had hesitated for a moment before he replied. 'There is a Jesuit mission station about eighty miles due north, over difficult country. Actually we never communicate. But the girls know they are there, and go in considerable awe of them.'

Appleby stared thoughtfully into the little fire. This was news. And clearly it was authentic – something, perhaps, which Wine thought it no longer necessary to conceal. But it would be better not to show too much curiosity. 'There was the girl called Eusapia –' he said tentatively.

'Aha!' Wine pointed his glass at Appleby with a gay and whimsical gesture. 'To be sure. Well, well, well.'

'But I rather wish I hadn't gone. Coming back I had a queer sort of feeling of something wrong. Not anything to do with those girls. Rather with this house.'

Wine's eyes narrowed suddenly. 'Wrong here?'

'Yes. As if something had happened. . . . I really can't explain.' Appleby paused, let his eyes travel uneasily round the little shadowy room . 'Funny thing, sex. Makes you feel guilty. Only the sense of guilt takes on all sorts of queer forms Doesn't it?'

'I suppose it does.' It was a cautious rather than the man-of-the-world Wine now.

'Sometimes you just fee. that everything has gone sinister.' Appleby frowned, nervous and puzzled. Would Hudspith, he was wondering, put up a better show than this? He doubted it. 'But, come to think of it, I had very much the same feeling earlier in the day. It was when we were walking through that little grove this morning.'

194

Wine was sitting very still in his chair. But his voice was casual still. 'My dear chap, it's probably nothing but liver. I wouldn't indulge these Freudian notions, if I were you. Guilty and creepy feelings because you've been kissing a girl behind a hedge is all nonsense. Have another drink.' He got up and reached for the decanter. 'And shall we turn out this lamp? I think few things are more soothing to the nerves than simple fire-light. We hardly need warmth tonight, but the glow and flicker are pleasing to exiles like ourselves.'

Exiles. That undiscovered country from whose bourn no traveller returns.... From the tessellated hall of 37 Hawke Square, gloomy beneath the frowning landings that led up to the nurseries of Mr Smart, came a faint and rapid whir – the sound of a grandfather clock preparing to strike. And then came the chime. It was midnight.

'Midnight!' said Wine. He set down his glass. 'Perhaps we ought to turn in. Hasn't the door blown open?' He twisted round in his chair. The door had certainly opened; it showed as a rectangle of darkness in the dimly fire-lit wall. And a breeze cool and faintly damp, as if it carried a fine spray; a breeze suddenly strangely chill....

'Odd,' said Appleby. 'The temperature does seem to drop at night. But such a really cold wind –'

He stopped. For the breeze was no longer chill merely; it was an arctic air, a wind chill as on a Russian steppe.... And abruptly Wine was on his feet. 'The smell,' he said hoarsely; 'my God, the smell!'

'Smell?' said Appleby. There was indeed a smell, a sudden indescribable reek as of the grave, a thick and seeping vapour as of vermiculation and decay. 'Smell? I don't notice anything. But it is uncommonly cold. And I do feel damned queer.'

Wine sat down again. 'You notice the cold, but not the smell?' he asked. In the flicker of the flame Appleby could see him frowning in some final effort of the dispassionate intelligence. Was the cold veridical – an objective fact? And was the smell a subjective concomitant? The fragmentary scientist that was in Wine could be seen on his features, doing battle with dismay. Everything was very quiet. From somewhere beyond the blackness of the open door came a long, deep sigh.

He was on his feet again and had swung round. 'Did you hear that?'

'I can't hear anything.'

'Look!'

There was a glimmer of greenish light in the doorway; it concentrated itself, took form and was a man. Or it was the phantasm of a man, immobile and framed in darkness. It was, thought Appleby, very like a good conjuring trick – dangerously so if the spectator's mind was cool. 'Wine!' he cried. 'What the hell are you staring at? Wine!'

The room reeked still. The phantasmal Hudspith advanced. Water dripped from his muddied and blooded tropical suit; one side of his face was a ghastly mush of orange and blue. Slowly, he was raising an arm.

'Can't you see?' Wine was clinging to the back of his chair.

'See?' Appleby stared blankly at the door. 'You're mad. I see nothing. There's nothing to see. Your blasted laboratory and your experiments have driven you out of your mind. Why couldn't you keep to the racket, you poor mut, and leave tinkering alone? Radbone credulous. Bah!'

The phantasm was pointing. And it spoke. 'I was murdered,' it said in a deep voice. 'I was murdered, Appleby, murdered –'

Wine screamed – screamed with his eyes strangely fixed on the phantasm's head. Part of the head was missing, as if it had been smashed or blasted or gnashed away. And yet not missing ... for a great fragment of skull, as if reluctant to accept dismemberment, floated in air above the wound, 'I was murdered,' said the phantasm; 'murdered by –'

Wine screamed again; he turned and stumbled towards a desk. He grabbed; he held a revolver in his hand and was firing; he was pulling the trigger wildly while the shaking and reeking barrel pointed aimlessly at the floor. There was a crash from behind Appleby and another door burst open. Two men were in the room; one of them the dark-visaged man who had trailed him all day. Heedless of him, they ran towards Wine; Wine was now lying on the floor; outside the nightmarish and flickering room the whole crazy house sounded of tumult and confusion. After all, thought Appleby, its whole constitution was such that it would go quickly on the jump. . . . He turned and slipped quickly into the darkness of the hall.

'It's only a rowing-boat,' said Hudspith. 'We might have managed to get one of the launches. But we'll be quieter in this.'

'I don't know that quiet is much needed.' Appleby mopped his forehead in the darkness as they pushed off. 'There's the deuce of a row.'

It was true. As if panic had propagated itself by mysterious means, the whole group of Happy Islands was in tumult. The clamour struck up to the stars and everywhere were strangely moving and darting lights. They pulled powerfully at the oars.

'Jacko' – Lucy's voice came from the darkness of the stern – 'your Italian friend did you proud.'

Appleby laughed softly. 'She certainly did. And on credit too.'

'What do you mean, on credit?'

'Never mind. How did she manage that cold wind?'

'Mr Hudspith understands it.'

'Ether.' Hudspith was peering anxiously up the river. 'Ether stolen from the medical stores and stood before a big electric fan. The alligator-stink disguised the smell.'

'And the alligator-stink?'

'Lucy will answer that one.'

'Never mind,' said Lucy.

They rowed on. Wine's collapse had caused a confusion almost unaccountably abundant; all the darkness was filled with tumult and cries and splashing. Appleby frowned into the night, opened his mouth to speak, changed his mind and was silent.

'I think it's the next creek,' Hudspith said.

'Good heavens! Wasn't it risky leaving it as close as that?'

Hudspith laughed shortly as he tugged at his oar. 'Not half so risky as trying to pilot the thing any farther.'

'Taxiing a hydroplane isn't all that difficult.'

'Lucy will tell you what it felt like.'

'It felt like death,' said Lucy briefly.

'Or like driving a racing car fitted with skates through a maze in the dark.' Hudspith turned round and peered ahead once more. 'Easy, all.'

They had taken two turns up a broad backwater, and the nearest island was now some distance behind them. But still the night was mysteriously alive and moving; the sky flickered oddly; there was a great deal of shouting from directions hard to place.

'If we can get it air-borne,' said Appleby, 'we shall do something.' His voice was anxious; the plane was their one hope; and still he was obscurely unable to feel faith in it. . . . The little boat drifted round a final gentle bend and he rubbed his eyes. For there the plane was – authentic, real and waiting. Only there was something odd about it. The night was starry as always, but here in the backwater it was very dark. What was odd about the plane was that it was *visible*.

It was silhouetted against a dull red glow. And in the sky were points and trails of light, shooting arcs of reddish fire. A cluster of these rose, fell. A tongue of flame shot from the tail of the plane; another rose beside it; there was a third in the cockpit. The plane was blazing.

And behind them as they rested on their oars there was a splashing in the river; Appleby turned to see a half-circle of dark bobbing heads. That, of course, was it. The general tumult was explained – as was the destruction of their only likely link with the outer world. But it was not a moment for reflection. He tapped Hudspith on the shoulder. 'Into the bank!' he cried. 'And out and up.'

The little boat grounded in mud; in a few seconds they were scrambling in a *monté* of tree-fern and bamboo, and it was very dark. But back a little from the water the terrain would be clearer, and it was necessary to see even at the risk of being seen. They were not being pursued, unless it was stealthily – and in that night's operations the period of stealth seemed to be over. From the Islands the clamour was now indescribable, and from somewhere farther along the bank came a savage and exultant singing. They stumbled on and were climbing; they were on the brow of a little hill, bare save for one vast tree, spreading and shadowy. They staggered under it and, momentarily safe from espial, looked back. Hudspith grunted.

Lucy gasped and laid a hand on Appleby's arm. It was an extraordinary sight.

Very clearly the assault, so strangely timed to coincide with the shock of domestic confusion on Europe Island, had been completely successful. The heritage of Schlumpf, the dominion of Emery Wine, was everywhere going up in flame; the sky already glowed as from one vast bonfire; a pall of smoke was gathering over the river. The windows of 37 Hawke Square glowed luridly – glowed as with an indignant glare at this second night of outrage within a mere fragment of time. The peace of the Augustans had seen its birth; it had known the long, strenuous tranquillity of Victorian days; now flame and destruction had pursued it from continent to continent.

The savages were intent to destroy. But they were not, it seemed, intent to kill. Clearly on the nearest Island – and distinguishably on Islands farther away – they could be seen bearing off, violently but with a sort of strange and ritualistic respect, the abundant and various stock-in-trade of Wine's now fallen and ruined enterprise. Naked and in groups, dark-skinned and powerful, they bore away billowy women and frightened girls and bewildered men. Mediums and palmists, thought-readers and scryers and astrologers; they were being borne away as by devils in an old window; were vanishing in a confusion of contorted limb and frantic gesture, like Sabine Women in a tapestry unrestrainedly Baroque. The clamour of the strange pervasive rape echoed over the river and the pampa; the flames waxed and mounted; the stars were dimmed.

'Look!'

Lucy was pointing. Just below them, and nearer the river, was another low hill. And in a sudden flare of light – it was probably the flame reaching the petrol in the plane – they saw a single figure standing immobile, surveying the scene.

'The witch,' Lucy said.

And it was Hannah Metcalfe. She stood very still and watched the bonfire with slightly parted lips. On Beaglehole and his whip, on Wine and the Isle of Capri, she had achieved her revenge.

Hudspith stirred sharply. 'My God!' he said. 'She's demented. Only a devil would plot such a thing.'

Appleby nodded. 'Perhaps so. And only a very powerful and talented person could carry it out. I believe –' He stopped and laid a warning hand on each of his companions. 'Listen,' he whispered.

The sound was very close. It came from the other side of the great tree. And it was the neigh of a horse.

In the flicker from the distant fires the creature showed cloud-like and uncertain. There was a flare of light, and they saw it clearly; it was erect, prancing and magnificent. Suddenly Lucy called out; of the three of them her senses appeared to be the keenest. 'Jacko, look!'

Appleby turned. The backwater was still behind them. And now, in front and steadily advancing, was a great sickle of dancing flames. Its significance was clear: a long line of savages was converging upon them with lighted torches, and there was no line of retreat. They must have been detected by those bobbing heads in the water; now they were to be rounded up. Appleby eyed the distance. 'Five minutes,' he said; 'we haven't got more than that.' There was a jerk at his shoulder; he turned and eyed the great horse; the animal was tossing its head strangely in air. 'One, two,' said Appleby; 'three, four, five – by the lord Harry, it's Daffodil!'

'Daffodil?' said Hudspith. 'Nonsense! Daffodil is a broken-down cab-horse. This is as fine a creature –'

'It's the pampa. It was the same with the Spaniards when they first came. They landed a lot of sorry jades –'

'They're nearer,' Lucy said warningly.

'– but after a month or so of the pampa air –' Appleby broke off; he was working at the horse's tether. 'Hudspith, I've rather lost my bearings. Which bank are we on?'

'North.'

'Then perhaps we can do it. Do you ride?'

'No.'

'But you can hang on to a stirrup-leather. Imagine you're an infantryman charging with the Scots Greys.' Appleby was in the saddle. 'Steady, Daffodil, steady! Lucy, up you come. And yell, all of you; yell like mad.' With difficulty he turned the horse's head towards the advancing line of fire. The creature reared, came down, curvetted like a colt. And Appleby gave it the rein. 'A Daffodil,' he shouted, 'a Daffodil!' They charged nightmarishly down the hill. Savages danced and yelled in front. The hooves of Daffodil thundered below and Hudspith held on as to a hurricane. Behind them the glare from the burning Happy Islands obscured Orion and climbed to touch the Southern Cross.

7

'Surprise me?' The Jesuit Father looked innocently at Appleby. 'No, I cannot say you do that. Except perhaps in the matter of the horse. It was an uncommon feat of endurance. One feels that he deserves a flagon of wine, like the animal in Browning's poem. You admire Browning? I think of him as an Elizabethan born out of time. He has that theatrical vision of Italy and the Papacy which is so essentially of the Elizabethan age.'

'I hate to think of all those poor creatures carried off by the savages.'

'It is curious that he could do so little in the dramatic form.' The priest shook his head, cultivated and austere and comfortable. No doubt, thought Appleby, he could discourse thus adequately on the poets of half a dozen semi-barbarous nations – and was glad to do so when the rare occasion should occur. 'But I beg your pardon. You were saying –? Ah, yes; about the poor people who have been carried off. There is little chance of rescuing them, I sadly fear. In any temporal sense, that is to say. You see, those tribes come from pretty far to the south-west. We never contact them. But I assure you that their prizes will be given a very comfortable time. They will be treated as gods.'

Hudspith took his eyes from the little sun-lit cloister-garth. 'Is that comfortable?'

'Humanly, it may not be so bad. We must pray for them, of course.' The priest was silent for a minute. 'You see, all the natives hereabouts have the most enormous appetite for marvels.

It amounts to an embarrassment at times, I do assure you.' He smiled gravely, a man who would not readily be put to a stand. 'And they are very numerous. They will absorb hundreds of holy men and miracle-workers without the least trace of spiritual or intellectual indigestion.'

'That,' said Appleby, 'is just what Wine believed the world at large was ripe to do.'

'I think we can look after the world at large.' The priest smiled again. 'You and I,' he said politely.

'It's an odd end to the thing. For a moment I was inclined to call it poetic justice. But it's not quite that.'

'It has a certain artistic fitness, Mr Appleby. To say more than that would be – injudicious.'

Lucy Rideout, rather alarmed in strange surroundings, looked timidly up. 'I'm dreadfully sorry for Mrs Nurse.'

'She shall be particularly remembered.'

Lucy blinked, very much at sea. 'And you think that Mr Wine – ?'

'It is likely that he will have been killed. We heard little of him, but undoubtedly he bore a bad name. And hereabouts, believe me, that is a fatal thing to do. I am wondering about the girl who was believed to be a witch. She must have obtained great power. Her, I believe we can rescue. In such matters, when they are important, we are not without means.'

'You think Hannah Metcalfe important?' asked Appleby.

'She has much talent, and among those people might be an instrument of much good. She shall be found. And instructed.' He smiled again and rose. 'And now you are tired, I am sure.'

Time had passed, and even Harrogate was not quite the same. Here and there a bit was missing. The enemy, uncertain of his reception in more martial quarters, was occasionally contriving to chasten the spas of England – chosen haunts of a warmongering plutocracy. And even Lady Caroline had changed with the times, wearing a steel helmet as she took her daily carriage-exercise in the open landau.

'Dear Miss Appleby,' said Lady Caroline as she stood on the steps of her modest but distinguished hotel, 'have you seen my muff? Maidment used to look after it for me.'

'No, my dear. I fear you have to look after it yourself now-adays. And you must not regret Miss Maidment too much. The auxiliary services do such wonderful work.'

'No doubt. But I fear that Maidment has been much actuated by a desire for the society of men.'

'Dear me!'

'I had frequently remarked it. Where is Bodfish?'

'Nowadays, Lady Caroline, he appears to like to walk Daffodil up and down before taking us up. Sometimes to *trot* him up and down. But here they are. Have you noticed that the carriage never seems to keep quite still?'

'Bodfish,' said Lady Caroline sternly, 'have a care.'

'How eager Daffodil is to be off!' said Miss Appleby. 'The carriage quite hits one in the back.'

'I am afraid,' said Lady Caroline, 'that this paltry bombing is having an undue effect upon the nerves of the populace. Have you noticed how nervous people appear to be in the streets? Our own modest progress might be a charge of cavalry. Did you notice that policeman at the corner? He positively leapt for the pavement as we passed.' Lady Caroline settled herself with some difficulty in her corner. 'I am not sure that the springs of this landau are quite as they were.'

'I agree with you.' Miss Appleby swayed in her seat. 'But it is a great comfort once more to be assured of a quiet horse.'

'Quite so,' said Lady Caroline. 'I declare there is quite a wind blowing; I had not remarked it before we started. And in what poor condition the street must be.'

'How fast we are going! Here is the Stray already.'

'To be sure it is. And the traffic is considerable. Have you noticed how red Bodfish seems to go sometimes round the neck? Can it be that he has returned to beer?'

'There *is* rather a lot of traffic. And do you notice how much of it appears to *swerve* at us? One could almost be alarmed.'

'My dear' – Lady Caroline swayed and bucketed and gasped – 'my dear, there is much comfort nowdays in a quiet horse.'

FOR THE BEST IN PAPERBACKS, LOOK FOR THE 🐧

In every corner of the world, on every subject under the sun, Penguin represents quality and variety – the very best in publishing today.

For complete information about books available from Penguin – including Pelicans, Puffins, Peregrines and Penguin Classics – and how to order them, write to us at the appropriate address below. Please note that for copyright reasons the selection of books varies from country to country.

In the United Kingdom: Please write to *Dept E.P., Penguin Books Ltd, Harmondsworth, Middlesex, UB7 0DA*

If you have any difficulty in obtaining a title, please send your order with the correct money, plus ten per cent for postage and packaging, to *PO Box No 11, West Drayton, Middlesex*

In the United States: Please write to *Dept BA, Penguin, 299 Murray Hill Parkway, East Rutherford, New Jersey 07073*

In Canada: Please write to *Penguin Books Canada Ltd, 2801 John Street, Markham, Ontario L3R 1B4*

In Australia: Please write to the *Marketing Department, Penguin Books Australia Ltd, P.O. Box 257, Ringwood, Victoria 3134*

In New Zealand: Please write to the *Marketing Department, Penguin Books (NZ) Ltd, Private Bag, Takapuna, Auckland 9*

In India: Please write to *Penguin Overseas Ltd, 706 Eros Apartments, 56 Nehru Place, New Delhi, 110019*

In Holland: Please write to *Penguin Books Nederland B.V., Postbus 195, NL–1380AD Weesp, Netherlands*

In Germany: Please write to *Penguin Books Ltd, Friedrichstrasse 10–12, D–6000 Frankfurt Main 1, Federal Republic of Germany*

In Spain: Please write to *Longman Penguin España, Calle San Nicolas 15, E–28013 Madrid, Spain*

In France: Please write to *Penguin Books Ltd, 39 Rue de Montmorency, F–75003, Paris, France*

In Japan: Please write to *Longman Penguin Japan Co Ltd, Yamaguchi Building, 2–12–9 Kanda Jimbocho, Chiyoda-Ku, Tokyo 101, Japan*